The Beautiful Ones

EMILY HAYSE

CONTENTS

*To all those who have inspired me creatively—
my Beautiful Ones.
Their number has swelled to too many to name over the years,
and many are no longer with us.
May their stories, their music, and their memories live long.*

THE PEOPLE

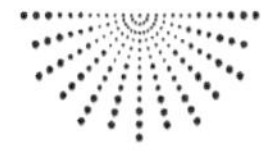

Doctor Sikes: Old as the hills with as many secrets. He set Archer Scott's life on its course and continues to watch him from afar.

Archer Scott: Governor of the Western Territory. After the defeat of the outlaw king, Alexander Mortimer, he looks forward to settling into his new duties as people flock westward.

Rosamund Lacey: Newly married to Archer Scott, Rosamund is eager to find her place in the Western Territory and the rapidly growing town of Glory Mesa.

Raymond Lacey: Now Marshal of the Western Territory, Rosamund's brother Raymond seeks to root out the rest of the outlaws scattered by Mortimer's defeat.

Jesse Thatcher: A rancher at heart, his loyalty to his cousin Archer lands him in trouble more often than not.

Lesley Gable: The new surveyor in Glory Mesa, he comes west with his wife Edith and is awestruck by the heroes that make up the town.

Edith Gable: Comes west with her surveyor husband. She has great hopes and plans for the place they will make for themselves in this wild land.

Kate Carnegie: Showed up in Glory Mesa and took a kitchen job a couple years back. No one knows where she came from or where she's going, only that she's young and strong and just passing through.

Irene Sandler: A newcomer to the territory, ready to make a new start after being widowed back East.

Cristobal Newton: One of the richest men in the West, he missed the last tumultuous year while on a prolonged business trip back East.

Maria Pike: Widow and businesswoman, she stands aloof from the rough dust of Glory Mesa.

Clay Carson: Owner of the only saloon in town. A hard man, but a good one to have at your side in a fight.

Peter: No-one's boy who cleans at the saloon and runs errands.

The Swift Brothers: Laughing blond fellows, hard to tell apart and settled on a large spread. One-quarter Auki on their mother's side.

Jack Selby: Rifleman, paid to guard sheep from the predators of the range. His shy demeanor and love of poetry belie his skill at tracking and killing.

Harrison Terhune: After nearly being hung, Harrison is determined to stay honest and stick to his ranch work as much as possible.

Blue Harding: Leader of the largest outlaw band since Mortimer's downfall.

Tagweiah: A member of the Auki nation and cousin to the Swifts, he frequently rides over the border to visit his cousins and his friend, Archer Scott.

Tora-Teth: Mortimer's former right-hand man and a dangerous hunter.

Britt and Buck April: Brothers and horsebreakers.

1

ALAN

THE SETTING SUN IS RUDDY, RIMMED WITH GOLD, turning the green hills and the cloudless blue into the colors of a dream I once had.

At least—I thought it was a dream.

I stare over the backs of the roving cattle, drinking in the light and color. Every day in this country is like watching poetry unfold over the hills in front of you. I wish I could come up with words for it like the poets do, but I reckon that's why I'm out here pushing cattle.

When Jem went to war, he sent Max to live with the Auki and left the ranch to me and the foreman. I wish he'd left Max with me, but he did what he thought was right.

I worked sunup to sundown those three, four years he was gone.

He and I, we never talk about those years. I reckon he thinks I'm respecting him, not wanting to pry into the war, not wanting to make him feel guilty for leaving. We're folk who tend to let bygones stay bygones.

But he doesn't know that I keep silence for my own reasons, too.

The warm evening breeze blows a strand of hair into my face—it catches gold in the sunlight before I brush it aside.

The cattle are bunching, rubbing long, angled horns against each other's hides, thrusting their heads up over the sea of milling backs as if swimming through it.

We'll have to make camp before long.

"Max!" I call, cupping one heavy-gloved hand to my mouth. He turns in the saddle—I'm amazed he can hear me— and I whistle, making a quick turning gesture with my hand.

He rides up to the front; he'll turn point riders in and we'll circle the herd for the night. Just ahead is a good spot.

The boys have the cattle well enough in hand. I peel my horse off the herd and canter up to the crest of the nearest hill.

The sun floods the valley between the hills like a mountain river after a storm. There's a wildness to the land. Even the peaceful moments mirror the deadly ones.

It was dusk then, too, when the dream happened.

There'd been trouble between a couple Eastern clans that year—nothing we wanted a corner of—so we had decided to drive the herd over the northwestern ridge-lands to a settlement beyond the territory borders. It was a promising settlement, sure to pay top dollar.

For a week we traveled through a strange territory. It was

timberland, mountain, and low barren places with rocks and pools that steamed.

The pools were made of nearly every color a man could think—yellow, orange, blue and green—and we kept the cattle steered clear of them.

I was scouting ahead and a little to the south of the herd, and I found myself up on a high ridge, looking down at the land around me.

To one side lay timberland, spotted with deep meadows; on the other lay a wide, flat stretch of land pocked with those hot holes, shooting boiling water, and pools of every color, steaming slowly.

And as I gazed down, I saw in the pools a simultaneous movement like the reflections of clouds moving across the sky above, but the sky was empty and blue.

It was a moment, a moment only, but I saw in the flat-lands the likeness of an eye, half a mile wide, the pools like golden flecks in the iris.

And then it was gone.

I was up on that ridge alone. I don't know that any living man had been up there or has been there since.

I look long at the fading valley below me.

I'll never know or understand what happened that day.

CAMP IS SET up by the time I ride down. The world is just blurred shadows as men move along the edge of the firelight, trail-dusted.

"Where were you?" Jem pours out coffee into a tin mug and hands it over. Always the eagle eye, Jem, watching for trouble.

"Just looking over the lay of the land." The coffee is good, hot and bitter and bracing.

"And?"

"We'll have good grazing."

"Good." Jem looks around the circle at the half dozen of us not on the herd. "Eat up. I want the riders out and the others in before it's too dark."

He turns to me. "You're on night hawk."

I only nod. I'm not tired anyway.

I finish my bacon and beans and pull a fresh horse from the string. The clear sky is darkening gently, the first of the stars coming out across it like markings on a map.

I've never been back there, to that ridge. But on nights like these, I think of it.

2

IRENE

It would not be ladylike to take my boots off
before this crackling fire, but I wish I could. Laura Baker has;
she is quietly massaging her sore toes in the safety of the
darkness.

But I carry the Sandler name. And even a displaced
Sandler, traveling by foot beside a worn wagon, no different
from the farmers, tradesmen, and trappers beside me, must
maintain her dignity.

Tim O'Blaines is picking at his guitar. The instrument is
so worn that it's hard to tell what it is, but he claims it is a
guitar.

Laura hums along, her voice low and rich. It reminds me
of the singing I've heard at concerts back East. Tim's picking
turns into a light, gentle tune—an invitation—and Laura's
sweet voice fills out the sound.

Come and see this distant mountain,
Standing high and proud alone;
Father says that we must climb it
If at home we would arrive.

Home is fair and home is pleasant—
Oft I dream, though ne'er I've seen
This good place that I belong in,
This good land of hope and peace.

The stars are bright, silver pinpricks in the wild night sky. Out here, away from the constant light of streetlamps, the stars are stronger. In High Park, anyone found out of doors at night staring at the stars would have been thought a lunatic.

"What do you think it'll be like?" Beside me, my cousin Arnold tilts his gaze upward. He is tall and fair, like all of us from the Davenport side. I always feared it made me look proud and distant, like my aunt; but it gives him a beautiful, wistful air.

"What?"

"Living out here. Glory Mesa. Land, if we can get it."

"Oh, I think we'll be able to get it if we want it." My mind goes to the thousand dollars in silver I have hidden in our medicine chest. My dowry, once upon a time. My husband, James, had never touched it.

Arnold doesn't know about the money, but it's safer that way until it's time to use it. With his soft heart, he'd probably find some poor soul in need and give it all away.

"I'd like a ranch. Or just—just a homestead." Arnold's face brightens at the thought. "A spot I could call all mine. Ours, that is. Oh, you know what I mean."

I smile.

"A place where I could look up at stars and belong," he goes on. "Where I could shut the door on a barn I'd built myself and hear the sounds of the horses and the milk cow and know all was well."

He has good dreams, Arnold.

Life has hardly turned out as I expected or wished, but I think I could be content working with my hands, living alongside my gentle cousin. After all, anything is better than my aunt and uncle.

I'm lucky Arnold wanted to escape them as much as I did. They never forgave me for spurning their inheritance to marry James, and for the last two years, they reminded me every day that my husband had been a failure, his great and final failure being to die and leave me alone.

A woman can only live with that so long, even if it comes dressed in velvet and diamonds.

A shriek rises beyond the fire, followed by a low, mean, bubbling sound.

The circle stirs uncomfortably. Our trail guide raises himself quietly and looks into the dark. His long face is grim, his eyes wary.

He isn't very old—late twenties, perhaps—but there's a

surprising depth to his eyes and an iron aspect to his lean face. He sinks back down. "Ain't coming thisaway."

"How do you know?" Arnold asks, looking more for reassurance than an argument.

"We've got a fire," the scout answers slowly.

"Still, gives me the shivers," Arnold mutters under his breath.

I reach over and pat his arm.

"Well, I'm turning in," he says to me, pushing his hat back. "If I can sleep."

"Go ahead. Don't worry about me."

He smiles briefly and leaves the circle.

His departure sparks a general exodus, and I find myself left alone with the scout, who is fortifying the fire for the night.

"Are you staying up?" I ask, rising from my place.

"Reckon so. We're in outlaw territory."

"I thought they were taken care of last year."

"Mortimer was, rest his soul." The scout gives a quiet, ironic laugh. "His leftovers weren't."

I wrap my shawl tighter around my shoulders. "The fire looks a little dull."

He squints up against the thin trail of smoke. "The brightest flames burn shortest. This'll last."

I stand and watch him at his work, trying to memorize the motions. I know very well that such skills may mean the difference between life and death out here, and though I love my cousin, Arnold could bear much improvement in that department.

"You should get your sleep, ma'am." The scout's keen eyes meet mine briefly.

"I like the night skies."

He looks at me with understanding. Whatever his life's given him, it hasn't been easy.

"I do too, ma'am."

When I set out to travel westward in a wagon, I never imagined the dust.

It is everywhere, stirred up by the wagons, by the stock driven along behind, by your own feet when you walk. Arnold and I take turns driving and walking, but you can't escape the dust either place. By the end of the day, it becomes a thick grime that can only be scrubbed off with the help of a rare stream.

I'm lucky enough, at least, to have three dresses with me. Most of the other women have only one.

Arnold is driving now, but it will be my turn in another hour. The wind blows my hair free and I step behind the wagon for a moment to fix it.

Gunshots split the air.

The scout's horse startles and bolts. I climb up and throw myself into the wagon among the stores.

Arnold is lying backward across them, his eyes unseeing,

blood from a wound below his collarbone trickling onto the floor of the wagon.

I reel back, a scream rising in my throat.

Shouts and more gunshots tear into my ears. The wagon in front of ours is on fire. Our oxen bawl, the wagon shaking as they barrel toward the rocks, toward the flaming wagon.

I have to get out. I've kept everything in our wagon as dry as possible, and it'll go up like kindling.

I reach for the gun propped up behind the seat. Arnold's gun. A bullet rips into the canvas above my head and leaves a tear out the other side.

It's now or never.

I jump out the back of the wagon and run for the rocks, a few yards away.

My skirt catches. I tumble, dropping the gun, scraping my hands and one knee on sharp rock. The wounds are numb and hot.

I jerk the offending skirt and it tears free. I drop behind the rock, out of sight. My heart pounds in my ears, in my throat, in my chest.

The gun is cocked now, and it has a full chamber. Poor Arnold, he never even had a chance to use it. I've never shot a gun in my life, but I've seen it done. If it comes to it, I'd rather try than not. I hold my breath to listen.

The air is full of screams, shouts, gunshots, splintering wood. I wouldn't be able to hear anyone coming until they were almost upon me. At that distance, I probably couldn't miss, but neither would they.

The gunshots die down, mixed with raucous laughs and the uncouth sounds of destruction.

I raise myself as high as I dare.

They've taken one prisoner—our tall scout. Scattered around are bodies I cannot bear to look at. A couple of the attackers hold the scout by the arms and another punches him, in the face and then in the stomach.

I sink slowly back down. There's nothing I can do against so many of them.

The sounds continue, flesh striking flesh and laughter. My skin crawls. I brace myself for the report of a gun.

And then I feel thunder.

Thunder, from the open blue sky. It encroaches on the sounds of reveling, and beneath me, the ground trembles.

Hooves.

Shots fill the air again, this time barking out with authority. A scramble, a scream, and then the gunshots again, one side volleying and another answering until they die away in a score of hoofbeats that pound away over the dusty ground.

I raise myself up again, just enough to look.

There are more men now, new men. Only about a dozen. They're surveying the wreck of the wagons, their voices audible, but the words lost at this distance. I notice one in particular—he is tall, wearing a navy blue shirt and high black boots.

From this distance, one could mistake him for a cavalry officer. But there's no military presence in these parts, the scout had told me, except for up north where the railroad runs out to the silver mines that dot the mountain country.

It can't be the army.

A couple men bend down to examine the sprawled bodies, shaking their heads. Another turns over a dead man—a man with a red handkerchief tied to his arm—with the toe of his boot.

No sign of our scout. I appear to be the sole survivor.

I try not to think of Arnold, of Laura Baker and her quiet husband, of Tim O'Blaines, and of the twin girls who translated everything for their immigrant parents.

But their faces come. I twist around, the smell of blood and gunpowder too much, and I am sick in the dust.

"Marshal!"

I hear footsteps running in my direction and I look up, my eyes blurred from the violence with which I am sick.

Two men, three, are standing over me.

"Well, what do we have here?" One of them is the tall man in the dark blue shirt. His voice is as low and deep as the rumbling of a train.

I only moan.

He reaches into his pocket and holds out a handkerchief.

I wipe my mouth with it. It smells of sage and soap. He extends a canteen. I rinse out my mouth and turn away to spit, then I drink as much as I dare.

"Are you hurt?"

I look at my scraped, bloody hands. The skin has curled like burned paper, leaving the hand below raw and slick.

The blood has dried, mingled with dust and particles of stone.

"No." It takes me too long to say it.

"Did you get a good look at them?"

I shake my head.

"They were a splinter of Abernathy's," says one of the other men. "The red horses and armbands."

The leader nods quietly.

I'm suddenly aware of my disheveled appearance. I start to get up but my boot is getting caught in my ripped hem. It's taking too long.

"Easy now, there's no hurry." He holds out his hand.

"Thank you." I take it, and his hand is gentle as he helps me to my feet.

The wreck of what used to be our wagon train fills my sight and I go dizzy. The man's hand holds my hand tighter and his arm reaches around me to steady me.

He leads me to a flat rock and eases me down.

"Have a little more." He extends the canteen again.

I drink again and feel a little better, but not much. I focus on the man's face, trying not to look at the smoldering ruins behind him.

He's a little weathered, but his gray eyes are sharp and intelligent, and the one distinct feature of his face is a long, heavy mustache.

"I'm Irene Sandler," I manage.

"I'm Raymond Lacey."

"Marshal," adds one of the men, as if to make up for his leader's modesty.

My lips try to form a proper greeting, but the world around his face swims again.

It is as if my body took every reserve and put it toward my survival, and now that the danger is over, it has nothing.

"Back up, boys," says Marshal Lacey in his low, rumbling voice. He wets a handkerchief down and hands it to me.

This revives me enough to sit straight on my own and collect my numb thoughts.

"You're the marshal of the territory?"

"Yes, ma'am."

"There's a few fine tales of you in the papers where I came from."

"None of them true, probably." The corner of his heavy mustache tilts upward.

He stands up. "Gentlemen, we'll be camping here tonight. Two of you get up on those rocks and keep an eye out. The rest of you, put out those fires and get on burying detail."

They obey immediately.

"I'm glad you came," I say, out of polite habit.

He doesn't answer, so I look up at his face. There's a surprising gentleness in the flinty gray of his eyes.

"I wish I could have come sooner." He looks over at the ruined wagons, some of them burning still. The smoke streams from the wreckage like a banner.

"Any of your folks here?"

I nod. "But he's dead. He was dead before I ran."

"I'm sorry."

I don't say anything. Words don't fit times like these.

THE HOT MIDDAY weakens to a windblown, cloudy afternoon. The cool air is a relief, as I am still shaky and faint if I stand too fast.

I go to our wagon to salvage what I can. Arnold isn't there anymore. There's a stain on the smashed boards. I turn my back to it and rifle through the mangled goods.

Our medicine chest is tipped on its side, covered in flour and molasses and dirt. I open it up and reach to the bottom.

The money is still there.

I tuck it quickly into my pocket. Better no one knows of this. The rest of our things are ruined; the dry goods are spread out across the boards of the wagon, my clothes are ripped and scorched. I cannot bear to look at Arnold's things.

"Ma'am." Quiet footsteps come up behind me. It's one of the men, his dusty hat pulled off, the wind playing in his stiff thatch of blond hair.

"Ma'am, the—the gentleman in the wagon, we buried him. If you want to see—"

I stand up, dust my hands off gently. "Yes, I'd like to."

He holds out a fistful of spindly yellow flowers. "I'll take you up there."

"Thank you." The words are barely a whisper. I take the flowers in numb fingers.

. . .

A LITTLE BEYOND the camp is a small overlook above a valley. It is dry and dusty up here, but the valley is dotted with green, and shining bands of light proclaim rivers twisting through it.

It's beautiful.

The man leads me to a raised mound of rocks with a cross made of sticks. There's an x marked in the dirt beside it, and the man smudges it out with the toe of his boot.

"What was his name?" he asks respectfully.

I kneel down, pick up a rock from the ground, and lay it gently on the mound.

"Arnold."

"Arnold," he echoes to himself. "Well—I'll let you be, ma'am."

I hear his footsteps retreat as I lay the yellow sprigs on the grave. They're not much. When James died, there were hothouse flowers and roses and everything money could buy.

Arnold gets a handful of desert flowers picked by a cowhand. He deserved better.

My fists clutch the dust, my breath comes in ragged sobs.

Arnold should have been able to have the life he wanted. Not have it taken like this, without even a chance to defend himself. For me, death would have not been so terrible. At least I would have been with James, but this was Arnold's dream.

What good is it to me now, without him?

I let out everything I've been holding back, cover my face and cry. Cry for my family, cry for all the hopes and dreams that can no longer be.

I cry until I'm spent. Until I can do nothing but lean my head against the rocks and breathe. It takes all of my energy just to keep breathing.

A crunch of boots on rock comes behind me, and I start up, off the grave.

It is the marshal.

He crouches down beside me. I turn away, trying to hide my face. "There now," he says softly. "It's all right."

I reach for his hand, craving the touch of another human being, and he gives it.

With his other hand, he takes his hat off, then gazes over the view before us quietly. "Was he your husband?"

I can barely draw breath to answer. "My cousin. My husband died two years ago."

"I'm sorry." He just keeps looking out at the expanse below.

"I was coming out here with him. He was the one who wanted it." My voice catches.

He shifts beside me. "Do you have any folks?"

I shake my head. I refuse to go back to my uncle and aunt, a second failure in their eyes. I'd rather die here, under these stark and beautifully unforgiving skies.

"No," I manage. "I want to keep going. I want to stay out here."

"This land's cruel," he says gently.

"It can't be worse than what's already behind me."

"We're starting back tonight, back towards Glory Mesa. We can't stay here."

I look up at him, wipe my eyes. "I couldn't have stayed here a moment longer anyway."

3

ROSAMUND

"Wʜᴀᴛ ᴅᴏ ʏᴏᴜ ᴛʜɪɴᴋ?"

I look over the wide, flat space, broken only by the skeleton of a rambling ranch house. Purple sagebrush has grown up around it, and cactus, round and dull green. But there's grass too, and around us, on a gently sloping hill, it carpets the ground and stretches into stands of pine that run all the way to the distant blue of the mountains.

"It's beautiful." I squeeze his hand. "Is this where you planned to live before the governorship?"

"Yes." Archer turns me gently and stretches his arm out to point to the expanse I've just observed. "And it's where I intend for us to live after I step down."

"When did you buy the land?"

"Right after I came home from the war." He sighs. "I just camped out here all that summer."

"Shame on you. You were nothing but bones."

He laughs wryly. "I needed to feel that I belonged someplace."

"Someplace all alone in the middle of nowhere?" I put my hand on my hip.

"Aw, I still ate well. This place is full of antelope. Besides, Thatcher rode out to check on me every couple weeks."

"You still wrote letters that summer."

"As I said, Thatcher checked on me on the fortnight."

"And you split that wood?"

"I did." His hand finds mine and his thumb strokes the back of my hand. "I was preparing this so that you could come out to me. But the territory had other plans."

He grins.

"Do you want to see the house?" His voice is eager, almost boyish. It was that eagerness that made me fall in love with him.

"What is there to see?"

He only smiles, mysteriously, and leads me to the doorway.

It has a partial roof, though the floor is just dirt with weeds growing in it. There's a large stone chimney, and stairs to an upper room with only the beginnings of a floor.

"The finest hearth," he announces, leaning into it. He can nearly stand in it, it's so large. "Even the coldest night cannot touch us." He reemerges with a smudge on the shoulder of his once-clean shirt.

He throws one arm wide. "This is the main room. We'll

host the best parties after the governorship is over and we have no one to impress."

I cover my mouth and laugh.

"And over there, the stairs to the bedrooms."

"Bedrooms?"

"Many. Enough for children, guests, family, anyone."

I take his hand and press it in mine. I can just imagine the halls filled with children, laughing and playing.

"It'll be a beautiful thing, one day," he says.

"One day soon," I reply.

"Over here's the kitchen. I was going to order in one of those newfangled stoves. And I thought the dining table would go here." He strides across the empty ground as if we are in the finished house.

"And the study? You have to have a study."

"Who needs a study if I'm finished governing?" he asks roguishly. "No, of course—it goes here." He steps between a couple brace beams and holds out his arms.

"It's perfect." I crane my neck upward at the dying red-gold light. "It's like a dream."

"I'd hoped you'd like it." He comes back and squeezes my hand. "This will be my first true home. The first place I've ever belonged."

"Surely not."

He nods, and his blue eyes are wistful. "I came here once when I was a boy, in Hector Muley's care, if care you could call it. And I swore to myself I'd come back and live here. That I wouldn't starve, that I'd make something better of myself, that I'd have children and I'd be good to them."

"And you will. You will have all that, and it will be true."

"Yes," he echoes softly, but the sadness in his eyes isn't gone.

"What is it, Archer?"

"Life doesn't give you what you want just because you try hard or want it badly enough. I'm afraid, sometimes, that I swore naively, and that one day I'll be forced to choose between my promise and what is right."

"Don't think about that."

He continues on as if he didn't even hear me. "My work in this territory is far from over, Rosamund. I feel the pressure mounting. It's like a storm gathering in the mountains. We don't know what is in the future. And I fear I am bound to this territory by far deeper things than the oaths of office I swore." His hand closes over mine. "Some days it's like I know—I'm sure—that this land will require my life of me."

"Archer, that's not going to happen."

"Promise me, Rose, that even if a storm comes, you'll stay by me?"

"Of course, Archer. That's why I'm here. After Mortimer, can you doubt it?"

I expect him to smile, agree with me, but instead his chin trembles.

"Darling, darling, what is it?" I take his face in my hands and kiss him.

"Sikes speaks of his land as cursed. The Far Hill Clan

tell beautiful stories about the cursing of the land and the heroes who will free it. They're just stories...but some days, I can almost feel it. The curse in the ground, in the air, in my bones. I felt it just now."

I run my hand through his hair soothingly, lean my head against his chest. I can hear his heart beating. "You are here with me. You are on the ground you have chosen, we are dreaming of our house and our children. It is a good night. You are only tired." I reach up and kiss him. "Let it go tonight."

He takes a deep breath and it's almost visible, moving across his face and down over his shoulders, the setting aside of his fears.

He looks over at me, his face serious but his eyebrows raised. "We should go surprise Thatcher."

"Should we?"

Archer smiles, his grin white against the dusk. "Of course we should. It'll be good for him. Besides, what kind of man would I be to keep you out in the night like this?"

"I don't care."

"I mean it, Rose—"

"No. I want to spend our first night in the house now. Tonight."

His eyes begin to sparkle as the idea sinks in. "Why wait?"

"My thoughts exactly."

He ties the horse up in the future kitchen and builds a fire in the hearth. We eat his dry provisions and drink from the same canteen, gazing into the flames and talking about our plans for the house. I'm curled against him, his arm around me, as the light dies away and night takes its place.

"Is it safe for us both to sleep?" I ask, suddenly realizing I may have doomed him to watch the night, as he wouldn't ask it of me.

"The bay's a wild-caught horse. She's sharper on the watch than Carson is."

I laugh and lean my head against him.

He bends down and kisses me.

"I'll get the bedroll," he says, and eases his hand out of mine.

He lays it out beside the remnants of the fire, where the oncoming chill of the night is not so strong. "Will you be comfortable?"

"Perfectly." I lay down and pull his woven blanket up to my chest. He feeds the fire and then pulls off his boots, lying down on the bare ground next to me.

"There's room for two," I whisper.

He moves closer, and I put my arm over him.

"This is it, Rosamund," he whispers.

"It?" I turn to look at him, but he's looking at the stars.

"When I dream, this is what I dream of. You and me, right here."

"And our children," I murmur.

"And our children. I don't think I want anything more."

"What about your dreams for the land?"

"It's my responsibility. Of course I believe in it. I believe in it enough to give all of this up, if it's required of me. But there's nothing I'd add to this right here. Nothing."

I tighten my hand on his. "Don't worry. We'll have this. All of it."

He presses my hand to his lips and kisses it.

We fall asleep with our fingers entwined.

4

GABLE

THE TRAIN PUMPS SMOKE AND THE WHISTLE SCREAMS. I step from the train and take in a long, deep breath of Western Territory air.

This Smith's Run is only the gateway, they tell me, but it's good enough for me. I turn around and reach up to give my wife a hand.

We have been married three years, but the touch of her fingers in my hand still makes me wonder how I ever got so lucky.

"So this is Smith's Run?" She looks around at the dirty buildings, at the horses standing and stamping their feet.

The streets are loud and dusty; I see the stage office, too many saloons, many wagons, and even more horses, tied at hitching rails.

I search her face, afraid of seeing distaste, but her face is as clear as a spring day.

"So they say."

"And we'll pick up the stage from here?"

"Yes. There's no railroad to Glory Mesa yet." I stride down the track, back towards the luggage cars.

"Isn't it risky still?" There isn't a hint of fear in her tone.

"Less than it was, or so the porter said," I reply, heaving our one shared trunk up over my shoulder. It's terribly heavy, but even so we could bring very little with us.

For the briefest moment, doubt flits across my mind. Perhaps I had no right to take this job, to bring Edith out to this place.

But she's staring up and down the street with interest, and as I pick up our satchels in my other hand, she turns to me with glowing eyes. "I'll take one, Les."

The stage station is not far. A block's worth of walking, and we're there.

"You must be Lesley Gable." The ticket officer looks me up and down. "They said to expect a man as tall as a telegraph pole."

I smile, not sure whether it was meant as a compliment, but choosing to take it as such. "That's me."

"Stage leaves in the morning, seven o'clock. We'll take good care of these." He nods to the luggage as we set it down.

"My tools are in there." I put my hand on one case. "Mind it's not dropped."

"Sure." He gives me a nod and then raises his cap to my wife. "Seven o'clock, remember."

We head down the street toward the lodging houses, and

my wife slips her arm into mine. "I'd dearly like to know what you're thinking," she says.

"I am thinking that perhaps we are about to begin the most wonderful time in our lives."

"Hm." She takes this with a smile.

"And you?"

"I am thinking how fine you look when you block the sun and it streams around you."

I bring her hand up and bend to kiss it.

WE ARE at the stage station half an hour before departure. Edith takes a seat inside, and I, unable to settle, go out onto the boardwalk and watch them load the stage.

The morning air is chilly and I tug at the collar of my coat. I smell the comforting homey smells of horse-worn leather and the coffee one of the drivers is pouring.

He glances over at me. "Want any?"

I shake my head.

They bring out the horses, six strong and wearing harness. I watch as they back the animals into place and get them hitched up. The driver comes out, his whip coiled in his hand, and begins to laugh and talk with one of the hands. The deference they show him is slight but unmistakable.

A man's got to have nerves of steel to be a driver, and everyone seems to understand that here.

A thrill runs through me. To be moving to a place where

legends are everyday men, where a heart has to be brave to survive—I don't think I could get any luckier.

My wife appears, looking fresh and strong and not at all like she has been traveling for weeks. I reach down and take her hand, giving it a gentle squeeze.

Another man joins us on the walk, satchel in hand, wearing a black cattleman's hat and a long tan duster.

He's a well-built man, neither too tall nor too stocky, with thick black hair. He tips his hat to my wife. "Going west?" he asks me, and his mouth gives an ironic sort of twist.

"To Glory Mesa." Even the name of the town sounds beautiful to me.

"Splendid. I'm headed that way myself." He heaves his satchel up. "After you, ma'am."

I climb in after my wife and the man takes the seat across from us, shutting the door. We make ourselves as comfortable as can be expected as the driver and the shotgun climb up.

The whip cracks and the stage pulls away with jolt.

"I'm Chris." Our fellow traveler holds out his hand.

I take it firmly. "Lesley Gable. My wife, Edith."

"Ma'am." He smiles with one side of his mouth, drawing out a dimple.

"Do you live in Glory Mesa?"

"Oh no, not me. I live much further west than that. I have my own ranch. You?"

"I'm a surveyor. A friend of mine knew the last surveyor

in town, a Garth Levine, and when Levine was killed, he offered me the job. He's got no taste for roughing it."

Chris's eyes go briefly to my wife and I feel a prickle of discomfort. Again, I wonder: Am I wrong in bringing her out here?

"So you've never been west?"

"No."

"How do you know you're going to like it?" He's looking at me quietly. There's an intelligence about this man that cannot be hidden. I've seen it in professors and the like, and some seamen, but never in a cattleman.

"I know." I smile, knowing how stupid it sounds. "I've heard it's hard, but I'm willing to put in the work, put up with trouble."

"Good." He pushes his hat back and looks lazily out the window at the passing rocks. "It's a new territory and it has land and it has trouble. Enough to keep you busy for a dozen lifetimes."

"What sorts of trouble?" asks my wife. She sounds more curious than afraid.

"Well, the land's hard and we've got more than our share of dangerous characters. But in Glory Mesa there's little danger, so long's you mind your own business. Things are safer since the incident near Shiloh Crossing last year. You hear about that?"

"I read about it in the paper," I reply. "What a man this Archer Scott must be."

"He's a good man."

"You've met him?"

"Course I have. He's been a fixture in the cattle market for years now. We used to drive stock together when our herds were smaller. But if you're headed for Glory Mesa, you'll meet him. The town's not that big yet."

Imagine that. Meeting our governor right in town.

Chris folds his arms and leans back, again regarding the passing landscape with some indifference.

Beside me, Edith sighs. Her eyes are fixed on the bright sky beyond the stage window.

"Are you tired?" I bend down to whisper the question.

She shakes her head.

I twine my fingers into hers, rub the back of her hand with my thumb. She's game for anything, this girl. She leans her dark head against my shoulder and my heart flutters.

I love her more every day that passes.

We try to rest, though the stage jolts and shakes. Chris sleeps.

The stage stops at a station around noon to water the horses. Even here in the yard, I can smell the fresh bread and hot beans. Chris heads inside as I climb down to give Edith a hand.

One of the hostlers jerks his head at Chris's retreating back and hisses to me with a grin, "That's Cristobal Newton, one of the wealthiest men in this territory. Runs an outfit bigger than most of the others put together."

A thrill runs down my spine as Edith and I share a smile. I was right. We are stepping into a world of legends.

. . .

THE STAGE PULLS into Glory Mesa at four o'clock one afternoon, less than a week after we left Smith's Run. It's large compared to the towns and encampments we've passed, but still small compared to the ones back East.

Chris opens the door of the stagecoach with a satisfied sigh. "Ah, Glory Mesa." He reaches up and pulls down his satchel.

"Excuse me," I say, before we lose him. "Can you tell me where I can find Carson?"

"Clay Carson?" Chris raises his eyebrows. "He's down this way. I'm headed to his saloon. You folks have a place to stay?"

"We've made arrangements to stay in one of his rooms. I need to talk business with him."

"Ah. Well, follow me, and don't worry about the luggage. They'll carry it down to Carson's for you. Looks like I haven't lost you folks' company quite yet." He throws a brief smile over his shoulder and sets off down the street.

Carson's saloon is moderately full. I feel a little conspicuous, ducking under the doorframe and watching eyes turn immediately to us.

Chris saunters up to the bar, where a young woman is serving drinks.

"Where's Carson?"

"In the back.

"Will you tell him that Chris Newton wants to see him?"

She looks up quickly, sets down her towel, and leaves.

Edith turns around and quietly surveys the saloon around us.

Less than a minute later, the girl reappears with a broad-shouldered, red-haired man at her heels.

"Newton! Well, this is a surprise." He holds out a broad hand and grasps Chris's.

"Carson. This is Lesley and Edith Gable."

"Gable, Lesley...ah, you must be the surveyor!"

"I am."

"Very good! Kate, show Mrs. Gable upstairs. Our best room's ready for you, ma'am."

Edith stands on tiptoe to kiss my cheek before she follows the girl up the stairs.

Carson goes on, his voice loud. "A pity about old Garth. A good man, he was. Now—drinks before business. I insist. What can I get you?"

"I'll take a beer," Chris replies in a reluctant tone that seems lost on Carson.

"Coffee?" I ask when he turns his questioning expression on me. "I'm a—teetotaler."

"Right." He pours out the drinks and I watch Chris brace himself as he tastes the beer.

I just turn my cup in my fingers.

"Say, has Sikes said anything to you?"

Chris barely shakes his head. "No, why?"

"He's all he was, and getting worse," Carson grunts.

"Just got into town." Chris's mouth gives that ironic twist. "But I'll be avoiding him."

"I swear, he was talking about you again just the other day, same old thing—'a woman'll be his death'."

"He always was one for the warnings."

Carson gives a scoffing laugh. "But he's been mostly harping on dry times. Says dry times are a comin' and beware."

"Who knows, maybe they are." Chris takes another sip of his drink.

"Now, Mr. Gable." Carson spreads his hands out on the bar. "About the surveyor's office—"

A voice outside the door breaks in. "Marshal's back! The marshal's back, and he's brought a girl!"

The room makes a general rush toward the door, but I have only to crane my neck a little and I can see: a dozen or so riders are coming in, dusty and worn, and there's a woman among them, wearing a slightly tattered dress.

"Hm." Carson shakes his head.

They ride on by and the men drift back to their tables or the bar.

"Who's the marshal?" asks Chris Newton, his voice slow —lazy, almost.

"Raymond Lacey. The governor's brother-in-law. And before you think it's a political move, Lacey's done this territory a sight of good since last year. I rode with him when he was starting out."

"But not anymore?" I hear a hint of amusement in Chris's tone.

"Newton, I'm a businessman. I'll ride posse if he asks, but I can't be outlaw-hunting all the time. This place can't get along without me too long."

Chris subtly looks past Carson to the girl he called Kate. She's smiling to herself.

"Now, to the business at hand, Mr. Gable," Carson says impatiently. "The survey office is all set up and ready as soon as you want to begin. I can help you find a place in town, or you can buy a plot at the land office. In the meantime, you're welcome to lodge here as long as you need to."

"When can I see my office?"

"I can show you tonight, if you'd like. Or tomorrow, if you're tired."

A figure pushes slowly through the saloon doors and my reply dies on my lips as the place hushes. He's tall and dust-covered, with a heavy mustache—one of the riders.

He moves to the bar, leans his arms against it, gives Newton and I a glance-over, and then looks to Carson.

"Can I get you something, Marshal?" Carson asks.

"Yeah." Raymond Lacey reaches into his pocket and counts out some money. "Anyone in your little place around the corner?"

"No, sir."

"Is she tidy?"

"I can have Kate bring some fresh linens out, but it's all

swept. No one's been in it since the Pearsons moved back East."

"Good. This should be a week's rent, give or take. You let me know when you need more."

"Sure, but don't you—?"

"It's for a woman. Raiders wiped out a wagon party, she's all that's left."

Carson swears under his breath.

"And make sure she gets a tab with Trasker. You let me know about that too."

"Anything you say, Marshal." Carson thumbs through the money and pockets it. "The poor woman."

Lacey gives a slow nod.

"Marshal, this is Cristobal Newton, from the Tall Tree ranch, and this here's Lesley Gable, the new surveyor."

"Nice to meet you gentlemen."

He shakes hands with both of us, then—to my surprise—turns to me. "You settin' up soon?"

"This week. As soon as I can." My mouth is dry.

"Well, I'll have some work for you when you want it."

"Stop in a couple days from now and I'll take it." My heart is beating fast in my throat. What luck—I come to Glory Mesa and Marshal Lacey himself wants my services.

This endeavor was blessed.

"Well, I'll see you." He touches the brim of his hat to all of us and strides out.

You can almost feel the tension in the room give when he's gone.

What a man.

I remember my coffee and gulp it down in one go. "Thank you, Mr. Carson. I'll see you tonight."

I push back from the bar and stride towards the stairs, trying not to let my shaking hands betray my excitement.

WE GO to the general store the next day, Edith and I. It's a short walk away, with a blue painted sign and well-kept wares on the walk out front. It looks distinctly more civilized than the rest of the town, with the exception, perhaps, of the restaurant.

The proprietor is sweeping the boardwalk. He straightens and holds out his hand. "You must be new in town? I'm Trasker, I run this mercantile."

"Lesley Gable. I'm the new surveyor. This is my wife, Edith."

"Pleased." She extends her hand.

He smiles and holds out his hand to her too. "Well, make yourselves at home, of course. Let me know if I can help." He goes on sweeping and I duck into the store after my wife.

Cloth goods are draped over one counter. Along the other are sacks of dry goods and glass jars of candy and dried fruits. Herbs and ropes and horse traces hang from the ceiling. In the back, I spy a plow.

Edith moves through the store comfortably, looking over everything with an experienced eye.

"Buck April!" I hear Trasker's voice outside. "What happened to you?"

"Had a tangle with some Red Arms. You got a problem if I restock?"

"No, go ahead." Trasker's voice sounds tight.

A young man comes in, flint-faced and chestnut-haired, with hard eyes that immediately take in the room. He's got a mean, half-healed cut and several bruises on his face.

He looks at me for a second longer than is normal, as if weighing me. Then he goes to the dry goods.

I return to Edith's side, just as a precaution.

Trasker comes back in and wipes the counter industriously, watching the newcomer out of the corner of his eye. "That's a nasty burn, son," he ventures after a minute. "You should have it looked at."

"It's healing," he says briefly.

A couple men stride in, their boots loud on the board floor. "Buck April, where'd you come from?"

Their tone is not friendly.

"A wagon train, east of here."

"You rode in alone."

"We were attacked by raiders. Don't think anyone made it."

"Except you."

"Yeah, except me." Buck sets down the cast-iron pot he was studying. "Only it's because they wanted me alive. A bullet was too quick for them."

"How do we know you didn't sell the others out?"

Buck stiffens like an animal sensing a fight. "There ain't a lick of sense in that, and you know it."

"Who says there ain't? You're an April, ain't you?"

"We're not thieves. I've never set foot inside a prison. As for a jail, you can't say the same for yourself."

There's a guffaw from the doorway. A crowd is gathering.

Buck picks up the pot and a bag of dry beans.

"You ain't sticking around, are you?"

Buck ignores this.

The troublemaker comes around and steps in his way. I shift so that if there's trouble, it'll hit me before it hits Edith.

She is, however, watching the whole scene with interest, as if hanging on every word that passes between these rough men.

"If you think you can walk straight into Glory Mesa after what your brother did—"

"Out of the way, Pete."

"No chance."

Buck's voice dips lower. "I said, out of the way."

"We got trouble here?" Marshal Lacey's tall form moves through the men in the doorway.

"No, sir." Every line in Buck's body is tense.

The marshal looks from man to man and settles on Trasker. "Is there trouble?"

"Buck's just getting supplies."

"What happened to your face, son?"

"Ran into Abernathy's men."

"Out above the creek valley?"

"Yeah. Were you the ones that chased them off?"

"Sure did. Where were you?"

"Tied to my bronc. They'd have finished me off in another couple minutes if you hadn't come. I reckon I owe you for that."

"Did you see where they went?"

"Yeah, they camped up on the gorge side of the Slate Shaft. That's where I got away from them." He shoves out a bloody, rope-burned wrist as if to prove it.

"How come you got away?"

This marshal is shrewd. I watch, unable to tear my gaze away.

"It's not the first time I've had trouble with their kind."

"Not your first time making a deal, eh?" shouts an onlooker.

Buck sways, not pushing, not giving. "I don't have to tell you my business. But we April boys have never been on good terms with the outlaw clans, you know that."

A tight silence hangs over the room.

"It's true," Trasker offers hesitantly.

Trasker's word must be good, because the marshal nods. "That's all," he says. "I want no fighting." His gaze hits the other men harder than Buck and they shrink, most of them heading toward the doorway.

Buck April pays for his things with a silver-studded belt buckle and heads out the door.

Trasker lets his breath out slowly.

"I think I may get a couple things," says Edith, calm as a summer's day, undoing the drawstrings of her purse.

"Go right ahead." I go to the door.

Buck is getting his horse, and a couple of the trouble-makers have circled back around like buzzards.

"Where's your brother, then? Heard he was released."

Buck doesn't answer, just stares the man down slowly. His eyes still on the man, he bends, picks up the sack, and heaves it onto his horse's back.

"You're hiding him somewhere, ain't you?"

"He's a free man," Buck says slowly. "Not that it's any of your business."

He thrusts his boot into the stirrup and hikes his long leg over the back of his rangy horse.

And then he's gone, just another milling figure in the hot streets of Glory Mesa.

5

THATCHER

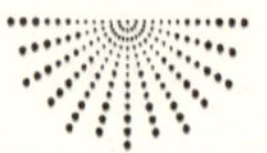

"Head 'em in!" I cup my worn glove to my mouth and shout. "Keep 'em crowded!"

A cow's breaking loose with a calf on her flank, and my horse hardly has to take my nudge. She cuts through and swings them back in.

I look across the sea of milling backs and can't help grinning to myself. Archer's across from me, hollering and swinging rope like he never left.

I've wondered all my life what marriage would do to him, and now I know. It's made him happy—happier than I've ever seen him. His face just lights at the littlest thing.

He needs it, too, because I think being governor is going to kill him if he keeps at it too long.

Rosamund is standing on the rails of the pen, her arms wrapped around the top rail. She's got eyes for Archer only, and they are shining eyes.

I suppose she's never seen him do this before.

The point of the herd is moving into the pens nicely. Once they've got an idea in their heads, the rest will all follow.

Works for and against you all the time.

Through the dust, I see a couple riders coming up the southern trail, trotting up past the buildings and towards the pens.

I peel my horse off the herd's flank and trot out to them. It's Raymond Lacey and a fellow I've never seen before.

"Raymond! What are you doing here?" I take off my hat and beat the dust out against my leg.

The stranger is a lean, long-legged man who makes his horse look small. He's wearing a satchel over his shoulder and his horse has a couple packs slung behind the saddle.

"Just passing through. Is my sister here?"

"Over there, by the pens." I jerk my head in her direction. "And where are you passing through to?"

"Out to that piece of land I was looking at last year. This is Lesley Gable, the new surveyor in town."

"Pleased." I reach across my horse's neck to shake hands. "So, you aiming to buy it?"

"Maybe." Raymond backs his horse. "Depends on if we get it surveyed before I get called back. Just brought in a survivor from a raided wagon train. Probably twenty dead."

I whistle. That's bad. Practically a massacre. "Abernathy?"

"Yup. We're getting close, Jesse, but there's still plenty to do."

The surveyor is paying keen attention to our conversation.

I scratch at my hairline. "I reckon. Look—if I'm remembering this piece of land, you're still half a day's ride away. Why don't you bunk here for the night? Toss a couple cattle, eat well. Get a fresh start tomorrow."

"What do you say, Gable?"

"Whatever you like," the man defers. "I am here to work, but I'll admit I have never seen a cattle operation up close."

"Come on, Raymond."

He glances at the lean surveyor, and I see in his face the moment he relents. "Very well."

Raymond dismounts and leads his horse off toward the pens where Rosamund watches.

I turn to Gable. "Come along! If you've never seen one of these operations before, it's bound to be interesting."

I trot back to the pens.

"All right, head them off, that's enough for now!"

A couple hands run over and shut the gate on the branding pen. Archer is inside, sorting, and I can't say what pleasure it gives me to see him eating dust with the rest of us. One of the hands makes a throw and drags out a strapping bull calf.

They pin him quick, slap a brand on, and he's up, dashing back to the herd. Once he gets there, he shakes himself off as if to rid himself of a bad association.

"Does it hurt them?" Gable's studying the process closely.

"Not much. They're single-minded beasts and they'll forget it fast."

"It's quite the herd you have."

"Thank you. Some of it belongs to that feller there, but since he's become a servant of the people, I'm running the outfit."

"The governor?" He sounds awed.

"Yep. My cousin. That one there in the blue shirt."

"You don't say." He shakes his head in wonder.

"Now, if you'll excuse me, I'd best get back in there before they accuse me of not doing my share."

He lets me go with a laugh.

"All right!" I swing over the fence and drop down. "This ain't a social, get them cows moving!"

I'M bent over a particularly brawny bull calf that's giving me a time of it. I straighten and let him up, and he aims a kick at me for good measure.

I look up and see Raymond watching, amusement in his eyes.

"Come on, Raymond, you come in here and try this."

He chuckles, low. "I'm getting enough enjoyment just out of seeing you sweat."

"Trust me, it's more fun in here."

"Come on, Marshal, try it!" shouts one the men, and it catches on.

"Marshal! Marshal!" the men chant. I haven't seen them enjoy themselves this much in ages.

Raymond's mouth gives a twist and he slowly sheds his jacket.

A cheer erupts.

One of the men drags a calf in with a whoop and Raymond wades in, deftly flipping it onto its side and pinning its neck.

"Are you a lawman or a cowpuncher?" shouts one of my hands, enjoying himself.

Gable is leaning against the rail, watching.

"Come on!" I wave him over. "Get in here and join us!"

He hesitates and looks around as if imagining I must be talking to someone else. When I keep waving, he takes off his jacket and vest and hangs them neatly over the top rail of the fence.

"Tenderfoot!" shouts one of my men.

Gable gives a sheepish smile and rolls up his sleeves. The hands whoop and shout appreciatively.

The next calf is a squirmy, quick-moving little thing. It takes Gable a moment to get his hands on her, but then he pitches her, deft and gentle as a mother.

"Who's the tenderfoot now?" laughs one of the hands to the other.

"I have no experience with cattle," Gable says with a shy smile, "but my uncle had sheep."

As far as I'm concerned, he's proven himself.

After that we all pitch in, laughing and roping and holding down calves until we're sweat-soaked and worn out.

It's nearing supper time.

I lean back and bawl, "All right, last set for today!" The men cheer and set to it with a will.

"Sir?" One of them comes up, twisting his glove in his hand.

"What is it?" I push my hat back and take advantage of the pause to scratch my head.

He nods toward the far end of the corral.

A stranger stands there, watching us. He's a hulk of a man, wearing a heavy, grease-stained green coat, and he has so much hair I can hardly see the face beneath the low brim of his hat. Behind him stand a scrubby-looking horse and a pack mule.

He's a mountain man, no doubt about it.

"Can I help you?" I ask, approaching him. Behind me laughs and whoops arise, probably as a steer breaks loose on someone.

"I remember when this place was empty. No ranch houses, no scrubby cattle knocking down good brush with their horns, no young men thinking themselves better than they were. This land used to teach young men like that a lesson. Now look."

His lip curls as he takes in my clothes. I wear good cloth and not bits of patchy animal skins, if that's what he means. But I was born on this land.

I figure it's best not to be offended on first acquaintance. I hold out my hand and smile. "There's good grub at the house. You're welcome to share it with us. There's more than enough."

He grunts. "I'll take it, but that ain't what I'm looking for."

"What is it, then?"

"I'll tell you. By and by. After I get some of that grub."

I glance back at the last bunch. There's only a dozen left.

"Howard, take this guest up to the house, he can—use the washhouse if he wants. I'll be in shortly."

From the look poor Howard gives me, I think he'd rather do all twelve of them steers on his own, but he says nothing, just heads towards the house, the strange guest in tow.

"Who's that?" Archer's leaning on the fence, one boot up.

"I don't know. Some trapper down from the mountains, I reckon."

I look back at the pens and the happy scene's gone sour somehow. I've got a funny feeling in my chest.

"Looks it. Otherwise you're taking in a grizzly."

I laugh briefly. "Sure hope not."

"Y'know, Jesse, I've missed this." Archer waves towards the milling cattle. "More than I thought I would. It's hard work, but I love it."

"Wish we could trade for a day."

He looks over at me, his eyebrows raised.

"Just—just a day." I grin. "Don't you get ideas."

Archer laughs. "I've never heard you complain about the ranching life before, Jesse."

I drape my arms over the rails of the pen, shove my hat back and remember, suddenly, how it felt to be a young sprout and watch my father drive the cattle in.

"I've never felt it before."

I'VE ALMOST SHAKEN off the feel of the mountain man's glower as we tramp up to the washhouse. We're covered in sweat and dust, and even with the army of washbasins and towels I instructed to be laid out, I know we don't ever get it all. Horse and cattle don't come off that easy.

I see the surveyor scrubbing his hands meticulously with a bar of soap, while at his side, one of my cowboys merely dips his hands, wets his neck, and dries his hands on his dirty jeans.

"Did I mention I forgot how good that felt?" says Archer, rubbing his neck with a towel.

He's missing the wide-open spaces, same as I would in his place.

The cook is out banging a pot with a spoon—not like we need the encouragement. I give my hands a vigorous drying and look down the line. "Hurry it up, men. I can smell that food!"

The ranch house looks homey in the dimming light. Rosamund is on the porch, waiting for Archer. Again, for just a moment, I remember being very young, when it was my mother waiting there.

Rosamund reaches out to take Archer's hand as he mounts the steps, and he kisses her softly on the cheek as they go in together.

They look happy.

The food is a spread worthy of a day's hard work. Thick slabs of beef that take up half the plate, mountains of greens and roasted potatoes, stacks of bread, rows of pies, a pot of beans so deep you'd drown if you fell in.

There's no talk, just the deafening sound of men moving quickly, the serving spoons and forks clanking as the men shovel the food into their mouths as if it's their last meal.

Archer and Rosamund sit together at the head of the table, eating and talking quietly together. Archer says something to make her laugh, and I swear, the lamps burn brighter when she laughs, her smile is so bright.

"Come back for more, there's plenty!" calls the cook, and a general cheer rises. Seconds and thirds go without saying, but cowhands are pretty uncomplicated and they'll cheer at any mention of food, even expected food.

The door flies open and slams against the wall.

The deafening room goes dead silent. It's that trapper. For a happy few minutes, I'd forgotten about him.

Beside me, I feel Raymond go very still. I've seen wild-cats do it—walking simple-like one moment, and the next, they're a hunter.

"Well," the stranger says, slowly, loudly. "I came down from the mountains to seek men and all I see are boys."

One of the hands has the gumption to laugh, just a bit breathless. The man has an unsheathed axe stuck in his belt, gun holsters over both hips, and a rifle in one hand. He doesn't look like a man who's come to eat. If he's washed, I can't tell the difference.

"I heard tell the gov'ner himself was coming to this here rowdy to-do."

"And what of it?" I answer, before Archer can react. He may be the governor, but this is my ranch and I will take responsibility for the rude vagrants that come onto my property.

"I came down to see men," he repeats. "And not a one of you—" He pauses, noting Raymond's face, and doesn't go on. "I want food."

"There's food." I shake my thumb over my shoulder in the right direction. "Help yourself."

He does. A plateful so high and so mixed together that I, a hardened man used to wilderness food and making do, can barely look at and keep my appetite.

The men eat in silence, like cowed dogs.

But Archer and Raymond and I don't, and neither does Rosamund. We watch him quietly, prepared for trouble.

He eats until the food is gone, and then he licks his plate.

He leans back and belches.

"I'll tell you what I want." He looks around at all of us. A muscle twitches in Archer's cheek. "I came here to look the man who calls himself gov'ner of the territory in the face and see what kind of man he is. I figure it's got to be one of you on that end of the table." He waves vaguely and dismissively at our end, where Archer and Rosamund sit.

"That would be me," says Archer.

"Huh." The trapper guffaws. "Should have known. You have a soft face, just like the rest of these boys."

No one in their right mind could fairly apply "soft face" to my cousin Archer. Sure, he's not bad to look at, but he's as trail-weathered as any of us—more, probably. This man is just throwing insults.

"I'll not permit this under my roof," I say sternly, fixing the man with a hard look. "You do not come as a guest and insult my kin."

"Kin, eh?" He wipes his mouth on the back of his sleeve.

"I'm giving you just enough time to get yourself on out of here. I fed you, and this is how you treat my guests?"

"You invited me in. I ain't moving."

"Does this mean anything?" I touch my gun on my hip.

He just laughs. "Well, son, look here. If you want me gone, how about you and I have ourselves a little shooting match? You win, I leave. I win, you come up to my place for a couple of days and I'll show you what a real man's work looks like."

"I don't have to do anything of the sort."

"Then prove me wrong."

I let my breath out hard. I'm angry now. "I'll do that."

He grins and rises from the table like a bear, sending his silverware clattering.

We go outside to an empty corral at the edge of the ranch yard and I gesture to a couple of the cowhands who follow us out to set up a few tin cans on the top rail.

"Cans are too big," the trapper grunts.

"We'll stand back then," I say.

"Set up six of 'em," he orders, as if the place is his. "We'll each try."

I draw my gun and feed a bullet into the chamber. "Guests first."

"Don't mind if I do." He spits into the dirt, wipes his mouth, and pulls his rifle up to his shoulder, cocking it.

The air explodes with the sound. One tin can goes flying.

One by one, all six of his bullets hit their mark.

"Try that," he smiles, blowing at the muzzle of his rifle.

I don't answer him. I step up to the mark, take a deep breath, and fire. Again and again. All six go flying.

He grunts. I'm not sure if he's impressed or bothered.

"Again," he demands, reloading his rifle.

I nod to my hand to go ahead.

The cans are hardly back up when the trapper lifts his rifle and shoots, sending my hand diving for cover.

"Easy, now! You shoot someone, the marshal's just inside."

He just guffaws and takes aim again.

Again, he hits every mark.

I finish reloading and fire swiftly, one after another. All six cans fall.

"Call it square?" I ask, shoving my hat back on my head. It's getting towards dusk. We're starting to lose the light, and my feet and eyes are sore after a long day of dust and sorting cattle.

"No," he growls. "Set it up again."

"Listen, you shoot near my cowhand again and it's over."

He grunts noncommittally, but he waits until the man is clear before cocking and taking aim. With frightening regularity, he nails each target again.

I sniff and stretch my neck before taking careful aim.

I hit five, swiftly, and the sixth stands—shaking, but it stands.

The trapper gives a slow laugh. "Well, son, I think you're beat."

I sigh, swallow my pride, and nod.

"Well, I've seen all I need to see. Now, are you coming up to my place or will I have to drag you with me?"

"I have things that need finishing up here. It might be a few days before I can spare the time."

His face darkens. "I say you come and come now."

"Look, I'll give you my word. Let me finish my work, and I'll keep my side of the bargain."

"How do I know you will?"

"It's called integrity."

"Integrity?" he snorts.

"Do you want something of mine as a pledge?" I take out my pocketwatch and hold it out. "Here."

He hesitates and rubs his beard, looking at me slowly. "You'll come?"

"I said I would." The words are dry as sawdust in my mouth.

"Keep your watch, son. I'll see you in the mountains." He trudges past me and heads for the barn.

He leaves that night.

THOUGH I AM TIRED, I don't sleep well. I toss and turn until the rooster crows outside, thin and defiant.

A soft knock, and my door creaks open.

"Jesse."

I roll over and squint. Raymond's face is covered in shadow, but I'd know his voice and his frame anywhere. A lantern is lit somewhere behind him.

"Jesse, I'd watch your back. I don't like the look of that man."

"I'll mind that."

The door shuts and it is dark again.

Hooves pound out of the yard a couple minutes later.

6

GABLE

The land Marshal Lacey is looking at is more than fine. It's a piece of highland with some valley connected, and it's one of the greenest spots of earth I've ever seen. I'd buy it in a heartbeat if I could.

"What do you think?" Marshal Lacey reins in his horse and leans on his saddle horn, surveying the land before us.

"You have an eye for land," I say. "And I promise, I don't say that to everyone."

"I thought it was pretty myself."

He's modest.

"Where does the line start?"

"Oh, I reckon about at that creek there." He points out a shining band of silver. "Everything west of that bend there isn't claimed."

"Who was the fool that stopped there?" I dismount and begin to unstrap my tripod.

"Probably someone who bought it sight unseen."

"Well, this won't take too long." I unbuckle the straps with fingers that don't need to think. I've done this part a thousand times, and any nervousness I felt in accompanying Marshal Lacey is melting away into the familiarity of my work.

My horse shifts away, not paying attention to me, its ears flicking north.

An ear-splitting crack. Something whines past my head.

The horse bolts.

"Gable, get down!"

I throw myself to the ground behind a rock as bullets whiz overhead. One hits the rocks above me, sending stinging pieces raining down.

I'm panting and there's dust in my mouth.

"You hurt?" Raymond crawls over to me.

"No, Marshal, just shaken up a mite."

"Just call me Raymond. Everyone does." He's got a sparkle in his eye as if we haven't just been sprayed with rock shards from unfriendly fire.

"Raymond." For a moment, I almost smile.

"Here." He produces a second gun and pushes it across the dust to me. "Can you shoot?"

"Only a little." I'm embarrassed to admit it. Here I am in a life and death gunfight alongside the marshal of the Western Territory and I have to tell him I can barely handle a firearm.

"Ain't nothing to it. You've got the eye, you're a surveyor.

You cock it—" He swipes with the heel of his hand and I hear the click. "Then you aim and shoot. And you make sure you get a good look at him. Most gunfights are won by aim, not speed, no matter what the papers say."

"A good look at him," I repeat, closing my fingers over the pistol. It feels foreign and heavy in my hand.

"Just not too good of a look, hm?"

I stop short. And then I laugh, realizing he's joking.

Imagine that. Less than a week in Glory Mesa, and I'm joking about life and death behind a rock with the marshal.

"What are we going to do?" I ask. Something warm and tickling is running down my neck. I reach up and put my fingers in a bloody cut. It stings, but that's good. If I were badly hurt I'd feel more or less.

"Well, I reckon whoever it is, they're after me. It was clever, catching me out here with just one man."

"But—do you think we'll get out of here?"

He looks over at me sharply, and again I see a gleam of amusement in his eyes. Whatever he's looking for in my face, he doesn't seem to find it.

"I figure we will. If we're careful, we can get up behind those rocks there." He twists around partway to point out the slope above us. "From there, they'll have to expose them- selves to get a shot at us. Think you can make it up there?"

I glance at the spot again. "Sure." My answer sounds more hopeful than I feel.

"All right. I'm going to cover you. Run like you're afire and don't stop to shoot."

"Now?"

His pistol clicks in his hand. "Now."

I lurch to my feet and take off running with everything in me. The only thing I feel is the cold iron of the gun I'm gripping. I mustn't drop it.

I fling myself behind the rock and the gunfire registers in my ears. My hands are scraped, but all I feel in them is heat.

I cock the gun. "I'm up here!" I shout.

"All right. You just keep your head down!" Raymond shouts, and the gunfire starts again in earnest.

Seconds later, he tumbles into me, panting.

"Well, our chances are better now." He wipes the sweat off his face with his sleeve and takes off his hat.

"What now?"

He lifts his head above the rocks cautiously. "We have better ground. Much better ground. Those fools should have rushed us when they had the chance." He ducks out from under the strap of his canteen and sets it gently against the rock.

"We're going to wait them out. Either we'll make it until nightfall and leg it when we get the chance, or—if they're impatient—we might be able to pick them off."

"What if they rush us?"

Raymond is checking the ammunition in his belt. "Long as we aim careful, that won't be a problem. There's only four or five of them, and like I said, we've got the good ground."

And then I see the blood. It's running down the bottom

of his right sleeve, dripping into the spindly grass, turning the dirt dark red.

"Your arm."

He looks down, catches a little at the ripped sleeve, and his hand comes away smeared in blood.

"Is it bad?"

He doesn't answer right away. He's examining it carefully as the blood runs down his other hand.

"Can you reach into my coat?" he asks, slowly. "Left side pocket. There's a handkerchief."

I oblige him.

He's wiping his bloody left hand on the grass, his eyes on the ground below.

"They're not coming yet," he mutters, maybe to himself, perhaps to me.

"All right." He looks at me, his eyes grave, and unbuttons his sleeve. "I want you to wet the end of that handkerchief for me."

"Is there a bullet in there?"

"Naw, this is just a mean crease."

He pulls his sleeve up. I dampen the handkerchief and hand it over. He sponges out the wound quickly. The water makes it clear for a moment, and I see he's right.

"All right—" He shoves the handkerchief back into my hand. "Tie it over, and do it tight."

I roll it a couple times, lay it over the wound, and pull it tight.

"Tighter," he grunts.

I oblige, then tie it off.

"That'll hold for a bit, I reckon." He gives me a grim, sideways smile. He shifts back up into a crouching position and peers over the rocks.

"Now do we just watch?" I squint over the rocks. From our vantage point, the men below can't take a shot without exposing themselves.

Raymond nods. "And save your energy. We'll likely be watching a long time."

I move into a more comfortable position and shift my gun so that my body blocks it from the sun. It is growing hot to the touch.

It's too warm up in these rocks. I try to keep myself from thinking of the cool river or the soft green grass below us. I'd do just about anything right now for a drink of that cold, clear water.

Raymond takes off his hat to wipe his forehead again.

"Do you reckon they'll try anything?" I ask, looking down at the empty ground below.

"Not unless they're stupid."

My eyes go to his arm. "How about you rest a little? We'll take turns watching."

"I reckon that makes sense." He pulls the plug out of the canteen and takes a tiny swallow. "You tell me if anyone makes a move, you hear?"

"Sure thing."

He rolls over with a hiss, fumbling with his belt. He pulls

it out with one hand. "Help me get this around my neck, will you?"

I reach up, buckle it across his shoulder, and help him ease his arm through.

He gives a long sigh and adjusts his hat over his eyes.

I turn my gaze back to the rocks and wait. The heat is vicious and I'm pretty sure I've sweat as much as I can sweat. I wipe away a trickle that is running into my eye and settle in for a long afternoon.

This is a test.

I'm going to rise to it, not fail it.

RAYMOND SPELLS me after a couple hours. I can't really rest, but I try. Relief from the heat comes at last when the sun goes down.

"We're not going anywhere," says Raymond slowly, when dusk falls. "That moon's going to be shining brighter than a lamp and there's no cloud cover. You can shoot a man clean and quick on a night like this."

I swallow my disappointment. He's not going to see any of that from me. "So we just keep watching?"

"Unless they'll get bold or stupid."

I hope not. Even with the bright light of the full moon, the idea of someone creeping up the rocks toward us at night makes my skin crawl.

"I'll take the first watch," I volunteer. I couldn't sleep right now if I tried, exhausted as I am.

"If you like. You have any doubts at all, wake me." He slaps my arm and eases himself down.

The night is still and the moon lights the world like a silver lantern. I watch and pray that no one stirs. Somewhere a coyote or a wolf howls—I can't tell the difference yet—and something larger snuffs and grunts. I have no idea what it is. I check the watch in my vest now and then, and though I can feel every second as it passes, unique and clear, the hours fly past.

Raymond spells me at one-thirty, but it's a long time before I sleep.

THE RICH, slanting light of the sun over the rocks wakes me before Raymond does. My neck is as stiff as a board, and when I move, a sharp pain shoots through my back. Raymond is sitting as grave and still as a statue with the light streaming around him, his eyes fixed on the rocks where our attackers hide.

I reach up and brush the grit out of my eyes with a finger.

"Mornin'." Raymond doesn't look my way.

"Morning." My tongue feels thick and swollen. My mouth is as dry as this dust.

"Take just a swallow. Helps when you first wake up." Raymond jerks his head in the direction of the canteen, which lies between us.

I take my permitted swallow and let it trickle slowly

down my throat. I lick my lips; they are already dry and cracking.

When we get out of this, I will never again take water for granted.

"How is your arm?"

"Fine," he says. "Hungry?"

"Enough."

"Eat then. They're stirring a mite; we may get some action soon."

He says it as calmly as if he is predicting rain. A knot forms in my stomach, but I reach for the pouch of provisions anyway. If we do have a fight, I'll be grateful for the strength.

The jerky is hard, but I let it sit in my mouth until it softens. The slow eating seems to give me a strength I wouldn't feel at a normal breakfast.

Raymond's gun fires with a thunderous bang that fills the rocks and sends the report echoing ten times over.

I whirl up into place. There's a man down there dragging his leg, moving for cover, and four more dodging from cover to cover towards us.

I try a shot at one and miss. "They're coming on us!"

"Steady." Raymond reaches into his belt and feeds a bullet into his rifle. "Just take aim and fire easy."

I take a breath and do as he says. I almost wing the man before he dives for cover. Beside me, Raymond's gun goes off again.

Another man staggers, hit.

Raymond narrows his eyes against the sunlight. "Put

your sights on one of those open spots and you wait until one of them makes a run for it."

I nod. I can do that.

I aim my sights at a gap about six feet wide, watch it like a hawk. One of the fellows is up and running, and he flashes past like a deer.

My gun thunders and bucks in my hand and the man gives a jerk before tumbling into safety.

"Well done," says Raymond. I must have actually hit him.

"Thanks." The acrid smell of gunsmoke is in the air. I cough once or twice, trying not to make too much sound.

A bullet whines overhead. I give myself a moment to wipe the sweat out of my eyes and then I get back in position, looking over the valley.

And it almost takes my breath away.

I'm inches from death, and yet all I see is the poetry of it: the dust from the spent bullets rising in the golden light of morning, the smoke from the guns hanging on the air over the rocks like mist, the green, beautiful land cut down the center with a golden stream.

The land we are, in a way, fighting for.

Raymond breathes heavily during the pause and leans his rifle against the rocks for a moment to adjust the belt around his neck. That arm must be bothering him awfully, but he's not showing it.

Nothing is showing on that iron face except the sweat trickling down it.

The air erupts with a string of six, ten shots maybe. The men below us whirl and shoot sideways, and then—just like that—they're down. Dead, I think.

A lone rider trots up below, leading a string of three horses. One hand is raised, and the other holds both rein and shotgun.

"Hold your fire, it's a friend!" he shouts.

"Who are you?"

"No friend of theirs." He waves to us with a lazy arm. "Come on down! That was the last of them."

Raymond heaves himself up leaning on his rifle before I can even offer to give him a hand. "Follow on behind and don't set that pistol down."

He starts down the rocks carefully, picking his way downward without hands. I glance toward the outlaws who had us pinned.

They are definitely dead.

I wish I hadn't looked, but I suppose I must get used to it.

The man who has come to our rescue is tall and lean, with a weathered face and narrow eyes as if he's looked at the sun most of his life. It seems to me I've seen him before, or someone like him.

"See you found our horses." Raymond gestures with the rifle.

"They're yours, hm?"

For a second, there's a strong silence, hard as a rock between them.

Then the newcomer reaches down and unties the rope

from his pommel. "It's your lucky day then." He tosses the rope over, and I start forward, barely catch it in time. Raymond doesn't have a hand free.

"Thanks." Raymond goes around to his horse and thrusts the rifle into the empty sheath behind the saddle. "You want to follow back into town?"

"Nah, just passin' through."

"You sure? There's probably more out there, and I saw you—you were heading Glory Mesa way."

"Well, you see, I'm not sure the law wants me in town. I ain't got no reward out or anything, but I just got out of prison."

"I'm the law." Raymond thrusts out his lean hand. "Marshal Raymond Lacey."

"Don't say." The man dusts off his hand and takes it. "In that case, I suppose there's no harm in riding in with you."

"Reckon not." A smile hitches up one side of the marshal's mouth as heaves into the saddle.

Out here, I suppose the line between life and death is as thin as a string. The two others seem unbothered by the swift change in our fortune, but I—I'm suddenly so relieved I can hardly stand.

7

IRENE

AT FIRST, I CAN'T TELL WHAT THE STIR IS. EVERYONE IS lining the boardwalks on Main Street, blocking the hot, dusty street from view.

I almost turn away. I've had too much excitement; I shouldn't go looking for more.

But I am also desperate for something—anything—to keep my hands busy and my mind off my grief. The little house the marshal found for me to stay in was neat and needed almost no cleaning. And I have little appetite at present.

I step up behind the gathering crowd and lift my head to see over their shoulders into the street.

It's the marshal, riding cool and easy, one arm cradled in a belt from his neck. The sleeve's torn away on that arm and there is a bloodstained bandage tied over it. Two other men are with him, both tall, but one of them has a hard face, like

72

he's done nothing but work in the sun for years, and the other looks simply bent, dirty, and tired.

I strain to listen to the talk as they rein in outside the governor's office.

"What happened?"

"Attacked by a few outlaws." Marshal Lacey's taciturn reply.

"Where? On the way in?"

"No, out on a claim spread. Nothing particular, only they knew somehow we'd be there." A murmur runs quickly through the crowd.

"Come on," he says to the man with the hard face, and ducks into the governor's office. The talk raises in volume. Questions are put to the third man, who looks sorely in need of a bath and rest.

"It happened so fast," he's saying in a soft, gentle sort of voice. He looks uncertain—a newcomer, perhaps, like myself. "No, I didn't really get a look." He scratches his bearded jaw. "Well, even if I did, I can't tell them apart."

He looks sheepish.

"You need a drink, man," calls someone in the crowd.

"Come on, wet your throat and tell us all about it," calls another.

He's protesting lightly—anyone should be able to see he's exhausted to the point of dropping—when a voice cuts through the crowd.

"Lesley!"

A beautiful, dark-haired woman runs through the crowd,

heedless of the people in her way. "My darling, are you all right?"

He catches her in his arms, lets her look at his face, then leans all the way down to kiss her. "Not hurt," he says gently.

The crowd begins to disperse. They've lost their chance at a story for the moment.

"When they said what happened—I felt so sure that you were the one hurt."

He reaches out and wipes away a tear from her face with his thumb.

"I'd have come back to you anyway," he says. "Don't doubt that."

I leave them then and follow the crowd's dispersal. This time, it seems, tragedy was averted, but my own is so fresh and keen in my mind that tears come to my eyes.

I wonder what she would have done, that beautiful dark woman, if they had brought him in over his saddle?

THE FULL STORY makes its rounds the next morning, as news does. Ambushed while looking at ranch land, trapped behind rocks for a day and a half, their last stand happened upon by one Britt April, an ex-convict who is now welcomed into town by the marshal himself, despite the mood of the town being clearly suspicious.

Marshal Lacey, it is clear, is a man of authority. The outlaws hate him for it, but the marshal says the man whom everyone hates is the one who will stick around, and he does.

That's the kind of person who makes me believe in Glory Mesa. This isn't someone's crazy dream that will fly away on the wind when trouble strikes. This place is here to stay.

I spend all morning baking and cooking. Finally I have some direction, a thing to do—albeit only for a few hours inside a long day, inside weeks and months to come.

Mr. Trasker is so kind as to point out the marshal's home, a small but well-built little green house a block past my own temporary place.

And I go, with my arms loaded.

On the doorstep, I knock, stand back, and wait. When the door opens, Marshal Lacey is still wearing boots, but no hat, and a white sling obscures most of his blue shirt.

"What's this?" There's a note of surprise in his voice.

"I came to see how you were getting on with that arm, and I brought—I brought some food."

"Why, that's mighty nice of you." He reaches out with his good hand for the pan and realizes how much I've brought.

"I'm sorry," I apologize, laughing in my embarrassment. I have a basket over one arm, a package under the other, and the pan in my hands.

"It's all right." It's amusement in his eyes now. "Come on in for a moment. You can set all this down."

"Thank you."

He holds the door for me and I step in. It's a neat, clean house, and the table is decorated with a tablecloth and a vase of cut flowers.

"My sister keeps this place looking civilized." He waves toward the table, the plates that hang on the wall, and a painting of an old white house. "She tells me I've got to go and get myself married one of these days or I won't survive."

I laugh and deposit the pan, the basket, and the package all on the table. "There's a chicken here, and preserves and a cake in the basket. Here's the bread, and some soup and some greens."

"You sure brought a lot. I'm obliged. You didn't need to."

But I did.

"I wanted to. What you did for me was—this is a thank-you, really. I felt—I wanted you to know how much your kindness meant. It was one of the worst days of my life."

"What I did was my job," he says gently.

"But—I'm very grateful." My thankless voice deserts me.

"Have a seat for a moment." He pulls out a chair with his good hand and then pulls out another for himself. "Those men are thieves and killers, and I am trying to root them out, not simply because they exist to be conquered, but because of people like you. You shouldn't have to feel like you owe me anything. It's enough that it happened to you. I don't want you living with any more burden than that."

I look at his face.

It's the first real look I have had at him when I wasn't mad with grief. He's handsome—not in a pretty way, but in a lean, well-made way. A face that would look just as fine whether he was smiling or angry or stern.

"Thank you," I say. He's being so gentle that I wish I

could just say yes and move on, but I want him to understand. "I wanted to be grateful. It's—" I compose myself carefully. I've been almost well today, and yet the grief rises so hard as I try to speak. "It's better than having nothing to be at all."

He nods, moves his hand toward mine in an understanding gesture. "Very well."

I stand up, mustering a smile, a real one. "Thank you for understanding, Marshal."

He just nods.

I STEP down from his porch a different woman than stepped onto it. I had been searching for something, someone to be when I came. Now there's a strange, dear warmth in my chest, something I hold onto like it's precious.

I'm still here, and I want to be myself again, and that's enough. It's enough to keep going on.

As I return to my house, I see the tall, weary surveyor standing out behind his place, tin cans set up along the water trough. He's in his suspenders and shirtsleeves, the sleeves rolled up. Even from here, I can see a long patch of scraped skin down one forearm.

He takes aim with a pistol, and the first piece of tin flies into the air with a sharp clang.

8

SELBY

IT'S A DESERT EVENING, DRY AND BRIGHT AND EVERY color known to nature. As much as my young, hot heart once hated warm, peaceful evenings, I find I look forward to nothing more these days.

Below me, the sheep graze, contented, shaking their heads over the tufts of grass they must wrestle from the ground. A couple have already come close to the cave and are lying with their legs tucked beneath them. Smoke from the shepherds' fire reaches me, envelops me for a moment, and moves on.

"Hey you, gunman!" The apprentice shepherd cups his hands to his mouth and shouts, "Supper is hot!"

I lift a hand so he knows I heard. They always tell me, but none of them has any grief if I come late and take my portion last.

From up here, I can see everything. The rocks are like

boats at harbor, moored among the swirling dust and cacti. Beyond our strange rocks and flatlands and *isark* breeding grounds rise the purple mountains. I have never been over them, and on these evenings, I think to myself what it would be like to cross them and live beyond. Perhaps I will, someday.

The smell of food and chickory coffee reaches my nose. They'll be moving the sheep in soon, and with the fading light, the *isarks* will be seeking shelter, not roaming about.

I draw my legs up under me and stand on the edge of the rock. It's a strange feeling to be here, only a few inches' difference between life and death, to be used to it.

I start on down.

I BUILD a fire away from the shepherds and take my ration over there. It's easier to keep watch when I'm away from their low stream of chatter, and they are still happier if I don't have much to do with them.

I've only begun to eat the mutton when the dog starts up, barking at the dim light. There's a horse and a man coming this way. He ties the horse to the sheep pen (no regard for safety) and comes over.

"Do you have a Jack Selby here?" His voice is loud in the stillness of the evening.

The shepherds go silent and their hands point like accusers in my direction. I stand up slowly, my hand inching toward my iron at my side.

"Jack, no need to be jumpy. It's me, Stanton. I own a spread northwest of here?"

"I remember." I let out my breath, let my hand fall away from my gun. I'm not overly fond of the man, but he's no threat.

"Can I share your fire?"

I just move aside and he takes that as an invitation.

"Been down Glory Mesa way?" he asks.

"Not since last summer."

"Missed a lot of to-do. That marshal, he had a right proper trial—tried and hung twenty men. They say he's got the fist of justice. And he's going after Abernathy's leftovers —oh, pardon."

I don't answer. As if he thinks I still care anything for that old part of my life.

He doesn't know what to do with my silence, so he plunges on.

"And you probably heard that Harrison Terhune was tried for trying to kill Rosamund Lacey."

"News came up to that effect. He was trying all last summer."

"Well, he got let go, after all that. Governor's wife spoke up to the effect that he was under duress, and seeing as he didn't do nothing, he got away with his neck and a promise not to meddle. Licking his wounds back home, I hear."

I did not invite this man to my fire for gossip, nor did he come for it. He likes me just as little as I like him. He wants something, and I wish he'd come to the point.

"Terhune was an idiot," he says with conviction.

"No, he was a clever man. I watched him for a summer." I pluck a couple stray pieces of grass and wind them around my fingers. "He simply chose the wrong side. A man's lucky if he does it and gets himself another chance."

"Speaking of that," Stanton breaks in. He's been waiting for a chance to broach whatever subject brought him here. "I am looking to hire a rifleman."

"You had words for Archer Scott last year when he hired me to track Mortimer. Did you forget those?"

"No." Stanton scratches the side of his head. "I didn't say I liked you."

"But you said you couldn't ever trust a man who'd fought on the wrong side of the war. Or did time for riding with Abernathy."

"Times are changing," he admits, leaning over to spit. "And you're the best shot I know."

"If you're thinking it's because I don't care who I shoot, you're wrong."

He scowls, but I know I'm right. When you see men at their highest points and lowest, you get so you can read a face, the line of their shoulders.

"You'd only be shooting those who asked for it," he continues, "We're going into a drought season and I need my water holes guarded."

"Shooting men over water has never been a good idea." I draw my knee up and rest my arm over it. "I thought you'd know that, Stanton."

"This isn't a time for what we like, Selby. We're coming up on desperate times."

"A principle isn't a principle if it gets thrown out in desperate times."

"Enough with that," he snarls. "You have no place to be talking to me like that."

I shrug, toss the grass into the fire.

"I'll pay you well. Really well. Enough that you can leave the territory if you want. Go anywhere."

I leave the silence between us, listen to the night sounds. Mostly friendly sounds—a cricket, a night bird, the breathing of the sheep.

One summer of this, and I could leave, go over the mountains, be my own man. Instead of shooting *isarks* year after year, avoiding the shepherds, eating their leavings, on and on, until my dream fades and dies with one bad shot from an indiscriminate tenderfoot.

But it's a temptation without teeth. If I'd wanted things the easy way, there'd have been a hundred lives better than this.

"Well?" It's the quietest I've heard him speak.

"I'm going to have to turn you down."

"I'll give you more. Has Terhune asked you already? Thatcher?"

I shake my head.

"If you take up someone else's offer, I'll make sure there's not a safe place you can hide."

I smile, slightly. His threats are just like any other cattle baron's.

"Rest assured, I am doing no one's killing for them."

He stiffens at my wording.

"Then goodnight," he spits out between his clenched teeth.

"Goodnight. Safe journey."

He doesn't answer. I watch him over the top of my fire as he collects his horse and rides off into the night. It's a pity that even when you run to the furthest corners of the earth, you find men like that.

But it's a disease, and it comes from inside.

Only a few of us are lucky enough to have it knocked out of us, and then we're called the unlucky ones.

9

THATCHER

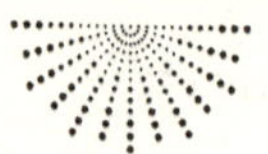

I WAKE TO THE HIGH, STEADY SOUND OF RAINFALL AND the swift drip of the water running off the shed's roof. Somewhere along its eaves, a metal bucket is in the way, and I can hear the dull *pang* as the rain hits it in a strange rhythm.

In my dream, I had been back in my bed at the ranch, under a real quilt, not in this forsaken spot halfway into the middle of nowhere.

I rub the sleep out of my eyes and shove my bedroll back. It's still darkish outside—the time of morning that would be showing the first rays of dawn, but for the storm clouds hanging dark and blue over us.

My horse stirs, shifting in the straw. It's all old and moldy, but he doesn't care. He's probably tried eating it, knowing him.

I bend down to roll my bedroll and sneeze hard.

I get my gear on my pinto's back and stump outside to see the day.

It's raining steady, perhaps a grumble of thunder here and there, but it ain't got too much bite to it.

Still, it's too wet to revive the fire I made in the dirt yard. The whole place, abandoned, run-down, looks sadder in the rain, and I wonder who the poor fool was who built this place and was gone from it so swiftly.

Anything can happen to a man out here.

The mountains are still a ways off. I almost thought I'd overtake the trapper with his pack animal, as I ride quick and light. But I haven't seen him, and that's powerful strange.

The mountains are mockers. They stay right there in your sights, never getting closer. I'm tired to my bones, and it's not trail-weariness.

The pinto has wandered out on his own and is picking at the stringy grass growing beside the shed. He ambles past me, unconcerned, and settles on the real grass ten yards out.

Well, there'll be no fire, so I might as well just ride.

I reach over and take my slicker off the saddle, thrust my arms in. Even just some canvas between me and the rain feels better.

I pull the reins up, and the pinto pulls against me in protest. I mount and reach into my saddlebag for some jerky.

He hops. I curse his fool head and leave the jerky be.

I move him off into a canter and he crow-hops and protests all the way across that rain-drenched field.

. . .

WE'RE MOVING FINE an hour out, and I'm finally eating—all these ponies come round after proving their wild streak in the mornings—when he plants his feet and goes bolt stiff, neck up, ears forward.

There's another rider, streaking across the plain. There's something strange about the way they're riding, and I puzzle it in my rain-dulled head a moment.

It's a woman.

By herself, riding like the devil was on her heels.

For a moment, I contemplate going after her, but that horse is quicker than a hare. Likely got some Auki stock, from the reach and set of the hindquarters.

She's gone in a matter of minutes, and the rain swallows up the dull thud of the hooves.

As if she'd never been. As if she was just a dream.

10

ALAN

Thunder rolls over the distant hill in dark clouds, low and threatening. The air is charged with electricity. The cows are bunched together, nervous, ready to bolt.

The rain is light and misting over us in sheets. It's no easier to see through it than through the dust.

In this territory, you never win.

"Ho!" Max calls, long and soothing. "Easy, cattle."

We're keeping them in with loose lariats swung along the edges, moving them forward, keeping their mind on moving, not bolting.

But all we need is one good crack of lightning and we'll have a stampede on our hands.

My slicker is buttoned up to my neck against the rain, the rope rough and slippery in my fingers. The wind presses and then retreats and tries again from another angle. If I was a cow, I'd be jumpy too.

I reach up and tighten my hat string, just in case. Max is up ahead, and I'm thinking he didn't put the strings I gave him on his hat. He says it ruins the look.

Trust me, he'll mind more when he loses it again in a strong wind.

Thunder cracks ahead, rolls down like an avalanche toward us, filling our ears. A flash of light sears the sky above us.

"Easy, cattle!" echoes from a dozen throats.

I feel it before it hits—the tightness, the wave rising like a shudder through the herd. It breaks, and we've lost them.

"Stampede!" Jem bellows from behind. The cows lunge forward and in the flashing rain I see Max bent over the neck of his pony, flying in a race for the lead. There's no chance I'd reach the head from my position; I wish him godspeed.

The rumble of hooves rivals the thunder. They seem to egg each other on. I hang on tight to my pony's slick back and keep at the side of the herd, bunching them in.

"Turn 'em!" someone is bawling, a thin sound above the heavy race of hooves. The cows begin to lean on my point as one. Max is turning them.

I keep my pony angling along, giving a little, pushing a little, keeping the cattle together. The world races in a rock-ing, flowing motion, so swift that time blurs and turns slow.

I'm seeing rocks flying through the air like ash, fire raining from the sky, and a world of black, scorched to the bare earth.

A roar drowns out all sound until all sound is gone and there is only silence—thin, piercing silence.

And I am there, alone. It's the end of the world.

The rain rises to my face as a steer slams into my pony and I'm jolted half out of the saddle. The vision is gone.

I grab a fistful of mane, twist it into my hand, and use it, with the slippery leather, to haul myself upright.

"Hyah!" I'm getting out before the cattle close in on me again.

We ride the herd out until they've settled. The storm broke hard and fast and blew itself out. Rain pelts us again, unpleasant, but nothing to the storm.

"Close one, Alan?" Max canters by, his form ghostly in the drizzle.

"Close one. Almost left you boys my third of the ranch."

"Naw, you're too good to die from a stampede. And that mare's too canny." He slaps my shoulder, his horse brushing against my chaps.

"You turned them."

I can see him better now that he's beside me, his fair hair plastered against his forehead, the rain running down his face. He's gone and lost his hat.

"Sure did."

"And your hat's gone. Didn't I tell you to put stampede strings on it?"

"I didn't want holes." He's grinning. When you cheat death like that, you laugh and nothing bothers you for a spell.

"Well, you'll have to get a new one. That one's probably in a thousand pieces."

"More'n likely. Hey, they're getting up a fire a half mile back. You want someone to spell you so you can grab something hot?"

"May as well, I just—" He's turned and loped off into the rain before I can finish.

Jem's looking at me sharp over the fire. Between us, deaf to our talk, is the cook, banging away with his pot, stirring the fire, keeping things going in the rain as only a good trail cook can.

"I saw you almost lost your pony." Jem's voice is gruff.

"Nearly."

"You're not rattled, are you?"

"It rattled me," Max volunteers with a laugh.

Jem hushes him.

"No, I'm fine." I flash a quick grin over the fire.

It isn't as if I'm done in or it'll keep me from work. Nor is there anything to say about it. I had a strange vision, and there's no place for it in my mind that I can think of.

Perhaps I just dream things. I wouldn't be the first.

I just can't shake this one yet, is all.

11

NEWTON

It's a strange feeling to stand in a place so familiar to yourself and speak to a stranger who is so at home in it as well.

There's a clock on the mantel, its ticking the only sound in the room as I take off my hat and shake hands with Marshal Lacey. He's made the old Miller place look downright civilized, which I never thought possible. Miller was a scoundrel, but he also killed more scaled varmints than any man I know. And, if you believe the charter documents, he helped found the town.

"Look, Chris, I'm going to be short and to the point." The marshal gestures to a seat across from him. "I've run myself into a little slow-down, and I need a man I can trust to keep an eye on things for the next week or so, including a nest of outlaws south of here."

"And you are asking me?"

91

"Yep."

"You don't even know me."

"Your reputation precedes you, Mr. Newton. I know you weren't in the territory last year when things were hot, but you're no stranger to the land or the folk in it. Ask anyone here, and you're pretty near the top of the list of men they'd trust with their town."

"I know," I chuckle. "They tried to rope me into your position a time or two."

"I'm asking for just a couple weeks."

"I'm honored, Marshal, that you'd think of me. I really am. But I respect you enough to not draw out what I've already set my mind on." My ranch has done without me long enough, and even two weeks' delay seems unbearable. I'm starved for the clean pine air, for the land that I belong to. I want to drink again from my own clear springs that taste like nothing else.

"I understand."

"If the time comes in the future when you need me again, I'll come."

"That's more than fair." He stands up. "Well, I appreciate your time."

"Marshal Lacey!" Someone bangs on the door and it flies open. It's Peter, the errand boy from the saloon, his cheeks flushed and his thick hair windblown.

"Marshal Lacey, there's a big fight down at the saloon. Kate said to come get you before everything gets smashed!"

"Who's in it?" The marshal stands up and reaches for the rifle over the door.

"It's the Aprils against everybody else." He grins. "But I think everybody else started it."

"All right."

I follow them into the street. The April boys are a couple of rowdy cowpunchers who made their names a few years back when they broke an untamable bronc and again when one of them killed a man. There was reasonable evidence for self-defense, so Britt went to prison on the Eastern-Western Territory border and Buck disappeared.

Seems they're back in town.

The sounds of the fight reach my ears before we've even turned the corner of the block—the crash of splintering wood and glass, the uncertain shuffle of stirred-up horses at the rail.

As we near the building, someone stumbles backwards out the door and falls on his back. He's got a mark on his face that's going to be quite the bruise in a few hours.

"Easy son, easy," rumbles Marshal Lacey, running up the steps to the saloon. "You just stay right there."

He pushes in between the swinging doors. "All right!" He bawls in a voice that silences the room. "What's this about?"

Britt April's got a man by the collar. He lets him slide to the floor like a dog relinquishing a bone. Buck collects his bony frame from the floor and gets slowly to his feet.

"I'm sorry, Marshal," he says, taking a rather shaky step forward. "I tried not to have a fight."

"We were just standing up for ourselves," says Britt, sounding considerably less contrite.

Lacey's eyes flick to Kate, who had the presence of mind to move the spirits under the bar and is already putting them back on their shelves with utter calm.

She nods.

"Who started it?" Lacey's face is like flint, but his voice is neutral.

There's an uncomfortable silence and the sound of boots dragging slowly against the floor. Without a word, Buck points to a figure sprawled in the corner.

"Jacks Hodge," Kate says, with whatever the opposite of good humor is. "About smashed his glass in Britt's face."

"Was there call?"

"No."

"Well, boys...." The marshal gives a sigh.

"It's all right." Britt's voice is grim and slow, as deliberate as his hands, brushing the glass off his sleeves. "We'll leave town."

"You're not leaving town unless you want." Lacey raises his voice. "Anyone got a problem with that, you come to me!"

"Come on, Buck." Britt casts his glance around the room and spits contemptuously. "Thanks for trying, Marshal."

"Look." Marshal Lacey steps up and holds out his hand. "If you boys change your minds, you tell me. I don't hold truck with fighting, but a man's got to stand up for himself."

Buck is just watching, dabbing at a cut with his sleeve.

"There's other places to find work than Glory Mesa. I'd rather be breaking horses anyway. Come on, Buck."

Buck goes over to the bar and grabs his gun belt. He seemed to have been prepared enough to take it off.

"Hey, you two boys looking for a job?" I step forward, eyeing the room, just daring someone to take issue with it.

"Reckon so."

"Horsebreaking?"

"Yep, if we can get it."

"There's a good herd, and I mean a good herd, out north of my place. I was thinking of rounding them up, pulling some of the best. Would you be interested?"

Britt looks over at Buck, who is squinting and grinning. "That's a yes from us, sir."

"I'm leaving town in two days. Any time you come out to the Tall Tree Ranch after then, I'll have a welcome for you."

The pair pass me, raising dust with their heavy boots, smelling of sweat and sharp alcohol.

Raymond Lacey just looks at me with a dimple in his cheek.

12

SIKES

THERE'S DESTINY IN THESE BOYS. IT'S AS THICK AS THE dust cloud around a herd of buffalo. They're wrapped in it, leave it at the corners and streets where they pause. It lingers in the air after they go.

Mark my words, the land has left its touch on the April brothers, and they'll leave theirs on it before they're nothing but dust and memory.

Not once do they look my way as they pack their horses and ride out of town. But I watch them from my porch until they are nothing but a little dust raised on the southern foothills.

I will go to them.

THEIR CAMP IS JUST a small flame standing against the blue night. There are two ponies and a pack horse staked just

96

outside the circle of flame, and the scent of roasted meat comes thin and smoke-tainted on the air.

It's a cold night.

They've built up a fire and it plays off their stony faces, drawing out every hard line. I'm only a wagon's length away before they both set their hands, still and quiet, on their rifles.

"No reason to fear, gentlemen," I greet, stepping into the light. "I don't carry iron."

The younger one lets go of his immediately; the older just watches me and doesn't relinquish his hold.

"You're probably the first one to ever call us gentlemen," he says with a harsh laugh.

The younger moves over so that I can share the log he's perched on.

"Who are you?"

"Doctor Sikes."

"From Glory Mesa," says the younger one. It's not a question. "I saw you last week." There's a spark of something in his eyes that pleases me. "Coffee?"

I nod and the younger throws out his coffee and refills the mug.

"What do you want?" asks the older one. He's staring at me with the deep eyes of a wild stallion—curious, cautious, angry, unafraid.

"I hear you are going west."

"Nothing for us here. What do you want?"

He's sharp.

"To talk."

The younger brother hands me the coffee. "Well, we got nothing else to do tonight. Though I fancied looking at the stars." The younger one leans back and stares at the expanse above with a contented sigh.

"There's nothing to talk about." The older one snaps a stick and throws it into the fire. He continues with a couple more, filling the silence with the harsh noise.

I let the silence drag. I am in no hurry.

The younger one busies himself with taking the meat off the spit and carving it roughly.

These boys. I can feel their power like the rumble of thunder in my hands. They are men of the land, whose beginning and end no man will know but themselves.

"Want something to eat?" The younger one holds out a tin plate.

"No, thank you."

"By the way, I'm Buck. That's Britt."

I nod slowly, first to Buck, then to his brother. "May I offer you one word of advice?"

"Sure." Buck cuts in before his brother can refuse.

"Stay out of the mountains to the northwest."

The older one doesn't take his narrow eyes from my face. "Well, we have business with the wild herd. It all depends on where they're ranging. I'm going to do my job."

"What is more important to you, the job or each other?"

"What kind of question is that?" Britt starts halfway to his feet. "Who do you think you are?"

Buck pulls at his brother's sleeve. "Easy, Britt," he murmurs.

"You don't have to listen." I stare into his troubled eyes. "But know that you are destined for great and terrible things. Often they go together."

"I've had my turn at that. I'm going out there to break horses and nothing else."

If only the boy knew what lies in those hills.

"More coffee?" Buck reaches for the pot.

"Thank you." I hold out my tin mug again.

"What is the trouble in those mountains?" Buck asks as he pours, not looking at my face.

"Buck!"

He ignores his older brother, reaches out with his long arm, and sets the pot back over the grate.

"There are ancient things in that hill, waiting for men with power to set them into motion."

"Then what do we have to worry about?" Britt's eyes are duller than a slate hill.

I stand up. Perhaps he wishes only to deny what he feels inside him. Or perhaps he no longer believes it.

But I saw it in his eye, that gleam. These two are as strong and beautiful and tragic as a storm that sweeps over a plain, razing tall-standing corn.

"If you go westward, you will only find grief."

I turn and leave their fire.

13

IRENE

HE RIDES BY EVERY MORNING RIGHT AROUND THE TIME
I'm pumping water for the day. Once or twice he's noticed
me and raised a hand in greeting, but most times he doesn't
see me.

I don't mind it.

Raymond Lacey certainly has more important things on
his mind. Outlaws down south near Anami Station, a band
of renegades stealing cattle from someone named Gilchrist.

Nevertheless, I've taken to hoping I see him in the mornings on his way by, the sun bright and gentle, his horse
casting shadows so long I can almost reach out and touch
them.

He rides differently from everyone else too. So straight
and so comfortable in the saddle. It's like he and the horse are
one and the same, not just in movement but in bearing.

Part of me hates myself for it, but my heart lifts when he

goes by. I've taken to looking for him, and the day is better if I happen to glimpse him passing by.

Perhaps it is dangerous to let this dream live. A wise woman, with so much loss behind her, should kill the dream when it is fresh and dear but not rooted.

But I am young and foolish and life has been cruel. A dream is a pain I can control, and I'd rather have it than not.

So I watch for him.

The sun is already up in warm, full rays by the time he rides by today. The dust curls around the slow, deliberate hooves of his horse—a sorrel—and when the wind picks up, it whisks it around him gently.

I move my bucket under the pump and return to work; it wouldn't do to be caught staring. He stops once in the street, leans his arms on the pommel of his saddle to talk with Peter from the saloon.

Peter is a shy boy, but when he talks to Raymond, he smiles. They converse like two men.

Raymond turns in the saddle and points beyond the town, to the south. Peter seems to agree with him and add a few comments of his own.

Instead of ending in a pleasant good-day, the conversation tightens into swift, short syllables and more earnest gesturing toward the south.

Raymond turns and urges his horse into a canter, back the way he came.

I stand still and listen until I cannot hear the hooves any longer. Then I lift my buckets and return to the house.

The next morning, he doesn't ride by.

I'm in the general store two days later, picking out cloth for a dress, when I hear a pair of boots on the boardwalk and one of the loafers outside the store says, "Morning, Marshal."

My heart jumps. It isn't supposed to do that outside of early mornings, when the air is full of mist and dreams.

I can't think of him in this way.

"Morning, Trasker." His voice is as unhurried as his step.

"Good morning, Marshal Lacey." Trasker steps up to the counter. "How may I help you?"

"I'm looking for flower seeds." His mustache tilts in a smile. "You got any of those?"

"Sure thing, and I can order in too." He sets down a heavy catalog. "Anything in particular you're looking for?"

"Lupine and hollyhock."

"Well, now, what's the occasion?"

"My sister's birthday. She's taken a shine to tall flowers."

Trasker smiles appreciatively. "I may have some of the lupine in the back. I'll go look, and if we need to, I will put in an order."

"Obliged."

Mr. Trasker disappears into the back, and I feel more than see Marshal Lacey taking slow stock of the store.

"Mrs. Sandler." He pulls the brim of his hat. "Afternoon."

"Afternoon. How is your arm?"

"Hardly need this thing," he replies, with a glance at the sling. "Just wearing it to please Rose."

"You're lucky to have an attentive sister."

"Don't I know it." His eyes take on a gleam.

"Is her birthday soon?"

"Next month. But I'll be riding out of town soon. I don't want to leave everything to the last minute."

"That's wise."

"And how are you getting on?" He narrows his eyes slightly. "Is your place comfortable?"

"Yes, quite."

"And you still mean to stay? If you ever change your mind, the stage is as safe as it's ever been."

He means to be kind and reassuring, but I wish he wouldn't ask me.

"Yes, I still intend to stay."

"Well, Glory Mesa is having its founding celebration in a couple months. If you wanted something to do here, you might speak to Rose—I mean, my sister, Mrs. Scott. There'll be a whole lot of preparation going into it, she tells me."

"I'd like that."

"Well, Marshal, here is the lupine, and I can order those others today. Would you like these wrapped?"

"Well, why don't you hang to it for a mite?" He rubs his chin. "Just in case, you know. Better someone's got it who knows what it's for."

"If you say so Marshal," says Trasker cheerfully. "I'll have it under the counter whenever you want it."

"Sure."

"Anything else I can do for you?"

The door opens with more authority than usual. If Marshal Lacey had an answer, he doesn't give it.

A tall woman enters, pale and fair-haired, a striking contrast with the black of her widow's garments.

"Mrs. Pike," Trasker greets in the same cheerful tone. "You're back in town! How was the trip?"

"Dusty," she says, drawing the word out just slightly. "And uncomfortable. But I was able to find the goods I was looking for, so—not a wasted trip."

"Glad to hear it, glad to hear it. What can I get you?"

"Did the candles come in? The white wax?"

"Yes, they did. They're just in back if you'll wait a moment, or—I can send Charlie over."

"Yes, send Charlie over. I'll expect him at three, if that is agreeable."

"Of course, no trouble at all. Good day, Mrs. Pike."

"Good day." She breezes past Raymond, who touches his brim, and out into the street.

"That woman always makes me feel like I've done something wrong." Raymond gives Trasker a slow smile.

"She has a way of her own, I'll give her that," admits Trasker. "It's helped her survive this long."

"You'd think a woman like that, with her resources, would move back East."

Trasker just shrugs.

"Well, good day." Raymond turns to me, touches his brim as he did with Mrs. Pike. "Ma'am."

I nod and smile in answer.

I wish my heart didn't warm so much when he did that. But oh—I feel alive again.

14

THATCHER

IT'S TWILIGHT BY THE TIME I FIND THE MOUNTAIN clearing where the trapper lives. I smell smoke and mountain pine, catch a whiff of vension. I've been dreading my arrival for the past two weeks, but now, with the warm light standing in the window of the small, dirty cabin, the strongest feeling in me is overwhelming hunger.

I ride down the strip of ground in front of his place. It's sandy and dusted with pine needles.

"Hey!" I cup one hand to my face. "Got a bed for a weary traveler?"

The door swings open so hard it slams against the wood of the outside wall. "Who's there?" The trapper stumps out of the cabin and peers into the dusk.

"It's me. I came." I dismount and lead my horse up to the door.

"So you did. Can you work?"

"That's what I came for, isn't it?" I force myself to laugh, move easy.

"Well, you can put your horse up in that corral there and come inside when you've a mind to. You can haul your kit in—sometimes we get frosts of nights."

"I'll do that. Any hay for him?"

"Sure. Just take a pile from the burro, he ain't particular." He shuts the door again, leaving the strong smell of roasting meat to linger.

I swallow and lead the horse away.

The corral is well-built. This man may be a stranger to soap and decent manners, but his work's nothing to scoff at. I steal hay from the burro's pile. He sniffs and pins his long corn-husk ears, but he doesn't make a move to fight for it.

I grab a fistful of hay and rub my horse down vigorously while he eats.

It's dark by the time I head up to the cabin. My feet are heavy and my shirt clings half-heartedly to my back where the sweat dried.

I knock.

"Come in!"

I pull the latch and step in. It's a rough place, but tidier than I expected. A bed stands in one corner, an assortment of stiff clothing hangs on a line across another corner, and there's venison hanging on a rough metal spit over a crackling hearthfire.

"There's a basin of water," he grins, jerking his head toward a table that stands by one wall. "Just this night you can wash inside like a tenderfoot. Rest of the time, you'll use the creek out back."

"Thank you." I ignore his insult and go over to the basin. The water is clear and cold. I scrub well. After weeks of travel, even a rough place like this feels homey.

There's a rag sitting beside the basin and I give it a quick sniff. It seems clean enough. I dry my face slowly and deliberately.

My host lumbers over to the fire. He cuts a hunk off the roast and slaps it onto a plate. "That's good deersteak. Stick to your ribs. I hope you're not too proud for that."

I wolf down the steak and he supplies another thick slice without a word.

He sets a pot of coffee on the table and pushes a worn tin cup my way. "You came a far piece," he says, pouring himself a cup.

"Far enough." It was weeks, weeks of cursing myself for doing this, trying to defend Archer's honor.

I reach over and pour myself a hot, black cup. It's piping, but I down it quick anyway.

"So do you mine or do you trap?"

"Both," he grunts, leaning back and putting his boots on the chair beside me. "Mine in the warmer months, trap in the colder months."

"Where do you haul your goods to?"

"You'd like to know, wouldn't you?" He narrows his eyes. Then he gives a sudden laugh, surprisingly merry. "Anywheres I get a good price, son. I've been in Glory Mesa a couple times, but I've never seen you."

"Ranch work." I pour out another cup of coffee.

"Well, I reckon it's good—you not being too proud to get your hands dirty." He's watching me keenly from under those bristling brows.

"Depends on the kind of dirt," I answer, with just a hint of stiffness.

I WAKE up in a chair with my slicker over me. Outside, I hear birds. It's dark yet. I throw my slicker off and stretch. I'm still wearing my boots.

The door opens with a long creak and my host shoulders his way in. He dwarfs the cabin with his hulking frame.

He goes directly to the fire and sets down a load of wood. Then he busies himself with stirring the fire vigorously to life.

"Better eat something," he says. "We start early."

"I can start now." I'm ready, after all, and I'm slightly nettled by this fellow.

"No need for that," he grins. "I've got some potatoes too."

"All right, then." I adjust my shirt and tuck it in properly.

"Have a seat. It'll be done shortly."

He roasts the potatoes, brews coffee, and cuts cold meat for us. Piles my plate high. He's generous with his food, I'll give him that.

"Mule's a bit sore today." He fixes me with a steely glare

over his coffee cup. "And this ore's got to get out. I'll be fair with ye, we'll share the load, but do you have any objection to being a pack animal, son?"

I swallow my bite. "No."

"Good. You got gloves?"

"Sure."

"Bring 'em. Less'n you want raw meat for hands."

I finish my coffee in one long swig and stand up. I pull my gloves from my pack and stuff an extra kerchief in my pocket. I've got one around my neck, but if we're pulling ore, I may want a second by midday.

"Ready?" My host is standing in the doorway already.

"Ready."

THE MINE IS about a mile off, up steep rock and twisting paths. A man could break his neck just walking here, let alone hauling a load.

The opening to the mine is set in the side of a rocky wall, above an area of gray dirt about the size of a breaking pen. A small lean-to shelters an array of tools.

"I'll pick and you haul. And then we'll switch." He shakes out a heavy canvas bag and tosses it into a wheelbarrow.

"Fine with me." I pull on my gloves and clap them together, sending dust into the air.

Mining is hard work. I see why my father turned down his partner's offer and took to ranching instead. It takes my host time to chip the ore out, takes me plenty more just to load it, and then it's nearly a quarter mile's haul up to the mouth of the mine, where I unload it in the baking sun, just to go back down and fill up again.

After one load, I'm covered in sweat. After the second, I'm covered in ore dust that sticks to the sweat. I cover my face with a handkerchief, but even that's hard to breathe through.

But I don't so much as make a remark. He can't find much fault with a man who works and doesn't speak.

Partway through the morning, we switch places. He spends a quarter of an hour teaching me how to swing. I've driven posts for days on end, so my hands know the feel of a heavy tool, but the angle takes me a few tries.

So we go on.

We break to eat around noon—the same haunch we've eaten off the last two meals, and tepid water.

I still finish it off in minutes. I'm famished.

When we start again, I'm the one shouldering the canvas bag and hauling. He's faster at working the rock than I am.

We don't talk—we're both working too hard for that—but I sense we're coming to an understanding. His eye has a rather merry gleam as he kicks more rock toward me, and once he stops to show me the vein of ore.

It's not so bad, after all.

We're near the end of the day when I go to shoulder another bag of rocks and something gives with a sharp, tearing sensation.

Searing pain shoots through my arm, down my back, forks up my neck. Everything goes bright and then still and hot.

I'm breathing slow, fighting against the sweat that breaks out fresh on my forehead. I'm trying to recover and move on, but my arm is not obeying. I count the seconds, willing myself to move.

My host notices.

He swings the pick down and comes over. "What is it?"

I shoulder the bag slowly as pain prickles over my body. It's no use.

"Hold on a minute." He takes the bag down, his gnarly hand ranging over the shoulder, probing until I stiffen under his touch.

"Well." He tsks, businesslike, and shoves his hat back on his greasy head. "Looks like you got a strained shoulder, son. You and the mule."

He laughs roughly, his eyes twinkling.

I muster a smile, but I'm not laughing.

15

SELBY

A NEW HERD APPEARS A COUPLE HOURS BEFORE DUSK, A gray-speckled herd of perhaps two hundred, the leader belled and a couple scrawny dogs keeping them in line.

The herders themselves are dressed in the woven colors of the Far Hill Clan, and half of them ride burros or scrub horses.

The horses alone are masterpieces of breeding, every line lean and hard. They can probably jump like antelopes.

Nothing is careless or a halfway job with the people of the Far Hill Clan.

I watch as the purple light overtakes the rocks, casting shadows until there is nothing but dark blue and the color of sagebrush.

The fires dot the landscape like stars in the night.

The shepherds called me ages ago for the food, but I

enjoy this time of the night, and I have little desire to return to their silent hostility.

Let me have the beauty of the night, there I find my solace; as one who dreams in broken days, I must see the stars.

I tilt my head to the sky and breathe deeply of the desert air.

A sheep bleats below and I hear the low murmur of the shepherds meeting and discussing arrangements.

New fires start up against the night and I sling my rifle across my back and start down. The others are so used to my perch on the rocks above that they don't even check to see if it is me or a puma descending, but one of the newcomers looks my way—an old man. He wears purple and blue, and a small feather dangles from his ear.

His gaze stays long on my face. I can feel it, like the rays of warm sunshine.

I wonder what he wants. He'll likely not find it with me.

I collect my leftovers and pour a cup of their bitter coffee. I put it up on the far end of the rock wall, out of reach of the dogs, and I build a small fire to stand against the night's chill.

I eat in silence and solitude, watched with some curiosity by the newcomers.

My rifle is against the rock beside me. As I finish and scrub my plate with sand, I hear the grind of footsteps approaching.

"Is there room at your fire?"

I glance up before answering. The man in purple and blue stands above me, pipe clenched in his teeth.

"Of course." I move over and give him room.

"I wondered. No one else wants your company, it seems."

"Perhaps it's because I'm not one of them."

"Perhaps," he echoes, noncommittal. He crouches down beside the fire and stares into the flames. Then he looks over at me. "You have lived a great deal."

"Is that so?"

He nods, closing his eyes and rocking back on his heels. "You have already seen more grief than some men see in a lifetime. But it has made you strong."

"I don't know about that." I fold my arms and lean my back against the cold stone of the cliff wall.

"No, you don't." He considers his words for a moment. "But you will."

"I'm Jack Selby." I thrust out my hand.

He takes it in his worn hand. It's strong, like tempered steel.

"My name is Ogbathashanach, but they call me Jackson, most men."

"Ogbathashanach is fine with me," I reply softly.

"Good." He takes his hand back and takes his pipe out of his mouth. "This is good land, mostly." He gestures out into the night. "Those herders—they will let us graze alongside. One of them is my brother's cousin."

"I'm surprised to see you so far south, away from your own lands."

"Our herds grow strong on the grasses of the south," he says simply.

"But is there not distaste for this land among your people?"

"Why are you on it?" His eyes are quiet, bright. The eyes, I think, of a poet.

I avert my gaze, more habit than anything. "I am already a cursed man. I figure another curse cannot take much more from me."

He just looks at me, deeply, almost fondly.

"So you do not believe the curse?" I ask.

"I believe that there are better things in life than to avoid trouble. There is grass here for the sheep, there is companionship. We are the keepers of the story. It is not our place to say what should and should not happen."

"Well, for the little it's worth, I think it's a good way to live."

He removes his pipe and offers it to me in a show of appreciation.

I take a draw and hand it back. I haven't smoked anything in years, but I know when it is well-grown and well-cured, and this is.

"Have you heard the story of this land?"

"Can't say I have—rightly. I've heard of the curse."

"It is a long story." The smoke from his pipe trails through the cooling night air. One of the herd dogs comes up with its long tail nearly between its legs. It scratches out a place in the unforgiving dirt and lays down with a sigh.

Ogbathashanach is in no hurry.

I fold my arms and lean back. He takes the unspoken invitation.

"The story begins when the land was young and warm and innocent. The game was plenty and gentle, and there was no need for fighting between clans and families, for what a man needed, he had freely. It was good.

"In that time, there lived a wise father—indeed, the father of all, a man who loved beautiful things and created them. His cloth was bright and strong and warm, his animals were well-bred and healthy, his home was full of laughter and friends and his sons and daughters. And to him were born two sons at one time: brothers, alike in looks and manner, so that none but their mother and father could tell one from the other. Their names were Abroska and Tamikan. They were handsome and strong, and when their father looked upon them, he said in his heart, 'I have been blessed with the best last of all, for these sons will be greatest among their brothers.' And it seemed so. For many years they were strong and their deeds were good.

"And the day came when they were to take wives, and Tamikan chose a woman of a neighboring family, a woman he had known since childhood, who was kind and fair-minded.

"But Abroska scoffed at his brother's choice and determined that he would seek a bold, beautiful wife from some far-off place. His brother begged him that he should not go, and his father spoke to him also, saying, 'It is not good for pride alone to lead you in this journey when there is more than enough good near at hand. In another matter you may go forth and seek adventure, but do not do this thing, my son. Behold, here is the sister of your brother's betrothed; ask for her hand.' But Abroska would not be turned. So he departed from his father's house and from his brother Tamikan and went into the wilds.

"And in time he came upon the clan of Hakar, a proud and warlike clan, and he found a woman of great beauty and fierceness and he wed her. And to him were born two sons, alike in face and bearing, even as he and his brother were. Then he scorned his father and his brother in his heart, for he saw naught but good in what he had done, even against their counsel.

"And it came to pass that he heard news of his brother traveling the roads that ran north of the Hakar, and he said to his wife, 'Now I shall go north to my family, and I shall bring you and my two sons, and they shall see with their own eyes that they were fools.' And his wife agreed, but in her heart she resented him.

"So when the time came to leave, she stole a relic of the Hakar and hid it in her husband's bag so that he would be killed and she and her sons would remain with the clan. But when the keepers of the relic discovered its absence and came to the tent of Abroska, he knew what his wife had done, and in his anger, he slew the keepers and his faithless wife.

"Then his heart failed him and he fled for his life, telling no one. And Tamikan, traveling home on the roads north of Hakar to his young bride, was set upon by the Hakar, who believed him to be his brother and killed him.

"So the innocent brother was slain for the guilty, and both the Hakar and Abroska were made guilty in that day of innocent blood. And from the ground there arose a great thunder, and from the sky fell flame, and the sky turned to ash; and the darkness from that calamity spread far and wide. And all who lived in that place died.

So it was said that everywhere the ash fell, the land should lie barren and unsettled until such as are chosen for the task come and break the curse. And if any comes and tries to break that curse who is not worthy, they shall die in fire and the people of the land with them."

"And the land knows?"

"The land has a guardian. An impartial guardian. And he will remain until such time as a successor comes."

"A successor?"

"At a time when great violence is not needed to keep peace." He nods with a smile. "And what a time it shall be."

The coals snap as if in agreement.

"The stories of what those chosen will do are long and beautiful. They are stories of beautiful souls. Worthy souls. They will suffer more than most. Their hearts will burn like fire. But they will be granted the sight of peace in the land, even though glimpsed as from afar."

"What a thing it must be to be one of those souls."

Ogbathashanach looks at me with dark eyes. "Indeed. But with the good come the bad, rising to meet them."

He takes a slow puff of his pipe and then bursts out softly, "Alas, how a man's heart must be guarded, for the smallest of wrongs, allowed indulgence, leads swiftly to evil."

"This I know, and I wish I had known sooner."

Ogbathashanach nods knowingly. "But your heart is clean, Jack Selby. When the time comes, you will stand and you will not run when a dozen good men turn back."

"How much you seem to know about me." I lean back against the wall of rock and fold my arms.

"I only know what is needed," he says quietly. "I will rest now. The night grows thin about the edges. I will tell you more of the legend and its chosen tomorrow, if you wish it."

"I wish it," I reply.

He rises and leaves the fire, which has sunk to glowing embers. I do not revive it, but I do not lie down to sleep.

I lean against the wall of rock and lay my rifle across my lap. There is comfort in its smooth, familiar feel beneath my calloused fingers.

I stare at the stars and listen to the sounds of the night.

16

THATCHER

I SNAP AWAKE. IT'S TOO BRIGHT AND TOO STILL. DUST motes stand in the red-gold light that stabs through the dirty windowpane.

I sit up and grimace as I move my shoulder. The memories of yesterday come back with the stiff ache—making do with one arm, my host treating my shoulder with wraps and poultice. The whole thing is dried and stiff and crackles when I move.

There is no sign of my host this morning.

I cross the room slowly. I'm a little sore, but the pain's not bad. A strained muscle hurts like fire when you get it, but it dies down fast enough.

On the table sits a note, scratched on a thin piece of hide and held down by the edge of a tin cup.

Mules feelin better so I figgerd you can rest. Gon on the far side of the ridge today so you wont see me. X

I set the note back down.

There is bread on the table and some butter. I cut a slice and butter it generously, shove half of it in my mouth as I search for more to eat. On the hearth I find a slightly warm pot of coffee and a pan of bacon and beans. Taking pains to go easy on my sore arm, I lay breakfast out on the table and pile my plate with beans and bread.

Honestly, I enjoy the quiet. Just the coffee and bread and bacon and the sounds of the birds outside.

I could get used to it. Trade in the ranch, the gunslinging on my cousin's behalf, the politics that follow civilization as sure as night follows day—

No, Jesse, you fool.

I can't do that.

I pile my dishes in the bowl where my host has left his. I'll find the stream by and by and wash them. If he's on the far side of the ridge, he likely won't be back until dark.

I head towards the door, but I'm stopped short.

There's a bag of raw mined silver sitting out near the window, a decent-sized one. I lift the edge of the bag and figure it in my head.

There's thousands of dollars worth, right here.

Maybe this is what living in the mountains can do to a man—you just leave money like that sitting out in the open while a stranger is staying, alone, in your home.

I close up the bag and tuck it under the corner of a nearby blanket. I really doubt there's anyone up here but me, but I'll be smart for him if he doesn't know better.

As I move the blanket to tuck the bag well under, my hand brushes something cold.

It's a silver locket, a bit tarnished, engraved with a lone mountain peak. I've never seen anything like it. Beneath it sits a note written on real paper.

As I move the locket back over the note, my eye catches one phrase: *kill the governor.*

I shift the locket over and smooth out the note with my thumb and forefinger. It's got a brown stain on one edge like blood.

Beginning to think you were dead, glad to see it isn't so. Meet the rifleman for me at the river fork between Givern Pass and Tall Rock. I cannot leave Glory Mesa at present. Give this locket as payment only when they've killed the governor.

My neck and ears are hot. I need to clear my head.

I step outside and take a deep breath. The air has the edge of a dying chill. Weather works differently up here in the mountains. This view, though—I'm not sure I've seen a spot of mountain land so green and wide and all-around beautiful.

I head down to the stream mid-morning to wash properly. It's cold. I undress and plunge in up to my waist, scrubbing with sand until my skin stings and tingles. I wish I had proper soap, but naturally, my host doesn't keep any.

Still, when I climb from the stream and put on a new shirt, my mind feels clear. I know what I have to do.

I gather up the note and locket and tuck them into my

pocket, hands shaking slightly. Under normal circumstances, I'd never take what's not mine. But this is important. This man could be deep in a scheme against Archer.

With another deep breath, I set to work on the dishes. Best to stay here and carry on as if I know nothing. Making a run for it would only rouse my host's suspicions, and I don't care to try my luck being hunted by a mountain man.

I scour the plates with sand until they're as fresh as they can be, considering that my host has probably had them for thirty years and not done much washing in between. If there's one thing that sets me apart from other bachelors, it's that I was raised by a fine mother who trained me to keep a tidy house.

As I set the dishes out in the sun beside the cabin to dry, I see a stack of unsplit wood and a chopping block with an axe stuck in it.

I lift the handle of the axe gingerly and then test my shoulder. If I go slow, I can split some without damaging it.

I roll up my sleeves and set the first piece on the block. I spit in my hands and grip the axe, and the first piece flies apart with a satisfactory *thwack*.

The longer I work, the better I feel. I go on and on until there's a goodly pile scattered about my feet. I'm sweating now and wishing for the stream again. I stack the split wood neatly—neater than his, anyway—and head back down.

It's been ages since I went swimming for the fun of it, but I'm doing it today.

. . .

My host reappears right around dusk.

"You get some rest?" he asks, fixing me with a grim expression, but I see his eyes are twinkling a little. He smiles as if he actually likes me, uncouth as he is.

I almost want to ask outright what his business is with my cousin, but I don't dare. Not yet.

"Yes, thanks." I stand up slowly. "Got washed up, managed to get some wood chopped."

"With that shoulder?"

"I hate to do nothing at all when I'm a guest in a man's house," I answer. "I figured it was at least worth a meal."

"A good answer. Though you fed me in your house without asking naught in return. Still—" He pauses by the window. I can't see what he's looking at, only his broad back. "Still, I'm glad for the wood."

He turns and smiles, and his eyes are merry.

"Will we be back to work tomorrow?" I ask.

"Naw. I figure our deal's nearly done."

"But I only worked one day for you."

"You worked today without my asking. I say that's as good as a whole day. I'll let you know what I want from you tomorrow." He slaps me friendly-like on the back, but not too hard, minding my shoulder.

The locket and note feel like lead in my pocket.

17

NEWTON

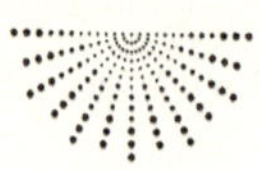

THE APRIL BROTHERS ARE SILENT MEN. THE YOUNGER, Buck, with the lanky, loose-limbed frame, occasionally leans over to murmur something to his brother, but he gets little answer besides a grunt or a nod. They're comfortable with each other, like a couple of mustangs who practically think as one. After traveling nigh on two weeks with them, I've grown used to their presence.

The horizon is dark and swollen with the promise of rain. My horse senses it. I can feel the way he wants to tend north to avoid it, the unease that makes him rise up under me.

"If we hurry, I know where there's shelter a ways up the trail," I say, gesturing to the storm. The brothers haven't even commented on it. I wonder if they'd plod on without complaint even if it broke over us.

"How far?" Britt eyes the horizon narrowly.

"Ten miles, maybe?"

"It'll be near dark by then." Buck shoves his hat back and wipes the sweat off his forehead.

"Then let's move." Britt gives his horse a kiss of the spur, and we follow.

THE WIND PICKS UP, roaring across the flat ground, whipping over the hills and pressing the grass to the ground. Thunder shakes the earth like a herd of buffalo. It's a terrible storm over beautiful land.

We're not going to reach shelter in time at this rate.

We're all moving at a quick lope, swift and easy, hoping to gain the rocks, at least, before the full fury of the storm hits us.

The rain comes, lashing, stinging like rock-spray against our faces and shoulders. Our horses shift a little, trying to angle their faces away from the wind, maintaining their speed.

Ahead of me I see a flash of slick saddle wrong way round, and my horse is sheering off, nearly unseating me.

Someone is down.

I circle back, peering through the rain, and see a tangle of horse and man scrambling up.

"Anyone hurt?" I fight to be heard over the storm. It's almost impossible to see through the lashing rain. I throw my leg over my horse's back and drop down.

It's Britt, his left side covered in mud, his horse hopping awkwardly on three feet as he lifts its left foreleg.

"What is it?" Buck appears at my elbow, squinting through the rain.

"His shoe."

"And?"

Britt straightens, shaking his head. "Can't salvage it. He'll limp the whole way."

I shield my eyes from the rain and peer through the gray curtain at the landmarks.

We're on Harrison Terhune's land, close to his ranch.

"Can he make it a few more miles?"

"Reckon so," Britt voice comes out from under the low brim of his hat.

"It isn't far." I nod northward, out of our way. "There's a place up that way, belongs to one of the cattlemen here. Two, three miles maybe. We're lucky. There's not another ranch house in a hundred miles."

"You know him?" Britt's looking at me keenly.

"Yes. Name's Terhune. Do you have a problem with him?"

Britt shrugs. "Don't know the man."

"Well, he got into some trouble last year, but he's got no quarrel with me."

"What trouble?" asks Buck.

"You didn't see any of the newspapers?"

"Weren't no newspapers where we were. Not me nor Britt."

"He nearly hung for some to-do last year during Mortimer's raids. Almost shot the governor's wife."

Britt whistles.

"How'd he talk his way out of that?" Buck leans over his pommel to catch my answer.

"He told the governor he was ready to face the gallows without a complaint, but Mrs. Scott spoke up for him, said he acted under duress. And Archer Scott has always respected a brave man."

"Under duress. He sounds like a coward." Britt gives a bitter laugh.

"A man can turn from his cowardice. It's not good to figure a man can't change."

Britt shrugs. "Well, I ain't a particular man, really." He looks to Buck. "Well?"

"Better than this rain," he says.

HARRISON TERHUNE's place materializes out of the rain as if from nowhere. There are multiple barns, long bunkhouses for the hands, and sprawling ranch house.

I trot ahead and rein in before the house. I pull my brim down hard and squint at the yellow windows beyond the dark porch. Someone's home, at least.

"Halloo the house!" I shout.

My horse jerks its head in protest. It wants out of the rain, and my voice is an annoyance.

The door opens and a figure with a lantern steps out.

"Who goes?" It's Harrison's own deep voice.

"Cristobal Newton and a couple horsebreakers. We threw a shoe!"

The lantern sways; I only catch a brief glimpse of the hard plane of a cheek in the flickering light.

"Chris Newton, huh? Put your horses in that corral up yonder by the barn and come on in out of the rain!"

That's good enough for me. I dismount, landing in about six inches of watery mud, and lead my horse off toward the shadowy outline of the corral.

My horse is more than happy to be let go. He shoots off the moment the bridle is gone and trots to the shelter at the side of the barn.

The April brothers are just blurs in the rain. One of them gives his horse a parting slap and takes the gate from my hand.

The door is standing open, warm and inviting against the cold darkness of the storm. I step in, peel off my hat, and unbutton my slicker. The brothers are ducking out from under their ponchos, wiping their boots industriously.

I forgot how well-off Harrison is—it's been a few years since I've been inside his house, and it's well, well furnished.

He stands watching us, one hand on the back of an armchair, a glass in the other. He's changed: his face is drawn, the lines around his eyes are deeper, and the hair at his temples is turning.

"Hello, Chris," he says slowly.

"Evening." I manage a smile.

"And you are?" His eyes go to the Aprils.

"Buck April," volunteers the younger. He points to his brother. "Britt."

"Pleasure." He switches his drink to his left hand and holds out his worn right. They shake it, one after the other, and then he approaches me.

I take his hand. "Been a while."

"Yeah." I can hear the strain in his voice.

He clears his throat. "Come on in, gentlemen, and have a seat. Hungry?"

Buck smiles. I don't think I've seen him do that yet. "Sure. Hungry enough to eat half a steer."

"Good. Should have half a steer around here somewhere. Henry!"

An older man comes into the room, quiet and well-dressed. "Sir?" He regards us with a suspicious glance.

"These friends are here for supper. Bring out what you have, and break into the pies."

"But sir—"

"I've got no better time for them. Go on."

The cook gives us another side-eye and disappears back into the kitchen.

"You'll have to excuse Henry, he's suspicious of everyone now. It's been a couple bad years and we're headed for a drought. There's talk of some of ranchers hiring gunmen for their water holes."

"The rain'll be welcome, then." Buck glances out the window.

"You thinking of hiring anyone?" I ask, slowly. We've been on decent terms in the past. I wouldn't want there to be trouble now.

He chuckles bitterly and straightens his fork. "Not me. Can't afford to step out of line now. You?"

I shake my head.

"In that case," he raises his eyebrows, "I'm turning over a new leaf as a neighbor. If you want to partner on the water, you just say. I figure two spreads will have enough together, here or there. I've got the Rockford running down from the mountains, and you have the lake."

"That's generous of you. I'll think about it."

The cook comes out with the food, and we dig in. The April brothers have surprisingly good manners for a couple of horsebreakers.

It's quiet around the table for some time.

"So—any news from out East?" Harrison wipes his mouth on his napkin. "Are the politics just as horrible as they used to be?"

"Unfortunately, yes." I smile wryly. "And prices are almost as high as they were during the war."

He tsks and takes a bite, washing it down with a drink. "And the railroad? How far did you make it on the rails?"

"Only to Smith's Run. There's a line all the way out to Saguaro City now, so I hear, and it's turning the place into a fine cattle town. But I had business in Glory Mesa."

Something closes off in Harrison's eyes.

"Well-concluded?"

"Yes. It's much more civilized than when I saw it last."

"It is." He forces a smile and takes a drink. He looks to the Aprils. "And you boys? You're horsebreakers?"

"Yes." It's Buck who answers, while Britt watches Harrison closely.

"You have the frame for it. You going for that northern herd?"

Buck looks to me.

"Figured on it," I say. "They look promising."

"You let me know if you bring in any good ones you'd be interested in selling. I could really use a couple good mares for breeding."

"To be sure."

The cook comes out with three pies and a grim expression. He sets them down quietly and starts out of the room.

"Henry, wait a moment." Harrison looks to us. "Something to drink?"

He motions to his cook with a couple fingers and I catch his low murmur. "Bring up the port from the cellar. And a bottle of whiskey."

"Sir."

The cook returns with the requested bottles and clears away our dinner plates.

"How are the efforts to clean up the outlaws?" Harrison asks, uncorking the whiskey decanter.

"They seem to be going well enough." I look to Buck for corroboration. "My trip out was uneventful."

"They're thinning," replies Buck. "I had a run-in with a

band not long ago. I was one of two survivors of a wagon train. But they're getting cleaned up."

"Glad to hear it." Harrison reaches for the port wine to open it when a knock comes at the front door. His fingers still on the bottle and the knuckles go white.

The door opens and a cowhand ducks in, dripping rain. "There's a man to see you, sir."

He pauses, sets the glass down. "A man?"

"Yes, sir. He says he'll stay outside and wait. He doesn't mean to stay."

Harrison glances out at the rain gushing down the eaves before giving the hand a meaningful look. "All right. Excuse me, gentlemen."

He folds his napkin deliberately and lays it beside his plate. Then he pushes back his chair, unhurried and regular, and goes to the door.

He reaches for the gun that hangs on the peg next to the door, then stops. He takes down his coat and leaves the gun. For a moment, the rain is loud, and then the door shuts firmly on it.

There's no sound except the brothers eating and a light clink as Britt pours himself a small glass of the whiskey.

I serve myself pie, but I'm unsettled now. Harrison seemed on edge, and anyone coming to see him in a downpour like this and not planning to stay....

I push my chair back.

I take my gun down from where it hangs beside the door

and shove my arms into my slicker. I step out onto the porch and peer against the rain as it runs and trickles from the roof.

Raised voices come from the direction of the corral.

"And I said no. You've got a lot of nerve to be coming here."

"Is it gold? Because we have—"

"It's not the money. I wouldn't take your filthy money."

"What did she say?"

"I told you, it's over. All of it. I don't want anyone speaking for me now."

I can make out two figures standing beside the corral, blurred by the rain.

"Terhune, we're getting close. You can come easy or you can come hard."

I hear a laugh, short and bitter. "I don't have to come at all. Get off my land."

The shadowy figure in the rain doesn't stir.

"I'm not saying it again."

The newcomer lunges and Terhune swings as if he was ready for it, catching him on the jaw with a crack I hear through the rain.

The newcomer scrambles up and lunges back in. They stumble backwards, both of them, and crash into the wooden slats of the corral.

They're up again, and I hear the dull thuds of kicks and punches thrown. I walk down the steps, ready to intervene if necessary.

Terhune throws him off again and they stand facing each other, panting.

"You fool!" growls the assailant.

"I already said I'm done. Get out before I have to put some lead behind my words. I'll do it."

"Try." He whips his knife out.

Terhune scrambles backwards, his hands outstretched as if to calm a wild colt. "Hey, hey—easy, now."

But the newcomer just laughs and throws his head. I catch the dull gleam of a claw against his throat.

It's Tora-Teth, one of Mortimer's outlaws. He's been a terror for the last five years or more, and that knife is almost as well-known as he is.

My gun is out and cocked in a single movement.

"Put it down and get out of here. He's got the law on his side."

"Not if he kills me." Tora-Teth's mouth is stretched into a nasty smile-like shape.

"It wouldn't matter. He's got witnesses. Besides, I'd be the one shooting you." I take a meaningful step towards him.

Beside me, I hear two more pistols cock. I'm suddenly thankful the April brothers are such bad men to tangle with. Even Tora-Teth would be a fool to pick a fight with all three of us.

He scrambles up from the mud, spits in our direction, and swings up onto his horse, all practically in one movement.

I watch to make sure he leaves.

As the thud of the horse's hooves fade into the pounding rain, Terhune reaches up with a muddy-knuckled hand and pushes back the hair that's plastered to his face.

"Thanks."

The Aprils holster their guns without a word and trudge back to the house. I glance back at the rain once more and duck under the streaming eaves.

In the doorway, Terhune's hand catches at my arm. "I'd have said no, even if you weren't here." His eyes tell me it's the truth.

"I've sent them packing before. I'm done. It's just the ranch now." His eyes search my face keenly.

"I believe you." We're facing the warm light, the two of us, with the cold rain at our backs. "A man'd be a fool to spit at a second chance. And you're no fool."

18

THATCHER

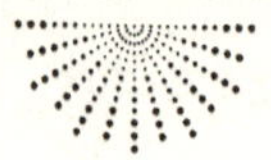

We're both up before the sun the next morning. My host is cooking up cornbread in a skillet, and the smell of it makes the whole cabin feel friendly and warm.

"Today's your last day, son." He looks almost disappointed.

"Last day?"

"I mean, we're done. You've held up your end of the bargain and I'm—nearly—satisfied."

Something in his tone makes me feel skittish.

"I'll be almost sorry to see you go," he says with a smile.

"But I thought—"

"You worked hard for me that first day. Mining's not for the weak. Then I left all that silver out and said I was on the far ridge. A dishonest man would have taken it and gone."

I did think it was a bit foolish to leave that silver out.

138

He chuckles. "If you had, I would have caught you and shot you."

"I see." The thought of the locket makes me gently sick.

"Well." He sighs and takes his hat off, beating it against his leg. "There's only one more thing. I just want to know—did you take anything from me?"

My ears start pounding like a storm on the prairie.

"Why do you ask that?"

"You heard the question."

My fingers twitch toward my gun. A prickle starts down my neck. I'm suddenly, unusually afraid.

"I took one thing," I hear myself saying. "A note that concerns my cousin. And something that was payment for his death." I pull out the locket and drop it on the table, hard.

"So you did steal from me." His eyes are hard and mean.

"It was because it concerned my cousin's safety, but it—it doesn't change the fact. Yes, I stole from you."

He scratches his beard. "I don't hold nothing for those men, but a thief's a thief and there's only one thing for them."

He picks up the rifle and gestures to the door. The world goes still.

"I need to say something." I stand my ground.

"Make it quick," he growls.

"This—isn't a reflection on my cousin. Archer wouldn't do something like this. I swear it. I just didn't trust you and—and I'd take a bullet for him any day."

"Well, you talk brave."

"You'll tell him I'm sorry?" I'm torn between him finding

out I was a thief and never know how I died at all, but that wouldn't be fair to him.

If it wasn't for Archer's honor, I probably wouldn't have given this man the time of day. Now it's going to be my death.

"Depends on if you actually know how to die brave. Better he doesn't know if he's got a coward for kin."

I knot my fist.

He stops and goes back to the hearth, still gripping the gun. He stokes up the fire and hangs a kettle over it with an unforgiving clang.

"Outside," he says brusquely.

I step outside. There's been a cold snap overnight, and all the trees and grasses are coated with thick frost.

For a brief moment, I contemplate running. I can see my horse in the corral. I could make a break for it, flee out of here bareback.

But I've come too far to turn yellow now. With his marksmanship, he'd pick me off easy, and I'd just prove to his mind that I'm a coward and a liar.

No. If it's death on either side, I'll face it head-on.

The trapper shuts the front door behind him. "Drop your gun belt. I won't have any tricks."

Slowly I reach down and unbuckle it, let it fall to the crackling grass.

"Get over there, in front of that wall." He gestures to the side of his shed with the end of his rifle.

I feel myself obey more than I will it.

Every breath I take stands on the chill air. All around me, the green of spring, paled with the recent mountain frost, mocks me.

He feeds a bullet into the chamber.

"Want a blindfold?" He glances up at me.

"No. I'd rather look you in the eye and make you earn it." My teeth are clenched and my breath's coming hard.

"I ain't the one who stole from a man under his own roof," is all he says, and he draws his rifle to his shoulder.

He takes aim directly at my chest and cocks.

The air splits with noise, and I flinch, but there's nothing.

"Misfire," he grunts. Then he looks up at me and there's a mean smile growing on his face. I was a fool to think there was any kindness in this man. "You talked brave, but you flinched. Are you that afraid to die?"

"I won't again." I grit my teeth.

He cocks his rifle and takes aim again, right at my chest.

I take a deep breath and hold it. Time seems to stop.

He whips the gun upwards and my hat goes flying.

He's playing. I'm angry now.

"Why are you toying with me?" I shout. "Can you not kill a man when he's looking in your eyes?"

"I won't miss this time." He cocks the rifle again.

Sweat trickles down my forehead and into my collar.

The world is so real, so still and alive. I draw a final, cold breath into my lungs, and it is sweet.

A crack breaks the stillness and the bullet slams me against the boards of the shed. Pain shoots through my neck.

But I'm standing, the world is here, clear and alive around me.

I reach up instinctively, feel the warm trickle of blood bathe my hand. He's nicked me, between the neck and shoulder.

Just a flesh wound.

I dive for my gun, bring it up with my shaking hand, slippery with blood.

"Don't fire again, or I'll shoot you square!"

"Put it down, son." There's a twinkle in the man's eyes. "You got more sand than any man I've seen in the last ten years. If your cousin's got half of that, this territory can count herself lucky."

Slowly, I lower the gun. The blood is running warm and wet down my back and my chest, staining my shirt.

"Let's get you inside, I'll bandage that up for you."

I buckle my gun belt back on but make no move to follow.

"Come on." It's his old, jovial tone. "I ain't raising my gun to you no more, no need to be skittish."

"But why—?"

His face turns grim—almost sad—for the briefest moment.

"I had to know what kind of man you were. Press you real hard. See how far your honesty would go."

"Why?"

"All that silver. I don't want it going to the animals or the outlaws when I die, and I'm no longer young. I had my doubts when I rode out of the mountains, and I had my doubts with you, but you're as worthy a man as ever lived. You'll be my heir, I reckon."

I feel myself swaying and manage to slump into a chair.

Sure death to untold riches is a bit much for one day.

He's got a kettle on the fire already, as if he knew how everything was going to turn out.

"Where'd you get that note, then," I manage, "if you don't hold nothing for those men?"

He chuckles low under his breath and applies a warm cloth to my cut, sponging away the already crusting blood.

"Got that off a body I found out by Givern Pass. Don't know what killed him, but he was a mean character and one I wasn't shedding a tear over, that's certain."

"Then I was right to be suspicious."

"I reckon you were. But he ain't getting anywhere with that note now."

He presses a folded cloth against the wound and winds a bandage around my chest to hold it in place. "I'll throw that in for free. Note, locket and all if you want."

"Thank you, I'll take it. The note was from someone in town. My cousin could be in danger."

"Then you'd best get back to him. You up to travelin'? You can stay another day."

"I'll be fine."

"Then I'll pack you to git goin'. I'll send word down the mountain from time to time. Just so's you know I'm alive."

"Thank you." I hold out my hand.

He grips it hard. "Stop by anytime, son."

Oddly, I find myself swallowing back a lump.

I pocket the locket and note and collect my things from the floor. Outside in the stark sunlight, I stop and breathe deeply of the chill morning air.

The birds are singing, and I don't think I've ever heard them sound so happy.

19

NEWTON

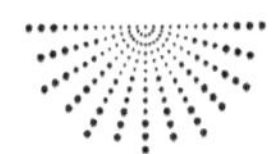

Morning is still and dark and damp. The ranch house is lit with oil lamps, displaying a rich spread, just the sort a man wants before a long journey.

Buck is at the table when I come out, halfway through a plate piled high with food. He pauses chewing long enough to give me a half smile.

"Excellent fare," he says.

"Looks like it." I pull out a chair and unfold my napkin.

"Are the others out yet?"

"They're out at the corral." He shovels another bite of grits into his mouth.

I pour a cup of coffee and fill my plate with hotcakes and apple butter, hot bread, pie, ham and bacon (hot and crackling at the edges), eggs stacked so high on the plate they're like a small mountain—it's food to stick to a traveling man's ribs.

"Ah, you're up." The door opens and Harrison strides in, pulling off heavy, dust-coated gloves. "Good morning."

I raise my coffee cup briefly.

"Cook came round," he notes, taking quick stock of the breakfast. He sits down and begins to pile food onto his plate.

He glances at Buck. "Your brother allows no grass to grow under his feet."

Buck shrugs his lean shoulders. "Reckon he's got the wander itch."

"Well, I can't blame him." Harrison gives a humorless smile and forks in a mouthful of hotcakes.

"Is he looking over the shoe?"

"Reckon so. My blacksmith's getting the forge hot. They'll see what's the matter when we have some light. If you need, I'll swap you a horse."

"Obliged," Buck replies around a mouthful of food. He washes it down with the rest of his coffee and stands up. "Thanks."

He goes out and it's quiet in the half-dark house, except for the ticking of the clock. Harrison and I eat in comfortable silence.

After a few minutes, He glances up and reaches for his napkin. "So—have you thought on my proposition?"

"About the water?"

He nods and leans forward for my answer.

"It would have to be even," I say.

"Certainly."

"Then it's a deal."

His face relaxes into a smile. "I am glad to hear it. And relieved. It's going to be bad one. I know Stanton and others are trying to hire gunmen."

I laugh grimly. "Well, I guess we've got no choice but to stick together." I drain my small coffee cup and set it down on the gingham tablecloth.

"The food was excellent, Harrison." I push my chair back and head for the door.

It's clear this morning, but hot already. A glance shows the April brothers leaning on the rails of the corral, as spare and long as the rails themselves.

The horse in question is tied in front of them.

I come over and drape my arm over the rough-hewn top rail. Harrison's man is bent against the side of the horse, the leg with the missing shoe cradled in his hands.

"What do you think?" I ask.

"It'll be a few hours," says the man, glancing up at Britt and then at me.

"I can catch up," says Britt.

"No need. We're not in a hurry," I reply. "We'll wait."

Behind me, I hear the ranch door shut and the scuff of boots striding out to us.

"What's the decision?" Harrison sets one foot on the lower rung of the corral and grips the rail in front of him.

"Just a few hours, sir," answers the blacksmith, setting the hoof down and giving the horse a genial slap. "I'll have to adjust a shoe and clip away some of this hoof."

"I can give you a horse," Harrison says to Britt.

"Nah," Britt shoves his hat back on his head. "We'll wait."

"In that case, I'll have the cook put up some provisions."

In the rising light I see a bruise on his jaw and a cut over one cheekbone.

"Your old friend's got a good fist," I comment.

He glances at me wryly and his hand goes to his jaw, covered in one day's stubble. "Not as good as I gave, and that was because of the rain."

"I heard he was running with Mortimer last year."

"He was. Longer than that—he'd been riding with him four, five years. I sort of hoped he'd gone down with the ship. Should have known he was too clever."

"He's a rough customer."

Harrison chuckles. "I know. The law's been better around here of late, but there's still pockets of outlaws around. Most got clear of this area, but if you go north or even south, they're still roaming. I'm afraid there might be a small band hiding out on my grazing land."

"Really?"

"We're missing cattle up in the northwest section. Just a trickle—three, four head every couple weeks. Enough to know someone's picking them off."

"I can ride up there and see. Scout around. I've got nothing else to do."

Harrison glances at the lightening horizon. "Well, I won't say no."

"I'll go saddle up. Borrow a rifle?"

MY HORSE, I think, is happy to be off again. He pops a couple easygoing bucks and snorts long as we go.

Harrison's range is good. I've ridden through it before, but not this direction. Green hill country with snow-fed streams from the mountains—he'll weather this drought better than most of us.

I follow the cattle signs, pass a stand of forty or fifty cows —more than half with calves on them—continue the way of the stragglers, spotting some here and there in the brush, but keep moving toward the water hole Harrison described for me before I left.

Near the hole, the earth dries out a bit. The sweet grass turns tough, choked with cantankerous weeds and sagebrush. Rocks and crags tower upward.

And then I smell it—death and decay. It stands heavy in the still air.

My horse snorts, gives an uneasy jerk on the bit.

A group of outlaws, if they were smart, would slaughter an animal and use it well. Whatever they didn't take would be quickly picked clean by scavengers.

This smells of rotting carcass, left for days untouched in the sun.

I come around one side of a deep-jutting rock face and see it. A half-eaten carcass, bloated and turned.

My horse snorts hard and side-steps, keeping its eyes on the body.

I ease the horse around to get a better look. Something's wrong about all of this. And another smell I can't place, thick and dank and heavy with musk.

There's a wide, smooth swath in the sand—like the slide of a traveling rattler, if the snake was the size of a horse.

A thin chill runs down my spine. This looks like everything I've ever heard about *darani*, the desert-dragons.

And then I hear a low burbling that seems to come from the ground itself.

I keep a tight hold on the horse and reach for my loaned rifle in its sheath.

My horse jerks and starts to tremble. I leave the gun and reach forward with one hand, patting the horse's neck. "Easy. I'm not going to let it get you," I murmur. One hand still firmly on the reins, I reach again for the rifle.

The low groaning comes again, louder. Closer.

My horse trembles so hard I feel every muscle jerking beneath me. I pull the rifle out, easy and slow.

I'm straining my eyes toward the rocks, looking for a place it could be holed up. I wonder, briefly, if I should just take off, but I hear they're fast, lightning fast when they want, and if I'm going to tangle with one, I want to be facing it.

Suddenly, my horse goes still and tight as a board.

In the shadows I've been searching, I see it, the dim

outline of a massive reptilian head, a bluish tongue flicking in and out, small beady eyes staring right at me.

Watching me.

It launches out like it was shot from a cannon and races towards me. I have just enough time to whip the rifle to my shoulder and fire.

The world upends. The horse is gone, streaking from me, leaving a patch of blood. The *darani* has a dazed look, shaking its head.

There's blood on its mouth from where its teeth grazed the horse, a dark hole in one shoulder from my shot.

I gather up the rifle and run for the rocks. I can't take the time to look back, but I hear a swift, uneven gait behind me. It's coming for me.

I scramble up, putting six, seven feet between me and the ground. I have just enough time to cock and fire again.

The shot glances off the raised ridge on its brownish-green head.

The *darani* rears up with a roar that shakes the ground. I've made him mad.

He's scrambling against the rock, trying to gain purchase on the rocks, but he's heavy and the ground is crumbling.

I reach into my pocket without taking my eyes off him and reload with one hand, but I'm using one hand to grip the rocks and I need both to cock the gun.

I wedge the rifle between my body and the rock and press myself against the surface as hard as I can. My fingers reach painfully. It clicks.

I take aim, but again, I'm gripping the rock. The rifle bucks so hard I nearly drop it and fall. I'm losing my footing and my grip.

The *darani* lashes his tail wildly. I hope it means I've hit him. His roaring fills the air.

I'm about to fall. I have one, maybe two shots left. I have to make them count. He's trailing dark blood, but he still looks too strong.

My fingers are failing me. I shove the gun between the rock and my body and reach with my other hand to gain purchase.

The rocks crumble away in my fingers.

I fall, the rifle slamming against my chest as I descend, both of us hitting the ground nearly on top of the beast.

I snatch the rifle up and fire right into his chest. He falters but doesn't stop. I cock again and then he seizes my shoulder with a score of heavy, needle-sharp teeth.

He shakes me, pounding me against the ground, tearing deep into the muscle. The world moves in close and dark and shies back again.

He stops for a moment, as wild animals do. I'm almost limp in his grasp, but the fight's not out of me.

I have just enough room to jam the muzzle deep against his throat and fire.

He jerks back and writhes, lashing me with his tail, his roaring so loud my ears ring and go thick.

He sinks to the ground, twitching.

My heart is pounding through my eyes; there's pain

exploding from me, I can't tell where. I'm fighting uncon-sciousness with every ounce of willpower I have.

The *darani* is still. The sun moves like I'm watching it through water.

I hear a distinct groan that must be me. Then everything goes still and painfully clear.

I must get back to the ranch house.

The world swims again—my arm's on fire. I pull myself up on one elbow and the world comes to a sudden, black halt.

20

ALAN

I LEAN DOWN IN THE SADDLE AND SCOOP UP A HANDFUL of water, bathing first my face, then my neck. The sky is blindingly bright, clear and hot without a cloud in the sky, the kind of heat that saps every ounce of damp from the earth.

The sun is angling off the moving river, casting broken sunshine across the water like the ripples of a skipped stone.

I stand and let my horse drink from the stomach-high water, his neck outstretched, pulsing slowly as he drinks.

"That's enough." I shift in the saddle and urge him forward. Slowly he picks his way forward, choosing his ground carefully. I can feel the pebbly bottom give way to shifting sand as he moves forward, then nothing as he starts to swim.

With the drought already in these parts, the river is low,

but it's running well enough that there's little danger of quicksand here.

Under me, my horse's hooves hit the riverbed again.

Too soon.

We make it across and my horse dips his head under the water and blows. He likes it, this cool break in the middle of the hot, dusty trail.

The crossing will do well enough.

From this side of the river, I can see our herd's dust rising like a brewing storm. I pull my hat off and wipe the sweat from my forehead.

In another minute, I'll have to ride back, talk to Jem, point out the crossing, but this moment is mine, caught clear and solid like one of those photographs they make of folks nowadays. The dust rising over the hill from the unseen herd, the bright sky standing behind, the muted green of the growing things that cling to the banks and shore, the deep and blinding blue of the river—all these things I've known since I could walk, and yet I'm as smitten with them today as I've ever been.

I was one of the first to be born on this land. I'm a lucky man to be here, to have this be my life.

I urge my horse back into the water and we cross.

I wave Jem aside and he peels off from the herd.

"I've got us a good ford."

"How low's the river?" He reaches up and jerks his bandanna down around his neck.

"Low, but I've seen it worse."

"Thank goodness we're crossing now, not later in the season." He lets out a sigh and wipes his face. "No quicksand?"

"None here. I imagine there might be some to the south, but we don't have a reason to go down there."

"Good." A quick grin transforms his grim face and he turns in the saddle, cupping his hand to his mouth. "Bring them down!"

He gives a tap of the spur and his horse springs away to the point.

Max is on the far end of the herd, a borrowed hat shoved back on his head. It's old and stained, a sore thing for his pride, but we're still weeks from the next town that would have a hat worth buying, so he's making do.

We drive the cattle in, whooping and calling. Max loves to really drive the flank, shouting and whooping, while Jem just leads them down with a few words of encouragement, given without an ounce of emotion. The cows seem to like that.

The water churns and swirls as we shove in. The cows lift their heads out of the water. In the clearer parts, where the sun penetrates, you can see their thick legs pumping as they swim. Splashes of water hit my face, lap at my legs, get in my mouth as I shout.

It's a beautiful day for a crossing.

Jem, near the head of the herd, is already climbing out of the water, turning his horse and minding the flank as the cattle scramble up onto the bank. A couple of the other men are minding the stragglers that try to head down the river instead of across.

Among cattle, you'll always get a few ornery ones that have individuality on their minds.

Max is still shouting on the flank, driving the cattle up, chasing them hard. My horse's hooves find purchase on the bank below and he heaves us up, shaking himself off a little.

I reach down out of habit, pat him appreciatively.

"Good ford." Jem nods to me as he takes his hat off and adjusts the brim.

"Thank you. It was a good crossing."

"No one lost, it looks like."

"And no dust!" Max grins, his face streaming water. He's below us, still in the shallows.

"Enjoy it now," says Jem, his grin dying. "It's going to be dry and hard for the last stretch."

Max's brow darkens a little, annoyed that Jem has to ruin good times with the promise of bad. He kisses to his horse and they scramble up the bank, dripping water.

Tagweiah is waiting for us, still as stone, under the hanging branches of a willow, just beyond the bank.

"My brother!" Max rides up and touches his forehead, pressing his hand to his shoulder in the Auki greeting. "How is the clan?"

"Well enough. When are you coming back to us, whelp?"

"Never." He grins savagely.

"Alas, I come to you with news I never thought to bring."

"What is it?" Jem is all business.

"The sign of the white stag has met with the lone mountain and the serpent in the sky. It is no longer foretold, but a thing come to us."

A chill runs up my arm.

Jem's face turns troubled. "Are you sure?"

"Yes. I am sure. And I do not say this, but there are those who say your father was warned of it when he brought your mother here and built on this land."

"Leave them out of this." Max's lip curls and he brushes past Tagweiah, spurring his horse up into the trees.

"Archer Scott should know this too," Jem says solemnly. "He was born on this land. It's his right." He looks at me. "The men can take the cattle up. If it truly is the sign of the coming of the end, we should be together."

"There's time yet," I reply.

But all I can think of are the memories and visions that have plagued me throughout this drive.

He's right. We brothers should be together.

21

NEWTON

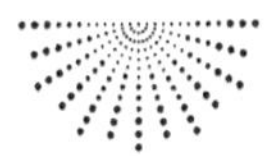

I WAKE IN A BEDROOM THAT SMELLS OF DRIED BLOOD and iodine. My head feels as if someone's kicked it a couple times. My entire right side feels distant, like it's lying six inches above me, but I can still feel the thin, mean pain lingering somewhere nearby.

Harrison Terhune's tired, cornflower-blue eyes are looking down at me. He reaches up to scratch his stubbled jaw.

Everything is slow, as if I've fallen out of time.

"What day is it?" I ask.

An ironic light comes into his eyes. "If you're asking how long it's been since we found you and that *darani* out by the rocks, it's been four. He was dead, by the way."

I groan out a wry laugh. "Figured I got him, but I figured he took me with him."

"Buck April tracked you when you didn't come back."

He chuckles low in his throat and shakes his head. "What were you thinking?"

"I wasn't thinking I'd meet a *darani*."

"I had the boys haul it back. I'm afraid it's gone now, but I saved the head and a claw. It's the biggest one I've ever seen or heard of."

"I guessed he was somewhere around fifteen, sixteen feet."

"Nineteen. It's a wonder you're alive."

I give a whistle—or try to. My lips are cracked and my mouth is dry. "Where am I hurt?"

"More than a few broken ribs, your shoulder's a mess. Burns down your side from—his saliva, I think. Did he breathe fire?"

"Not that I recall."

"Half my hands want to go work for you now, dragon-killer." He gives another dry chuckle.

"And I wanted to get home," I groan.

"Well, I'm afraid you're stuck here with me a little longer, though I'll make you as comfortable as I can. I have the doctor fetched out from Glory Mesa. We're not in the wilderness yet."

"Sikes is here?"

"Yep. And he says you're staying put for a bit. Tall Tree is going to have to wait."

"What's a bit?"

Harrison just shrugs. "I'll get him if you like." He starts towards the door.

"I'd rather you didn't."

He smiles slowly. "Well, I can't stop him if he tries, but—I won't mention you're awake."

The door shuts behind him.

I DON'T KNOW if Harrison kept his word or not because I cannot tell if Sikes comes in right away or if I've been asleep. Time's all blurred right now.

He's unchanged since the last time I saw him, two, three years ago.

"Terhune showed me the beast. You're a lucky man, Newton."

I don't say anything.

"Where does it hurt?" He pulls the sheet back partly, exposing my shoulder.

"Everywhere?"

He chuckles under his breath. "I have no doubt. In a little while, you'll start feeling it more in your side and arm and back. It appears he shook you like a rat."

"I think he did."

"And you still shot him." A gleam almost like a smile comes into his eyes. He reaches down and moves some of the wrapping on my shoulder.

I draw my breath in with a hiss at the sudden, throbbing pain that washes over me.

"Very few living souls know how to treat the *darani*

poison." He winks conspiratorially. "But I'm one of them. Hold still."

I'm not going anywhere, though if I could pick anywhere to be, it certainly wouldn't be in Harrison Terhune's bed with a *darani* bite and Doctor Sikes hovering over me.

A terrible smell fills the room as he uncovers a bowl filled with poultice.

He unwraps my arm and applies it thickly. It smells terrible and stings a little on the open wounds. He gives me something strong and bitter to drink before he puts away his things.

I'm starting to drift when I become aware that Sikes is still standing there, staring at me grimly, almost sadly.

"What?"

"You are a good man," he says, regretfully, and turns away.

Odd, I think, and then everything grows warm and dull and dark.

A STIR SOUNDS in the hall outside; a lamp is flickering. I have no idea of the time, but by the brightness of the moon, it has to be the middle of the night.

"There was someone, I'm sure of it." It's an April's voice —Britt's, I think.

"Where?" Harrison.

"First, in the corral. Then on the porch. Carrying iron."

A chill hits me like a shock of water.

"Did you get a look at him?"

"Not a good one. He was quiet, whoever he is. But the moon—you can't erase every shadow."

"Thank you. I'll stand watch tonight. I figured they'd come for me, sooner or later."

"You know who it is?"

A deep sigh from Harrison. "I know."

22

THATCHER

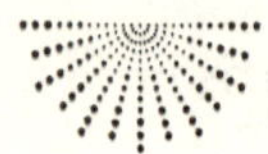

WHEN PETER RUNS UP BESIDE ME, I DON'T KNOW WHAT he's smiling about.

"Mr. Thatcher, I knew it was you!" he crows, catching my horse's bridle as I rein in to talk. "They said it was a stranger, but I even with that beard and the mud on your horse, I knew it was you."

I reach up and touch the growth on my face, suddenly self-conscious. Kate Carnegie and Carson stand watching from the doorway of the saloon, and Carson's not even trying to hide his curiosity.

I turn back to Peter. "And how'd you know?"

He shrugs. "Just the way you ride."

He's a sharp kid. I reach down and pat his shoulder. He's noticeably taller now than when I last saw him, and that was only a matter of months ago.

"Is the governor in?"

"In his office." He turns and looks down the street. The street has far more people in it than I remember being normal, and there are buildings and signs I've never seen before.

"Thanks." I kick my tired horse and head up the street. We didn't stop for anything but food and brief sleep on the trail back.

I suppose I look a bit like my host now.

I tie my horse up outside the building that now has a sign proclaiming it the Territorial Governor's Office.

It looks nice. A bit stiff and official, but I'd bet anything Rosamund is happy about it. And if she's happy, so is Archer.

I open the door and step in.

Archer is there with a couple men in suits, who look at me as if I'm Mortimer risen from the dead.

My cousin's brows draw together in what looks to be mild consternation and concern.

"Excuse me, gentlemen."

He comes over, ducking his head low to mine. "Thatcher, what you are you doing in town? What happened to you?"

"Long story."

"Well, go, clean up and I'll—get rid of these men and we can talk." He starts to dig in his pocket.

"I've got money." I reach out to stop him. "It can't wait."

He closes his mouth and nods. "I'll get rid of them."

I stand in a quiet daze as he talks to them in a low voice, hear their murmurs of assent and the scrape of chairs as they stand up and shake hands, the brief gust of fresh air as they go out.

"Who were they?" I ask.

"Railroad men. They're hoping to lay track into Glory Mesa by winter."

"What's the world coming to?"

My wry comment falls flat. Archer's standing with his hands braced on the back of his chair, his expression dark. I must look worse than I thought—he's looks like I'm preparing to tell him the end of the world.

"What in blazes happened to you, Jesse?"

"I haven't been home for a month," I say ruefully, feeling the beard.

"Why? What happened?"

I push my hat back on my head, try to line the story up in my head. "I went out to that trapper's cabin. I worked for him. But while I was there, I got some information. Someone in Glory Mesa wants you dead, Archer."

"Well." Archer lets out his breath in a whistle. "Did he say who it was?"

"He didn't know." I hold out the locket. "All he had was this."

Archer takes the locket with cold fingers. He looks up sharply. "They gave him this?"

"Do you recognize it?"

"Not exactly." He turns it round a couple times. "But Hector Muley used to tell of a man he met once in the middle of nowhere—a wild place he thought no man had set foot in but himself—who wore a locket like this."

A chill runs up my spine. "What was he like?"

"That's the strangest part. Muley said he'd never seen a man so handsome and well-dressed. Seemed uncanny. He always made the sign against evil when he talked about him."

"But that must have been ages ago."

"Certainly. But a thing may change hands many times." He rubs the locket's engraving with his thumb. "It's not a common design for a locket, a single mountain. It almost looks like a crest."

"Someone has to know something about it. I'm worried, Archer."

His blue eyes fix on my face as if he's suddenly remembering I'm here. "Well, whoever it is, he's obviously too scared to take me himself." He winks. "Meantime, you should get a shave and bath."

He sets his hand on my hurt shoulder and I almost flinch away.

"You hurt?" Concern crosses his face.

I pull back my collar to reveal the mostly-healed bullet crease. "It's nothing. See?"

"Who?" His face turns dark. "That mountain man?"

"I told you, it's nothing."

"He shot you!"

"It was—more complicated than that."

He rubs his jaw then looks at me, stern and sincere. "Well, don't you ever do that again. Next time there's an insult meant for me, let me take responsibility for it."

I snort. "Like blazes I will."

23

IRENE

I turn the thick bunting on the table in front of me and bring the next portion down into my lap as I reach for my threaded needle.

Edith Gable leans over to speak to me, her dark eyes dancing. "Mrs. Sandler, please tell me you intend to come to the dance after the ceremony. It simply will not be the same without you."

"I intend to."

"You must be good if you came from East Rutherford."

"Their skill is rather exaggerated," I smile. "But I can dance." I tie off the knot and snip the string. "I hear your husband is an excellent dancer?"

"He is." Edith's face lights up with pride. "And he's coming with me."

"Hmm," Maria intones from across the circle. She bites

her knot serenely. "It seems he's entered Glory Mesa with both feet."

"Yes, Raymond Lacey seems to find him indispensable," laughs Edith. "I thought the stories in the papers about the marshal couldn't possibly all be true, but from what Lesley tells me, they fall short of the reality."

"Raymond Lacey seems exciting in the papers," Maria says coolly. "But whatever they may say, he is not always capable and he certainly isn't 'Glory Mesa's Great Hope.' Take that wagon train massacre, for example."

I go numb, but my fingers are still moving, somehow.

"Mistakes aside, every man has a choice whether or not to be a coward, and Marshal Lacey is not a coward," Edith insists brightly.

Maria seems about to answer, and something in me cannot bear to hear her reply.

"The marshal did nothing but right that day," I speak up, willing my voice to be loud enough and my words disconnected from the memories I cannot bear. "He saved my life. In a newspaper, it sounds like nothing—one soul saved. But to me, it's everything."

Edith shoots a genuinely sympathetic glance in my direction and then looks down at her work.

Maria sews on more swiftly than before, her rich red lips pressed together. "A harsher hand is needed in dealing with these outlaws, or we will never settle this territory properly. Archer and Raymond let Harrison Terhune go free last year when that man should have hung. It was an outrage."

"I spoke for him." Rosamund comes over from the table, her strong mouth curving into a gracious smile. She has the presence of a queen; I can see why Archer wanted her at his side here. "If I can forgive him, shouldn't anyone be able to?"

"There's more work here," invites Edith, handing over a tablecloth to be hemmed.

Rosamund drapes it over her lap and opens the nearest sewing box, selecting a needle.

"It is not a matter of forgiveness," continues Maria. "Harrison Terhune was responsible for what he did. Showing mercy to a man like that only invites more wrongdoing into a society that desperately needs order." Her tone takes on a slight tartness.

"I am more than proud of the work my husband and brother are doing," Rosamund says pointedly.

Maria shakes her head regretfully. "Wait long enough and you will feel otherwise, mark my words. Men like that will always choose ambition over the good of their personal households. My husband was that way—killed himself with work, really."

"What did your husband do, Maria?" Edith asks quickly.

"He was a businessman. He started the mercantile, he owned the livery stable, and we established the restaurant together before he died. I sold the mercantile to Trasker and the stable to Jensen and carried on the restaurant alone." She sighs. "Poor Thomas. He simply couldn't bear the strain."

"I am sorry for your husband," answers Rosamund,

slightly cold. She looks unconvinced, I think, that it was the work that killed Mr. Pike. "But not every man is like that."

Edith leans forward. "It must have been wonderful, though—the years when you were building all that from nothing."

"It was." Maria smiles, as if amused by the younger woman's eagerness. "But in time, you will see. All of you. Sometimes the things you most want and the people you most love are like roses that prick you when you pluck them. They are beautiful, but you bleed nonetheless."

"Sometimes, Maria," Rosamund says, jabbing her needle into the tablecloth again, "to bleed is to remember that you are alive."

24

CARNEGIE

Founding Day starts before dawn for me, fresh and charged with anticipation. It takes me mere minutes to be ready for the day. I dress, wash my face, tie my hair back, and button up my boots.

It's quiet in the dark streets, though I hear horses down by the stage station. The station men are always up early, getting ready for the morning run.

I dream sometimes of having my own horse to ride, but it would do me little good in Glory Mesa. The day I get a horse is the day I ride out of here.

A whisper of excitement rests in my stomach. It's going to be nothing but a long day of work, with perhaps—if Carson feels generous—an hour or two of my own, but I am looking forward to it, somehow.

It's like I can sense something right around the corner, something good.

The lights are on in the saloon when I arrive, though it is rare that anyone arrives before me.

Carson must be excited too.

"Good morning," he greets, looking up from his books. He keeps his voice low, as we are full up with boarders. "Get breakfast going—our guests will be up soon and needing a hearty meal to start the day."

I take down my apron without a word.

He doesn't have to tell me. Hearty means more. Beans, porridge, bacon, cornbread, and eggs, all of it. Maybe ham, if he's got it.

I step into the kitchen in the back, and sure enough, he's stocked everything.

Quick steps out back signal Peter's arrival. He comes blinking into the kitchen.

"Mornin', Kate," he grins. He's not even totally awake, but he's rarin' and ready.

"Fill this with water?" I hold out the big pot.

He takes the pot silently and hurries outside. I hear the pump going like there's a fire.

I open up the big barrel of cornmeal and start to measure out enough to feed an army. Like as not I'll need it just as much or more than the boarders.

By mid-morning, as I clean up from breakfast and start the chores at the bar, I can hear a band playing somewhere down the street. The town raised a pavilion down by the Tippins barn, and that is where most of the festivities will take place —the dance tonight, the speech from our governor this afternoon, the celebration picnic. There will be food from every household and business in town, spread out as far as the eye can see.

I saw the tables being set up on my way home last night; Gable, the new surveyor, was supervising, and the other men were giving him a time of it. But he seemed to be taking it with fine good humor.

Jesse Thatcher comes sauntering in, looking both stronger and thinner than he should. A man gets to look that way when he's been on the trail a while.

He leans his arms on the bar.

"Coffee?"

"Lucky for you, I just made more." I pull out a tin cup and set it with a clank on the counter.

"I've never seen Glory Mesa so full," he groans.

I pick up the pot from the range with a towel and pour out a full cup. "Me neither. We're big doins' now."

He laughs, or rather scoffs, through his nose.

"What—or should I say who—convinced you to be in town this week, Jesse Thatcher?"

He smiles, but his heart's not in it. His eyes take on a grim glint. "Business. I had to talk to Archer." He sips his coffee and grimaces. "Say, you haven't seen any bad characters around?"

"What do you mean?"

"Anyone who'd kill—you know—for money?"

I shake my head. "I've seen a sight of men I hope never to clap eyes on again, but no one like that."

He nods, brief thanks. "Just figured I'd ask."

"If I see anyone, who should I tell?"

He looks back at me with a touch of admiration in his glance. "Raymond. Tell the marshal."

"Kate!" Carson's voice booms from down the bar. "I ain't payin' you to talk!"

I swallow my annoyance and push myself back from the counter.

Without a word, Thatcher sets a coin on the counter and slips out.

With a glance at Carson, I dip the washrag in my bucket of suds and wring it out hard. If he could know what we were talking about, he'd not be so sharp; but from the way he sounded, I reckon Thatcher doesn't even want Carson knowing.

Something warms inside me, right in my middle, that I'm the one they'd look to for information.

I'll keep a sharp eye out now, that's for certain. If Thatcher's worried about someone coming and shooting up the governor, then there must be something to it.

A patron comes up to the bar. From the grin on his face, I reckon he's aiming to celebrate hard from the start.

I drop my rag back over the edge of the bucket and turn to him. "What'll it be?"

"Rye?"

I thin my lips and set a bottle and a glass on the bar in front of him.

Someday, someday, someday I'll get out of this hole.

I turn around as the man uncorks the bottle and reach for the towel and coffee pot as another patron comes up and points to it.

It's going to be a long day of smelling cheap spirits and smiling. I want the fresh air and the glad music of the band down the street and the lemonade, which I hear is going to be cold, if one gets there fast enough.

I just want to be free.

IT'S ALMOST AFTERNOON, and hot outside. One the patrons is mighty tipsy already, and—just my luck—it's the one who wants more and is broke.

"Sorry, sir." I give him my sincerest, sorriest expression. "No money, no whiskey."

He swears under his breath, rifling his person again for a coin.

If he had it, it would be used by now.

Peter is leaning on his broom, grinning with delight at the man's trials and tribulations.

I take the broom from him. "Go on, get yourself some fun while you can."

"You mean it?" His eyes light up with hope.

"Sure." I reach into my pocket and give him a dollar.

He sticks the coin in his pocket and throws his arms around me in an uncommon show of affection.

Then he's gone out the back door. If I can't go, at least I can enjoy his excitement.

The patron is glaring at me as if I should have shelled out for him too. But it's short-lived, as his attention is redirected by a murmur from the doorway, men parting in an uncommon show of respect as a woman enters.

It's Rosamund Lacey.

"Kate!" I can smell the scent of warm vanilla and lavender as she steps up beside me and lowers her voice. "You should be enjoying yourself."

I reach down and wipe my hands on my apron. "Well, Carson can't pass up the opportunity to make money."

"It's a celebration day. Close the bar and slip away for a few minutes when you can—I'll talk to Carson."

"I'll try."

"Come by when Archer makes his speech. It's at four o'clock. Carson can't say no then. Find me and I'll have lemonade and cake." She winks.

"Lemonade and cake sounds perfect," I say, tucking away a stray, damp curl. I think it comes out sadder than I mean it to.

"Carson can't keep you all day." She leans closer and presses my hand. "I'll be watching for you."

. . .

THE STREET IS ODDLY QUIET, but far away, I can hear the hum of hundreds of voices. It's five minutes to four, and I gather my skirts and break into a run. Rosamund must have talked to Carson, because when I asked to go hear the speech, he said yes immediately, though with great reluctance.

A crowd is gathered all around the low stage. Archer stands atop, talking quietly and comfortably with Raymond Lacey. I'm not sure if I've ever seen the marshal in such nice, clean clothes. They almost look wrong on him.

"Kate!" Rosamund spots me and waves for me to come over. I push carefully through the crowd to join her near the punch table.

"I was worried that you weren't coming." She smiles, fresh and ladylike.

"Carson wanted the bar open until the last possible minute."

"That boar," she chides, though the smile doesn't disappear. "He was down here himself earlier."

I glance back up the street out of habit and see him coming down now.

"Have some cake." Rosamund bends down and cuts a thick, yellow slice, covered in pink frosting. I've never had a piece of cake this big in my life.

"Lemonade?" She hands me the cake and reaches for a pitcher.

"Please."

I take a bite of the cake and taste lemon.

"It's lemon?"

"Glory Mesa is the capitol of the Western Territory. We thought we should be grand if we could. There will be champagne tonight."

Champagne. I haven't thought about that stuff in ages, but I remember the way it tasted.

"Have you ever had it?"

A nod, vaguely. Memories I've kept back are swimming around in my head. I stare at my reddened hands.

They used to be soft and white as milk.

Hang it all, I'm not thinking about this now. I shove my fork into the cake and take a huge bite. It's beautifully made, buttery and light as air, and the frosting is rich and sweet.

"Good?"

"Very good." I take another large, cantankerous bite.

Archer is walking to the edge of the low platform, holding up one hand, an almost shy smile on his face. "Hold? Hold the music?"

The band plays on with cheerful abandon, and he has to shout to be heard.

The music breaks off awkwardly.

"Thank you, people of Glory Mesa and the Western Territory, for coming together to celebrate today. Twenty-two years ago, this town was founded as a bastion of hope in the middle of a barren land."

The crowd breaks out in applause.

"There was talk out East about the impossibility of this

venture. But brave souls would not be deterred, and here we are."

More applause.

"However," —he holds up his hand, breaking the claps and cheers— "this success is not to be attributed to human stubborness alone. We, as a people, as a town, have cared for one another, we have protected one another, we have fought for one another. It's the people of Glory Mesa who have made this town the heart of the Western Territory. And that is something each and every one of you should be proud of."

As I stand there in the press of people, something, I'll never know what, makes me look away toward the open land past the end of main street, and I see him coming as if out of a dream—a boy, not much older than Peter, galloping into town from the shimmering beyond, he and his horse lathered and wavering.

I count the seconds until the sound of the hoofbeats disrupts Archer's speech. The people are turning now, murmuring, looking to see who could be riding into town at this moment, of all times.

I notice how Raymond Lacey steps closer to his brother-in-law, his hand on his gun.

Jesse's not the only one on edge.

The boy reins in so sharply the horse almost loses its balance. "Where is Governor Scott?" he demands in a voice that is only on the cusp of manhood.

Archer takes a step forward and Raymond catches him

by the arm. But the boy seems harmless. He's dirty and weaponless and riding a cowpony.

"I need him...is he here?"

"He's here," says Archer. "What can he do for you?"

The boy looks at him for a long moment.

"I came for help. I heard tell you're settin' down the law sure as the rail ties."

"How can I help you?"

The boy throws his leg over his pony's back and drops to the ground. He looks ready to faint. "Got anything to drink?"

Maria Pike swiftly brings over a brimming glass of lemonade, her black silks rustling. The lad's hands shake as he takes the cup, and he drinks half of it in a few ragged, desperate gulps.

He takes a long breath like a man coming up for air.

"It's my brother. We're cowpunchers and we own our own herd." A defensive note enters his voice. "It's not the biggest around, but they're good cows. We drove about sixty head to the railhead in Saguaro City a week ago. But someone's out for our cattle."

"Tell me," says Archer.

"The Cattleman's Association said our herd had ticks, which it didn't, and we proved it. Then they offered to buy them at half price, and we refused. My brother, he knows what good stock is worth. He's no fool. Next morning, the sheriff came and charged us with murder."

"Murder?" Archer's eyebrow raises. "Of who?"

"Dunno. A man I never saw before. My brother Luke

never saw him either. But we didn't do it, we were both in the boarding house all night. The clerk saw us, our other puncher saw us."

"What about them?"

"The puncher's dead, the clerk changed his mind. And they took Luke to jail. They'd have taken me, but I got away. They're going to kill us for our cattle. If we'd known—well, someone told me you're holding down justice."

"Yes, we are." The governor's voice is hard. "What's your name, son?"

"Ted."

"Ted, I reckon I can go down there and straighten things out."

Raymond Lacey takes a step closer. "A deputy could." He speaks under his breath, but his voice carries. "I'll swear someone in, you send them with a letter and gun."

Archer's opening his mouth to answer, and then it hits me strong as a gunshot.

"Governor!"

I push my way past the handful of people between me and the stage. Archer is looking at me with astonishment.

"Governor, you promised me a favor."

"I did." He remembers, thank goodness for that.

"Let me go." I hold his gaze and refuse to look at Marshal Lacey. I have nothing but respect for that man, but my appeal is to Archer and Archer alone.

"I'm a good shot, you know that. I'm careful and smart and I'm not afraid of rough characters."

I see it in his face; he's weighing it.

"I can do it."

"I know." The words are reassuring, not in the least impatient.

The world stands hot and still.

Archer turns to his brother-in-law. "Raymond, will you do it?"

"Come by the office tonight." Raymond winks at me. I almost can't believe my eyes.

"Thank you." I seize Archer's hand in mine.

I turn to the boy, but he's staring at me with a face of white, stricken horror.

"You can't do that," he whispers. The words seem to drive home to him the thing he can hardly comprehend. "You can't do that!"

"I can," I say quietly. "I swear I'll get your brother out." I can't hold his doubts against him, but I have no doubt in my own mind. This is the thing I've been waiting for, the thing that's been waiting for me.

"I wouldn't agree to this, Ted, if I didn't have complete confidence in her. I promise you that," Archer assures him.

"I came to you for help." His voice breaks.

"I'm giving it."

"But he won't listen to a woman. They told me if I asked for you by name—" Something breaks in his face. He jams his fists down at his sides and stalks back through the crowd.

He swings up and kicks his horse into a gallop, going back the way he came.

Archer looks to me, a question in his face.

"It'll be all right," I reply. "I'll catch up to him tomorrow."

"Good. Don't let me down, Kate." He shakes my hand. I'd rather he'd slap me on the shoulder like a man, but he's a gentleman all the way through.

I let out a deep breath and become aware of the crowd again.

They're stirred up. I hear a voice that sounds too much like Carson's shouting words like "preposterous" and "ridiculous." A woman's voice agrees with him.

I pick up my lemonade and duck back into the press of people, blessing my short stature. I'll keep my distance from Carson until he's had time to cool down.

Jesse Thatcher is there, irony in his eyes. I can't tell what he's thinking, but he is thinking something.

He reaches over and clinks my lemonade glass with his.

"Sorrel or pinto? It's yours."

I glance up at him, confused.

He's got a little smile on his face as he looks over at Carson, who is fuming and scanning the crowd for me.

"They're both pretty little mares. Can't go wrong with either."

"Jesse..."

"Come on, quick, before Carson gets over here."

"Pinto."

"Done." He tips his head back and drains the last of his lemonade. "Good stuff, this."

And he drifts off into the crowd.

25

IRENE

THE OPEN BARN IS FILLED WITH A PLEASANT HAZE. I've been to a few dances in the fine ballrooms of the Eastern mansions, wearing black, drinking punch in a corner, listening to my aunt hold court among the rest of the women who were too old and comfortable to dance.

This is entirely different.

The lanterns illuminate fresh-cut beams that still smell of wood and not hay. Laughter, real laughter, fills the air; and the music—stringed instruments, mostly—is wistful and strong and alive, not musty and stiff like inherited lace.

I decided to wear colors tonight. I've worn mourning since Arnold died, but he was the one who convinced me to put off my widow's clothes before we came west. He wouldn't want me to wear black to a dance.

The dress is green—bright, living green—and it hangs

about my shoulders, leaving my neck free under my pinned-up curls.

I see Edith across the room, her arm tucked through the arm of her tall husband. They look so happy together, so comfortable.

I used to be that way with James.

Maria Pike is at the punch bowl, her gloved hand curved elegantly around the glass. The woman knows how to make even a punch glass look like it's in the hand of a queen.

Rosamund is standing along the wall talking with Jesse Thatcher and Mr. Trasker. They laugh—it must be a fine thing to fit so smoothly into this place as Rosamund Scott has. Kidnappings, desperate rides, near death, and she still looks like she's fresh from the East, her eye unclouded and her smile glad.

I wish I could be her. It is a silly thought, but I envy the poise with which she has moved through the tragedy that has swirled around her from her first days in the territory.

We are not unalike in that respect—the tragedy. But I feel already that I have been tainted by it forever, and she appears untouched.

My eyes stray to the doors that stand open to the fresh air. Raymond Lacey steps in and I feel the air change.

I did not know if he would come.

He looks around the room slowly, reaching up absently to straighten his tie. His hair is combed and parted to one side. There's something young and almost cavalier about it.

I wrest my gaze from him and go to get a glass of punch. I'm feeling the heat of the room.

"How are you enjoying the celebration?" asks the young woman with the ladle.

"Very well." I smile.

"You're the woman who survived that massacre, aren't you?"

"Yes."

She smiles. "I'm glad." She means nothing more and nothing less.

I move along to the wall, watch as one dance ends and another begins. Jesse Thatcher is ten feet from me, politely excusing himself from a dance with a young lady who is desperately trying to catch him.

When she has been successfully dissuaded, he leans over and says to Rosamund, "I think I'll go find Archer."

"He's outside. Talking with one of the heads of the mining syndicate, I think." Her lips curve into a wry half-smile.

"Perfect." Jesse gives a short laugh and heads out, nodding to me on his way past.

"I figure he's about to go break up a mighty important conversation," remarks Raymond with a sly smile. "Wouldn't mind watching that."

"If that's what you consider entertaining, you've been out in the desert too long." Rosamund laughs softly and reaches up to brush something out of her brother's hair.

"Nonsense."

"Raymond, really. Enjoy yourself."

"I am enjoying myself." There's a hint of amusement in his tone.

"You don't look it. Standing on the edge of the crowd, arms folded, wearing that gun. You look like you're standing guard."

He turns to face her. His eyes twinkle gently, as if just looking at her makes him happy. "What do you want me to do, Rose?"

"You could try dancing."

"Dancing?" He looks out at the glowing room.

"You're the people's marshal, after all."

"They'll excuse me for standing guard, then."

"Just one, Raymond."

"With you?"

"No. I promised Archer I'd wait for him. There's no lack of ladies here."

I drink my punch and turn my attention to the dancers and musicians. The fiddle is going at a heartstopping rate and dust rises from the floorboards as the dancers keep up.

The song stops with a swift-flung chord, perhaps a little out of tune, but very enthusiastic, and the dance ends.

The talk rises in volume and the musicians regroup and start again.

It's "Rover's Widow," a gentle, lilting waltz.

I catch a movement in the corner of my eye. It's Raymond Lacey.

He's moving slowly toward me, and the people make way

for him. The light catches the dust in the air and the motes move slowly, as if caught in this dream of mine.

I'm sure he's walking past. I do not turn to face him.

But he's here, right here at my elbow, close enough that I catch the scent of soap and worn leather.

"May I have this dance, Mrs. Sandler?" His voice is deep, courteous.

"Yes." My voice almost fails me as I turn to face him. "Of course. I'd be honored."

"The honor is all mine." He extends his hand, and I put mine into his, suddenly cold. His grip, calloused and strong, closes gently over my hand, gentler than I've ever felt. He leads me toward the center of the room. My heart is beating loud and quick in my chest.

I'm afraid he'll feel it in my hand.

The musicians are still playing the introduction; time must have slowed, for it can only have been a matter of seconds since they began.

He puts his hand on my waist and I reach up to put mine on his shoulder. The introduction gently gives way to the melody.

Raymond smiles, just a little, and then we're off, swept along the way grass bends to the breeze.

I was expecting something less than what I was accustomed to back East. But I think he's better. I feel light in his arms, free.

He guides me across the floor, his strong hands tender, and he gives me his full attention, his eyes smiling politely.

It's almost too much, his gaze on me like this. He's put his vigilance on hold just for this dance, but I still feel his other self lurking underneath, the man who can face a storm of bullets without flinching. What he is now, tender and charming and so gentlemanly, will disappear again like a sheathed saber.

I've only seen it a few times—when there's someone in distress, or with his sister, or here, in this moment.

"You're so serious." He raises his eyebrows. "Am I that rusty?"

"No." I force myself to smile and look him in the eye. "I was actually thinking the opposite. You must have had practice once."

"A long time ago." He draws out the second word.

"Well, you sell yourself short. I think you're better than any partner I've had. You'll probably have a line clear to the door after this is done."

He chuckles low in his throat. "How you settlin'? Is Carson being fair?"

"Yes." I avoid answering the settling question. I'm well, but my heart aches for something it can't reach, something I cannot even decipher myself.

"And the settling?"

"I think it'll be a little longer," I admit, the truth coming out on its own. "But—I think I'm ready to earn my way."

"No hurry." He looks at me with an expression that almost could be a smile, but isn't. "No hurry."

"It may as well be sooner rather than later. I want something to do."

He nods slowly, and perhaps it is my imagination, but I think his hand tightens gently on mine. "Do what you will," he says. "But do not feel uneasy about money. Your place here is secure as long as you need it."

"Marshal—" I draw in my breath, trying to find words to protest firmly but politely. I can only guess that he's the one who pays for it, as Carson is too hard a businessman to give away lodging out of the kindness of his heart.

"My sister was nearly in your position." He looks at me knowingly. "If I hadn't made it, I'd have wanted to know she was safe and not driven desperate."

My protest dies, and with it, our conversation.

It's just the music and us, moving slow and gentle across the fresh floorboards.

Then the music ends and the moment is over. It's glow remains, gold and thick as the haze in the air.

"Thank you, Mrs. Sandler," he says in his molasses voice. He bends to kiss my hand, and something in the motion takes my breath away.

The room slows around me.

"Thank you, Marshal Lacey." I try to smile.

"My pleasure." He gives me a nod and disappears into the crowd.

It doesn't matter that he thinks no more of it now that it's over, or that he doesn't realize how wondrously gentle and charming he is compared to the rest of this wilderness—my heart sings, and I let it.

It's late. I close the door behind me and go upstairs to my small bedroom. There's a little light from the street below, and by it I light my candle.

Slowly—I cannot tell if I am dreamy or just weary—I take my wrap off, unbutton my boots, and set them aside.

The candlelight flickers against the wall. I go to the window and open it, letting in the warm summer breeze and the music from the barn across the street.

They're playing "Rover's Widow" again.

I close my eyes, let the music drift in and surround me. I wrap my arms around myself and dance, quietly, in the darkness between the music and the stars.

26

CARNEGIE

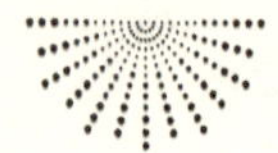

IT'S LATE AND THE CELEBRATION IS NEARLY OVER BY THE time I go to the marshal's office. There's a lamp on in the front room.

I knock and then open the door. The marshal doesn't stand on ceremony.

He's sitting at his desk, his collar open, his tie hanging undone over his shoulders. He looks up.

"Kate, I was hoping you'd come. Carson hasn't talked you out of it?"

I laugh quietly through my nose. "I haven't seen Carson. Besides, he can't talk me out of anything."

"I'm glad to hear it. And you're still determined?"

"Yes, if you're not having second thoughts." I hold my breath. I want this so badly.

"I have no doubt you'll manage." He smiles slightly. "Do you want another to ride with you?"

"I'll have Ted to travel with when I catch up."

"Very well. It goes without saying that as a deputy under me, you'll not use that gun unless it's truly needed."

"No, sir."

"Good." He stands up, unfolding his long length until he casts strange shadows on the far wall. "Do you, Kate Carnegie, swear to uphold the laws of this territory, to administer justice, and to defend this land from wrongdoers and outlaws?"

"I do."

"Do you swear to conduct yourself with honor, remaining subject to the laws you uphold, and to act with courage and conduct befitting a deputy of this territory?"

"I swear it."

"That's good enough for me." A line appears along one side of his cheek. He opens the drawer in his desk and pulls out a small tin star.

"This is yours." He sets it into my palm. "Bring it honor."

I run my finger over the smooth, shiny tin. The words *deputy marshal* seem to mock me. It seems pretentious all of a sudden.

Quietly I hand the star back.

"I'd look ridiculous wearing it," I say.

"Don't wear it, then. Just keep it." He presses it into my hand and closes my fingers over it. "You'll want the tin before you're through, even if it's to flash over the top of a saloon bar."

"I'm finished with those," I grin.

"Those fools you're after won't be. Just watch your back, now."

"Thanks. I will."

I slip the star into my pocket.

"Now." Marshal Lacey moves across the room to a rack of rifles. "I seem to remember you prefer pistols."

"Yes. But I have one."

"What year?"

"Thirty-one."

He shakes his head. "I'll get you a new issue. You'll like it. Try it out a little when you get out on the range, get a feel for her. I'll get you some cartridges to go with it."

He reaches up and takes down a couple boxes. "Do you have a belt?"

I shake my head.

"Well—" He takes a couple down off the wall. "Try these. You may have to cut another notch to fit."

I try them around my hips. One's better than the other, but he's right; I'll probably have to cut another hole for it to stay on.

"I'm also giving you a rifle and kit. As I recall, that kid wasn't armed."

"Thanks."

"I'll the bring the rifle around. Do you have a horse yet?"

"Jesse's lending me his pinto."

"I'll see him tonight, then, if he hasn't turned in. Get the sheath put on the saddle for you."

I give him a nod of thanks.

"And one last thing." He goes back to his desk, pulls out a sheet of paper with writing on it, and signs his name.

"This is from the governor, with both our signatures. You give it to the sheriff there and that'll put things straight. If there's reasonable evidence that the boy has lied or that the brother is guilty, you wire me and I'll come up and get him, understand?"

"Yes."

"Good. Here's that, then." He folds it up, stuffs it in an envelope, and hands it over. "Godspeed, Deputy."

I'M up in the dark before dawn. I know Carson's still hopping mad, and I'd rather avoid a scene in front of his boarders.

A lantern glows in the livery stable. I shove the saddlebags back up onto my shoulder and quicken my steps toward it. Jesse said the pinto would be there.

"Kate." It's Peter, standing in the shadows. His hand is cupped around a half mug of coffee he must have gotten off the hostlers. "You know, you shouldn't go alone."

"Why not? I'm catching up with the boy. I won't be alone for long."

"I should come with you." He glances up at me.

"I don't know, Peter."

"It might be a trap, you know." His dark eyes are serious. It's like there's a man trapped in that boy's face, under his solemn boy's voice.

"Better me than the governor, then."

"You don't mean that."

"Yes, I do!"

"You're too nice, Kate."

I laugh. I don't go putting my thumbs in people's eyes, but nice is not exactly the first thing most folks call me.

He relents at last. "You can go alone if you're careful."

"I'm always careful."

He laughs. It echoes in the tin cup as he raises it and takes a drink.

"You be careful too, Peter."

"Sure." He shrugs. "There won't be any trouble here while you're gone."

He says it like he's sure somehow.

I reach out, catch his shoulder, and give him a hug. "I'm going to miss you."

"Me too, Kate." He pats me on the back and then he's gone, heading down the street the way a wild thing goes about its business on the mesas.

He's something different, that boy.

Maybe it's why we fit together so well.

Jesse's waiting inside. The pinto is already saddled. The rifle hangs from its sheath, strapped tight against the saddle.

"Morning," Jesse says from the other side of the horse. There's a grunt and I figure he's giving the cinch another check.

He comes around, giving her forehead a brief, friendly

rub. "She's the nicest thing you could ask for, not a bit sour. She'll take care of you if you're good to her."

"Jesse, I can't tell you how much—"

My thanks dies as he waves me off. "You really don't have to thank me. It was due you from one corner or another." He chuckles. "Besides, I see it in your eyes—that trapped feeling town gives a body who's made for the open spaces."

I run my hand up the mare's cheek. "I'll take good care of her."

"I'm sure you will." He steps closer, lowers his voice. "Look, Kate. You recall what I was saying yesterday?"

I nod.

"You keep your eye out. It may be that the letter and the tin star will settle this just fine, but there's something afoot. Haven't got it figured, exactly, but there's something. Watch your back."

"Thanks. I will." I untie the mare's reins from the ring on the wall.

My heart's pounding with excitement. I am finally free from Carson, on my way to an adventure.

The whole Western Territory lies before me.

I check my saddlebags again. The provisions I packed, the flint, the tin star, the letter, it's all there. I reach up and throw the saddlebags over the horn.

I shove my foot in the stirrup and swing up.

"Godspeed." Jesse pulls his brim, a shadowy gesture against the dim light of the stable.

I brush a stray hair out of my mouth and pull my brim in

return.

I'm off.

I give the pinto a touch with my heel and she shoots forward like an antelope.

A shout reaches my ears over the sound of her breath and hooves. I hear Jesse's voice raised. "Clay, don't—it's too late. Let her go!"

I pause, swing the mare around.

I hear hooves clattering over the hard dust, and Clay Carson rides up beside me in the dim morning light, his horse snorting and fighting him. He saws the bit, turns it in a couple circles, and swears at it as I wait for him to sit still enough to talk to me. The horse doesn't even have a saddle on, and Carson's shirt's is half untucked.

He's panting and out of breath by the time the horse stands still. "Kate, you know this is plumb loco. Come on back."

"I gave my word to the boy. He's in trouble."

"It's the marshal's business."

"He deputized me."

He mutters something under his breath.

"Carson, I'm done at your place."

"I've had no time to find other help!"

"Peter knows the ropes."

"It's a long ride to Saguaro City. And what'll you do after this is all over?"

I press my lips together. "Don't worry about me. What I do is no longer your responsibility or your business."

He flushes red. Even in the dim light, I can see it. "If you think you can walk in there like the governor himself and they'll listen to you" —he shakes his finger at me, leaning into my face— "you're dead wrong, Kate. You'll see. You got these tom-fool dreams of glory, but mark my words, you'll be disappointed. Or worse, dead."

"I'm the messenger. The badge and the letter will do the talking. Now, I must be on my way, and if I'm pretty sure you have a saloon to mind."

"I won't let you throw your life away." He pulls his gun.

I let my breath out slowly. Perhaps I should have kept riding, let him fester and fume but not make a scene like this.

I look down at his gun. "I'm not drawing on you, Carson. You're tired, you had some drink last night. But I'm not going back. I've been deputized, and that's my job now."

He doesn't move.

I take in my breath again and whip my hand out like lightning, knocking the gun out of his hand. It happens so quick he doesn't have time to grip or react.

A girl learns things in a saloon.

"Carson," I say gently, "never draw on me again."

His face is flushed with anger as he dismounts to search for his gun among the dark sagebrush.

I turn my horse northwards and my heart nearly jumps to my throat.

There's a rider sitting there watching, beside the old oak.

Marshal Lacey. He merely pulls the brim of his hat and turns back toward Glory Mesa.

27

NEWTON

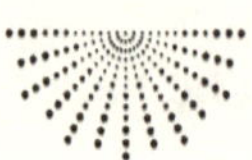

The warm, late-summer breeze pushes the curtains in the window across from my bed in a gentle ebb and flow, like sea waves.

Through the open window, I can hear the comings and goings of the ranch below, the clang of the hammer as a horse is reshod, the bellowing of cows near the barn.

Harrison may have the finest spread this side of the Rio Jefe, but with every day of my convalescence, my longing grows for my own tall pines and icy mountain streams and the wild horses that range the hills.

Below me on the porch I hear Sikes's voice, matter-of-fact and a little dismissive.

Despite his giving the distinct impression that he doesn't enjoy his stay here, he has remained for nearly two weeks. I tell him I am improving very well and that Glory Mesa should not be without its doctor, but he dismisses my excuses without bothering to refute them.

Strangely, the slowest thing to heal has been the burns from the *darani's* mouth. A couple places on my side may scar, Sikes says.

But a scar is just that. If I can return to riding and managing the ranch, I'll take it.

The April brothers are working for a hand's wage while they wait. I suggested a few days back that they go on without me, but the whole ranch is on edge after the night they spotted a man in the shadows of the porch. Buck says neither of them are in a hurry, and Harrison tells me they're the best horsebreakers he's seen in twenty years.

Slow steps sound on the porch below my window, the sound of boots wearing spurs.

"Afternoon, Doctor." It's Buck's voice, respectful and genial.

"Afternoon."

"Warm day, huh?"

If Sikes replies, I don't hear it.

"Say, how's Newton?"

"He'll be back on his feet before long."

"Glad to hear it. I'm itching to see that herd—there's a herd of mustangs out northwest of his place. We're going to get some stock to break."

"I've been there," says Sikes. "If you go after them, it will bring you sorrow."

"I think you've said something to that tune before." I hear

a scrape as if Buck's pulled out a chair. "But a man's got to make a living."

"What things men have justified with those words."

"Britt and me, we don't go on the wrong side of the law. Leastwise, besides the occasional dust-up. We go straight, and that's a fact."

"I mean only that a man may always choose a different path from what lies before him, and yet he refuses in the name of what he must do."

"And you want me to choose a different path?"

"Buck April, if there is one thing I cannot do, it is change your path for you. Not even if I tried. You and your brother, you are like those mountain stallions. You cannot be turned, you cannot be broken. Yet it is my wish that you make your choice with eyes open rather than walking into it blind."

"Into what?"

A pause. "This land is cursed. And it will require its toll of good men before the curse can be broken."

A shot cuts through the peaceful noise like a knife. A horse screams and there are shouts coming from everywhere below.

Two, three more shots follow.

I'm done being in bed.

I throw back the blanket and jerk on my boots. I grab my gun belt off the back of the chair against the wall and pull my pistol out. I spin the chamber. Someone's reloaded it.

The front door is open, the porch framed in the doorway.

Three or four men are crowded around Harrison, half-dragging him back into the safety of the house.

"I'm fine, I'm fine!" he's bellowing, shoving off the men as they haul him into the room. There's blood on his fingers.

He pushes them off and pulls up his shirt with a grimace. There's a nick above his right hip, bleeding down his side, but he stuffs a handkerchief against it.

"Son of a gun missed." His voice is wry.

Britt strides in slowly and leans one hand against the wall, looking at the scene with an iron face. "He's lit out. Might have grazed his pony, but nothing real."

"Did you get a look at him?"

"Not much. He had his face covered. Quick as a cougar."

"Where was he?" I lower myself into Harrison's blue armchair. It's a strange feeling, being weak.

"In the bunkhouse," replies Harrison. "Shot right through the window."

"One of the hands?"

"No, I think he stole into there during the roundup. That gunshot gave him away. He only had one chance and he missed." Harrison grimaces.

Buck comes running up the porch steps and through the open door. "Britt, the horses are ready."

"We're going to track him a piece." Britt looks at Harrison and then at me. "He can't have gone far, and his horse had shoes."

"My blessing," I reply with a mock salute. "I'd come along if I could. Go get him."

2 8

CARNEGIE

I CATCH UP TO THE BOY THAT EVENING, FOLLOWING THE flicker of his campfire against the craggy hills and the scent of smoke in the clean night air.

He hears me coming, but cannot tell the direction. I see him start to his feet, draw his knife, and turn slowly, first towards me and then away.

"Evening," I greet, stepping into the light, leading Thatcher's pinto by the bridle.

The boy whips around. His eyes take me in, head to toe, from my father's army jacket I'm wearing against the cold to the trousers I borrowed from one of the young hands at the livery.

"Get out of here. I already said I didn't want you."

"May I share your fire? It's too dark to be traveling anywhere tonight."

His eyes narrow. He's too much of a man already to turn

a woman away from his fire, but too much of a boy still not to take offense at my presence.

"Go ahead."

"Thanks." I hobble the pinto next to his horse and approach the fire. A pot with coffee sits on an iron trail range, but I don't see evidence of food.

"You eat already?"

He gives me a nod. I think perhaps he didn't eat at all.

"You mind if I cook something? I'm famished."

"Nope." He shifts and pulls his canvas coat tighter around him.

I cook up a pot of beans with some salt pork and I make extra. Poor boy is swallowing and trying to keep his eyes off the food.

"Do you have a plate? I won't eat all this." I don't look at him as I say this, just plate up my own, business-like.

"Sure, somewhere," he says carelessly.

"Go get it." I glance up at him and smile. "I'd hate to waste any of this."

He scrambles up and disappears to the shadow side of his horse.

"You're Ted, right?"

"That's my name." He returns, plate in hand.

I give him the spoon handle-first and start into my supper. "I'm Kate."

"Hm," he grunts as fills his plate.

"Do you—just have that knife?"

"Yeah. I had a pistol, but they took all our weapons back

in Saguaro City." His eyes go to my gun, still belted around my waist.

"I have one for you. Ever shot a rifle?"

"I'm good at it." He shoves a spoonful of beans into his mouth.

"Good, because I could really use a good shot backing me up."

"I didn't say you were coming with me," he says quickly. "You can share my fire, but you're not coming with me tomorrow."

"We're going the same direction, pal."

"It's a free country." He shoves the last bite of his food into his mouth and puts down his plate with a clatter.

"Well," I say, "you can have me and the rifle, but if we split up, the rifle stays with me. It's the marshal's, so it's territory property."

He stares at me long and hard. I stare back quietly. If there's anyone I know how to deal with, it's boys on the edge of manhood.

"I reckon you can come with me. But mind, I'm still looking for a real gunman."

I pick up a fistful of sand to scour off my plate. "Well, like you said, it's a free country."

WE'RE in the saddle by the time the first hint of light streaks across the horizon. Ted may be a boy yet, but he's a cowhand, and he has no trouble being up before the sun.

"Why are you doing this?" he asks as we leave the camp-site behind.

"I have a letter from the marshal. It's going to help free your brother."

"They ain't going to listen to a letter."

"Well, that's all anyone else would have done."

"The governor could have done better if you'd have let him."

A tiny whisper of doubt settles in my stomach. Had I been rash?

I know Archer Scott would have gone himself in a heart-beat, heedless of the danger. But he has too many people concerned for his safety now.

"It's not that simple," I answer quietly.

"Well, it'll be pretty simple when we get there. You'll see. They won't listen to you, letter or no."

We ride in silence until the trail goes golden-red in the rising sun. The wind is cool but the light of the sun is warm already. I can sense the boy continually weighing the annoy-ance of my presence against the loss of the rifle.

I can't be too hard on him. If I had a brother I loved, I'd wish for only the best champion. And he doesn't know what I'm capable of.

"Son, where do you think you're going?"

I look up swiftly. A rider blocks the trail at the next bend, beneath a tall, spreading tree. He's mounted on a black horse. His dusty jacket is black under the light trail dust, and he wears multiple gun belts strapped across his chest and hips.

His eyes light on me and he tips his hat with a dark, muscular hand. "Ma'am."

I give him the barest nod.

"Might I ask your business?" His voice is rich and thick like good trail coffee.

"Our business is our own," I reply.

"Indeed?" He's amused, not offended at my coldness. "Well, you see, I was paid for a job. I'm looking out for a boy of this description and his companion—a man about thirty with a bay and a .45 Croix-Savannah commission."

That description fits Archer Scott like a glove. A prickle runs up my back and I glance at Ted. I've stepped into a trap.

"Well, that's not us." I spur my mare forward a couple steps.

The gunslinger shifts his horse further into the trail, moves his gun up. "Hold it. The boy fits the description."

"We'll fight you then," bristles Ted.

"Easy, son." The gunslinger grins. It's a nice smile, white and quick. "You can go on. My quarrel's with your companion."

"I'm not the man you described," I say, setting my hand on my gun. "Let us by."

He looks to Ted, not me. "Go on, son. Now or not at all."

Ted doesn't meet my eyes. He spurs his horse forward and disappears up the trail.

It's silent except for the wind rustling the leaves of the tree and the impatient stamp of my pinto, annoyed at the delay and at being left behind by Ted's horse.

After the silence has gone on too long, the gunslinger says, "I don't make a habit of fighting women, though I won't say I never have. But if you tell me why you're here and where to find the man I was expecting, and leave your guns, I'll let you go on by."

"No chance."

He laughs, the first sign of impatience I've seen out of him. "Look, miss, I'm being a gentleman. I don't have to ask."

"Well, I ain't telling and I'm certainly not dropping my guns."

He shrugs. "Your choice."

He spurs his horse forward, coming for me, ready to wrest my iron right out of my holster.

I draw on him.

He wasn't expecting that. He reins in sharply, only five or six yards away. "Easy, girl! Don't you go drawing. It's just business."

"Too late for that." I cock my pistol.

He remains as still as an oak, his eyes on me, trying to gauge my mettle. "Won't you tell me what I need to know?"

"Ain't your business."

"Well, then." He turns his horse for a clean shot, but I'm ready for him.

My gun barks out, hits him square in the shoulder. His horse kites into the air and shoots away across the hard, dusty ground, leaving the man on the ground, gasping.

He fumbles for one of his holstered guns, but I cock mine again. "Hands off. Guns on the ground."

He looks at me hard, but he believes me now. He empties his belts; three guns lie in the dust.

"Now back up, slow."

He obeys. He's gripping his wounded arm with a shaking hand. I think that and his runaway horse will be his primary concerns from here on out.

I dismount, keeping my gun on him, and collect his two spares and the pistol with one chamber empty—a hardy, ten-year-old model with a bullet scar on the barrel.

I shove that one into my belt and drop the others into my saddlebags. "Your belts too."

He drops the ones across his hips.

"That one." I gesture to his chest.

With one hand, he unbuckles the last belt and throws it on the ground with an oath. A knife gleams in it.

I take that belt and leave him the other two.

"Good day to you too." I pull my brim in farewell and clap spurs to my pinto, riding hard after the boy with a smile on my lips.

TED'S LOOK is one of disgust when I lope up behind him half an hour later. "Did you bribe him?"

"No."

He just raises his eyebrows at me like I'm stupid.

"Do you want a pistol, a real one?"

He looks at me with his eyebrows drawn. I glance behind

me and rein in. I dig in my saddlebags and pull out the belt and one of the pistols.

"May as well put this to use."

His expression only darkens further.

"Where'd you get those?"

"From the gunslinger, back there."

"He gave them to you?"

"No, I disarmed him, couldn't leave him with his iron. Only a fool does that." I hold out the belt and gun again.

"You expect me to believe that?"

"You should have stuck around, then. Something you'll learn about me is that I am not a liar. You really think he'd have lost these any other way?"

Ted accepts it quietly. I think he sees the sense in it.

29

SELBY

In my days following the herd, watching for *isarks* and coyotes, I rarely see riders. Most men will cross the flatlands or take the trail that follows the Rio Jefe. Traveling through the hills brings you near the *isark* breeding grounds, and most men don't fancy that.

So when a cloud of dust rises in the distance, the sort that only comes from a group of riders, I draw back up onto the high rocks to watch their approach and clean my rifle.

"What is it?" shouts one of the shepherds, when the cloud grows enough to be seen from the ground by an untrained eye.

"Riders," I call down.

"Shouldn't you be loading that thing, not taking it apart?"

I wave him away. He goes, muttering. They pay me to shoot *isarks*, not men.

My rifle is cleaned, put together, and loaded by the time

the newcomers draw close enough to put them in my sights, but by then, it doesn't matter. I can see there are four of them, all riding with the long-legged ease of the Auki, but three are fair-haired and ride roans.

It's the Swifts.

Jem's the first one to see me—he always has an eye out for danger.

"Well, Jack." He takes off his hat and beats it against his leg. "Fancy meeting you here."

I salute casually with two fingers.

Max cranes his neck and squints up at me. "You shoot down any *isarks*?"

"Not today."

"Do you have room at your fire for a few travelers?" Jem asks. "We're looking to bed down soon."

"You are welcome to share my fire. The shepherds—they keep to themselves." I stand up and gesture southwestward with my arm. "Camp's thataway."

Jem smiles broadly. "Thanks."

The four ride on.

I'M SITTING and watching the sun sink half an hour later when I hear the scrape of boots on the rocks behind me.

It's Alan.

"Evening." He swings his arms idly. "Mind if I share the view?"

"Go ahead."

He settles on the rock beside me and takes off his hat. "No wonder you came back to this," he remarks after a few minutes. "There's no landscape quite like it."

"I could do without the sheep."

He snorts appreciatively. "Yeah, I suppose there's that."

The shepherds are bringing in the stragglers and strays, settling the flock for the night. Soon the dogs will take over the watch from me.

"Jack, I want to ask you something."

"Me?"

"Do you believe in the curse on the land? That without the chosen one, all will end in destruction?"

"That's quite the question."

"You've lived here a long time, but you also spent a great deal of time in the East. I think a man like you must have some perspective."

"I reckon I believe it's true in one way or another. But sometimes those things are fulfilled right in front of you and you don't know it." I rub my hand along the stock of my gun. "So I guess I don't believe in chasing signs too close."

"Yes." He sounds relieved. "I feel the same way."

"Is there a concern?"

He hesitates. "Not really."

I stand up and sling my rifle over my back. "Good. But if there's trouble—you call. Not many men I'd lend my rifle to, but I would for you."

Alan smiles, a lean, halfway smile that leave a deep wing-line up one cheek. "I will remember that."

. . .

DOWN IN THE CAMP, a little distance from the shepherds' fire, a second fire already burns. To my surprise, a sheep is roasting.

It's been so long since I've had good fresh meat, the smell is almost painful.

One of Ogbathashanach's shepherds slips past me, away from the fire, with a respectful nod. I catch his arm in passing.

"Where did the meat come from?"

"Ogbathashanach welcomes your guests as brothers," he says, not meeting my eyes—no one around here does but Ogbathashanach himself. "He will come himself in short time."

"You didn't tell me that you had a friend among the Far Hill clan," says Max, from beyond a veil of blue smoke. "I was expecting beans and fry bread."

"You'll have that too, if you like." I duck out from under the strap of my rifle and lean it against the wall of the steep rocks behind us. "There's some supplies in my pack over there."

Max jumps up and goes to my buckskin, hobbled and contentedly picking at a spot of grass. He lifts his head and briefly pins his ears in warning to Max.

"I see you have the same horse," says Max, making peace with it before skirting around it to my supplies.

"He's given me no reason to trade him."

Max chuckles appreciatively and comes over. "I'll do the bread, you can do the beans." He shoves the flour and soda tin into my arms.

THE MEAL IS ready before Ogbathashanach comes, dressed in woven purple and red.

"As far kin greets far kin, so I greet you," Tagweiah touches his forehead. "Are these your herds?"

"Some of them," replies Ogbathashanach. "I sojourn with my far kin and their companions. We have traveled alone and without protection for two years and it is good to rest with larger herds for a time."

"It is our honor and pleasure to share your fire," continues Tagweiah.

Ogbathashanach smiles, his dark eyes twinkling.

"It's his fire, and we are his guests, all. The meat alone is mine to share. Come, sit." He motions to all of us.

"Do you not live in the north, you half sons of Auki?" asks Ogbathashanach as the food is passed around.

"We do," says Jem. "But Tagweiah brought us news from the south where his people study the stars, so we're heading down to Glory Mesa to speak with Governor Archer."

"What news?" I lean my arms on my knees and rest my head against the rock wall behind me.

"The Auki constellations tell stories, and it is foretold that when the sign of the white stag meets with the lone mountain and serpent, that the chosen one is at hand."

"The curse? As in the end of the land's curse?" I glance at Alan, who is eating quietly.

"Even so," says Ogbathashanach, with interest. "Yet, the end could be a while off yet. Is it not said that the white stag must be slain in the skies?"

"So it shall be. But after thousands of years, the coming together of these stars is event enough to tell the governor of. For who can tell if the curse is over or if it will bring destruction?"

"And if it brings destruction?" I take a piece of fry bread and tear it in half. "What then?"

"We will worry about that, if it happens. For the time being, it is perhaps a good sign."

"Perhaps the heroes are coming at last," says Ogbathashanach approvingly. "The stars tell their stories as well. They will help bring the curse to its end. Do you know the stories?"

"We keep the stars," says Tagweiah. "The stories are not so often spoken over our fires as they are over yours."

"Then I shall tell you of some of them, that in your memory they may live as well." He closes his eyes and takes a deep breath of the night air.

"The chosen men are fair and good men, ones who could be kings and captains in their own right. Instead, they shall follow a man of war, who loves the land with his heart as a man might a woman. And this man of war shall be good and his cause shall only be for right. He will win in what he sets his hand to do. And those who make him their foe shall fall, be they good or evil."

Max offers me a thick slab of mutton from the end of his knife and I thank him softly under my breath.

"They tell of one man, a slayer of fearsome beasts, who will be beloved of all men and so skilled as a warrior that news of his fame will reach far and wide, and that by his hand will the bringers of the end be brought forth. But he will die by the hand of a friend. They also tell of a man with a good heart who will suffer great pain, both in body and spirit, and it will make him changed and burn with anger. And woe to him, for he will ask for death and will not receive it. But even in that, he will have grace, for he will bring an end to great evil."

Somewhere a coyote yips and I start up, but a herd dog barks sharply and the sound of the coyote moves away.

Ogbathashanach resumes in his still, warm voice. "And there is yet another, who will be likened to the white stag in the heavens—who, indeed, will see heaven. And if he dies, the world shall live."

"These sound a bit like downers," says Max with a concerned scowl. "Do any of these chosen men end happy?"

"Legends such as these view men from the eye of an eagle. It is not for us to say if any of these men die unhappy. They die. So do we all." He shrugs and begins to fill his pipe.

"And yet, there is one the legends speak of—a man with blood-stained hands. But his heart yearns for a good thing, and in the end, he receives what his heart desires."

Ogbathashanach lights his pipe and takes a long draw.

"I suppose, if any man were to be happy, perhaps it would be him."

30

CARNEGIE

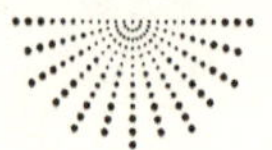

THERE'S A CAMP PITCHED RIGHT NEXT TO THE TRAIL below us, in an otherwise quiet, rocky valley. The quiet breeze carries the busy sounds of men and horses to my ears.

"Who are they?"

"It's Blue Harding's gang," Ted replies, leaning forward on his saddle horn to peer down into the valley. "If they find out you're coming from Glory Mesa and the marshal, you're dead."

"I've never even heard of him." I shade my eyes and peer up the trail.

"He used to camp out in the northern mountains. Luke and I used to ride for an outfit up there."

"What feud does he have with our marshal?"

"He's just got a problem with government out here. Figures it'll be the death of life as we know it."

"It'll also be the end of a lot of lawlessness."

"That's exactly his problem." Ted shoves his hat back on his head.

"Is there a way around his camp?"

"Not less'n we go far out of the way."

"Nothing for it, then. Let's go." I spur my horse forward, up the trail.

"But if he finds out—"

"If he finds out, so be it. I won't volunteer information, but I'm not running either, not when we have a life depending on us."

Ted turns to look at me. "You mean it, don't you?"

"Do I look like the sort of person to say what I don't mean?" I raise my eyebrows and slow my horse to match his pace.

"No. Sorry." He glances at the camp and then back at me. "I just—I know some men a lot bigger and stronger who'd go around. You got guts."

And I need them.

I quicken my horse to a trot as we approach the camp. It's sprawled out in a collection of tents and fires and anchored by a line of picketed horses. A faded blue handkerchief tied to the line blows wistfully in the dusty wind.

The smell of horse and sweat and smoke are over-powering.

A strongly-built, lean fellow with a thatch of blond hair going gray gets to his feet and comes to the edge of the trail, pulling a cigar out of his mouth.

"Well, well, well, what have we here?" His voice is slow and easy, like molasses.

"Just passing through."

"Through my camp, you see."

"Your camp has blocked the trail," I reply, reining my horse in.

"That may have been deliberate." He bites off the end of his cigar and spits.

"Seems an odd place to set up camp."

"Well, here's the trouble." He saunters over until he's standing about ten feet from me. He walks like a man accustomed to calling the shots. "I'm looking for a pair, supposed to be coming this way from Glory Mesa, due right about this time. I can't afford not to."

I stiffen. Again, we're expected.

His roving eyes settle thoughtfully on my face and his voice dips low and gentle. "You know anything about that?"

"I reckon maybe we have enemies," I say calmly.

"You're saying you came from there?"

"I reckon so."

"Hmm." He takes a draw on his cigar and folds his arms. "Now, what I want to know is if you think you have enemies, why didn't you just—" He gestures in a circular motion with the cigar. "You know—go around?"

"I can't afford the time. I don't want any trouble, just let us through and we'll leave you be." I glance at Ted then at the rifle hanging in its sheath inches from his shoulder. I just hope he gets the idea.

"And I say it'll probably be in your best interest to drop your weapons and come with us," drawls the man.

"No chance." I set my hand over my gun.

"Well, then, I'm sorry I have to do this—" He reaches for his gun. I've been waiting for this moment.

His bullet cuts a furrow in the dust two feet from my horse's hooves. Mine goes into his calf. He's on the ground before he knows what hit him.

He looks up at me, his mouth jammed into a tight line. He doesn't move.

I dismount slowly, painfully aware of the men around us, hands floating above their guns. Ted is backing me up with the rifle, his finger on the trigger. This is a powder keg about to blow.

I take a couple of slow easy steps until I'm practically standing over the man. I cock my gun with a hard click. The sound's clear as day in the tight silence.

"That was a warning shot. Twitch and the next one goes somewhere more important."

I raise it and aim it right at his heart.

"Blue." One of his men takes an involuntary step in his direction.

Blue Harding has his men too well in hand for them to interfere unbidden, but they're ready to jump as soon as he gives the word.

Then Blue laughs.

"Easy, easy now, ma'am." He holds up his hands in a placating gesture. "You've got pluck, and it's true—I underestimated you."

I glance over at Ted.

"I know when I've been had, and I'm not too proud to admit it. So you let me up, put that gun away, and I'll leave you be. The boys'll leave you be. You're even welcome to share some grub, no hard feelings."

"You're an outlaw."

"And you said you wanted no trouble," he replies, wry amusement in his face.

I don't know why he was called Blue in the first place, but I swear I've never seen a brighter pair of blue eyes. And they are not intimidated by me, but they are sincere.

"Fair enough."

One of his men comes over and gives him a hand up.

"If you'll excuse me, I'm going to get this tended. Make yourselves comfortable." He throws his arm over his man's shoulder and starts to limp away. "And if I see a man pull iron, I will be the one to shoot him!" He taps his chest with a blood stained hand.

Beside me Ted lets his breath out, small and sharp.

"Kate...."

I reach out and clap his shoulder.

I'LL SAY this for Blue Harding, he's tough. Not half an hour passed before he was back out to the nearest fire, limping on a cane.

"Come on, come on!" He waves us over. "Like I said, you

have nothing to fear from the boys." We come over, but Ted doesn't put the rifle down when we sit. It stays across his knees.

There's food cooking, beans and beef and pan bread. They don't even ask us if we want to partake, they just dish up the grub and pass it out, to us same as the rest.

Blue pushes his beans around on his plate and looks up at me. "I have just one question for you, ma'am. What are you doing out here with a boy for company, carrying tin and lead for the marshal? It just ain't—pardon me—what folks like you tend to do."

"It's a job. I'm just a messenger, I wasn't expecting to get into a fight."

Blue chuckles under his breath. "Well, for not expecting it, you are quick."

I give him a nod of thanks.

"I assume you're headed north. Saguaro City or Tapo Junction?"

"Saguaro City. I am looking for their sheriff."

Blue shakes his head and clucks his tongue. "Look, you don't want nothing to do with him. He's a real rough character."

"I don't have a choice." I glance at Ted, who is shoveling beans into his mouth industriously. "The boy's brother has been accused of murder."

Blue whistles long. "Then you got a storm ahead of you and no doubt. If you're smart, you won't turn your back on that man for one second."

"Do you know him?" I take a bite of the fresh beef. It's a little tough, but I'm famished.

"Enough to know he's more a scoundrel than half the outlaws left out here. He came west after the war like a good many of us, looking for opportunity. It's men like him who turned us to the wrong side of the law."

"There's still time to turn back," I reply. "The marshal's granting amnesty to men like you."

"An interesting decision on his part." Blue's eyes take on an amused gleam. "But most of that talk's hot air."

"Not with Marshal Lacey." I scrape the last of my beans off the plate with my spoon. "He's true to his last word. If you tell him I sent you, he'll listen."

Blue just chuckles, short, under his breath. He leans down to put his empty plate on the ground, and the movement makes him grimace.

"If you weren't a lady, I'd have words with you about my leg."

"I'm sorry I had to do it."

He waves me off like it's inconsequential. "Look here." He reaches up and rubs the back of his head. "I got this tip— no name, mind you, but a hefty sum involved—for a boy and a little lawman coming up from Glory Mesa, and I figured it was the governor. I used to give the territory a lick of trouble back in the day, and I got rather notorious for calling him the 'little lawman,' since he didn't have a badge or nothin'." He chuckles under his breath. "No offense, but I took one look at you and nearly laughed out loud."

There's an appreciative laugh from the men gathered around the fire.

I don't laugh, good-naturedly or otherwise. His first guess was right.

If the lone gunslinger we'd met had been told to expect Archer, why not this man?

"Is something the matter?"

"You're not the only person looking for him along this trail." I set my plate down with a clatter and stand up. "We should be going, before dark sets in."

"You're more than welcome to lay your bedrolls here," Blue says, with a nod to the empty ground beyond the fire. "Especially if there's like to be trouble up the trail."

"Thanks, but we'll move on." I nod for Ted to follow. "We can make another hour before dark, get in by mid-morning."

"You're plucky, Miss Kate." Blue holds out his hand. "I sincerely hope we meet again sometime, under different circumstances."

"Only if they're pleasant."

"To be sure. And one more thing—" He draws his .45 and holds it out to me, standing silent for a moment. "She's a good one and she's got luck. It's never a bad idea to pack an extra if you're going up against someone crooked. Put old Rojo down her sights just once for me, huh?"

I swallow. "My father had a .45 like that. Officer's commission."

"That so?" Blue holds it up and then spins it. "It's a good gun. Saved my life a time or two. Maybe she'll save yours."

"Thanks. I'll use her." I take my old gun out of the belt where it's jammed against my hipbone and thrust the lucky .45 down across the front of my belt. Ted is already heading to get the horses.

I pause at the edge of the fire. "And Blue, about the marshal? Remember what I said."

I pull my brim in farewell and he salutes me.

3 1

NEWTON

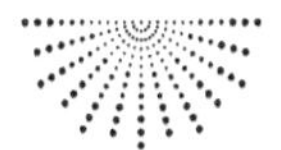

It's purple dusk when the April brothers return two and a half days later. They are tall silhouettes against the gentle sky, nearly identical in shadow, coming over the far hills beyond the barns and corrals.

Harrison and Sikes are sitting out on the porch with me, enjoying an evening smoke. Harrison leans forward and takes his cigarette out of his mouth.

"This soon. They either caught their man or they lost him fast."

Sikes stands up and goes to the edge of the porch to knock the ashes out of his pipe. The dying light slants across his face and pierces the depths of one gray-blue eye.

He puts his pipe away, sticks his hands in his pockets, and stays there at the edge of the porch, watching the Aprils ride in.

They stop at the corral first and strip the tack off their

231

horses, then saunter over with the stride of men whose legs only remember the shape of a saddle.

Buck sits down on the edge of the porch and pulls out a handkerchief, wiping the dust off his face with an equally dusty hand.

Britt leans one hand against the post of the porch and spits. "We lost him in the rocks near where that *darani* was holed up. But he was heading due northwest. The skill it took to disappear, good odds it's Tora-Teth."

He spits again. "I figure we'll catch up with him one of these days."

"You're not hurt bad?" Buck asks Harrison politely, his eyes scanning the man's body.

"Nah. Just a scratch." Harrison grimaces. "I do wish someone would catch that renegade, though. He's made enough trouble around these parts."

"He won't be in these parts long," Buck says.

"And we'll keep an eye out for him when we head out to that mustang herd," adds his brother. "Seems he was heading thataway."

"What's thataway that he'd have business up there?" asks Harrison. "It's wild country, isn't it?"

"A lot of mountains, yes," I offer. "And hot springs. His people, historically, don't touch that ground. But he's never been one to follow the ways of his clan."

Sikes takes his hands out of his pockets suddenly and turns to look at us. He regards each one of us slowly, as if committing us to memory.

Then he goes inside.

SIKES LEAVES THE NEXT MORNING, without announcement or warning. He simply comes down to the breakfast table around sunrise, bag in hand, and requests his horse.

Buck wipes his mouth with his napkin and pushes his chair back. "I'm finished. I'll do it."

Sikes follows him out.

The rest of us finish breakfast and head out into the yard. Sikes is standing on the porch, watching the sunrise with a solemn air.

I move to stand beside him and regard the young light of day. "Thank you, Doctor. I'm obliged."

"If you meet another *darani*, just send for me." A glimmer of humor appears in his steely eye.

Buck comes out of the barn with the horse, tacked up and still chewing. "Your horse, sir."

"Farewell," Sikes says briefly to me, and starts across the yard to his horse.

"Strange man." Behind me, Britt gives a small laugh. "Very strange."

"He's seen more than any of us will in our lifetimes," I reply softly. "I suppose that can make a man seem strange."

Sikes takes the reins from Buck's hand. "I do not think that I will see you again in this life."

He holds out his hand and waits as Buck comes around

the other side of the horse. "I wish you strength and courage in the task you must do."

"And to you, good doctor." Buck grins and gives him a firm handshake. "Good times and long life."

Sikes smiles, a little thinly, and mounts up. Then he reaches down and clasps Buck's hand one last time. His voice is thick.

"Godspeed, my boy. Godspeed."

32

CARNEGIE

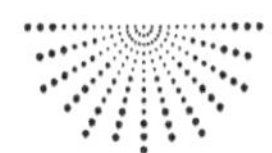

Saguaro City is three streets made up of slat-board businesses, cattle corrals, and dust. On the far end of the main street, I see the unnatural flash of silver running across the desert like quicksilver.

The railroad.

"You're sure this is it?" I push my hat back a little and look around.

Ted raises an eyebrow. "Of course."

It's a nondescript town; the only thing I can manage to make stand out is the crudely painted steer on the Cattle-man's Association sign. Whoever painted it hadn't ever looked at a steer properly.

"It's so quiet," whispers Ted. "It shouldn't be this quiet."

The dull sound of our horses' slow, deliberate hooves echo against the buildings lining the narrow street.

He's right. A town like this should be filled with shouts

and cattle bawling and the hiss and grind of steam engines and boxcars.

I see a man sitting in the shade of a porch across the street, his worn boots up on a hitching rail.

I ride over and rein in. He looks rough and his white beard is stained with tobacco, but he's what I've got.

"Excuse me, where is everyone?"

He looks at me slowly with narrow eyes that look like he's gone and squinted at the sun once too often. "Well, if it ain't a *lady*. Been a long time since I've seen one of your kind."

I'm tempted to flash my tin at him. "I said, where is everyone?"

The fellow is chewing slowly, taking his time. "Down at the courthouse." He overpronounces the word, as if it's foreign. "There's a trial on."

"A trial?"

"Murder and theft. But I'm too old for such goings on. Too old to care if the young or old die."

"Where is the courthouse?"

"It's the Broken Wheel saloon. Can't miss that." He chuckles. "Why, there was one fellow who came in one day —a real rogue, he was...."

I don't wait for him to trail on and on. I turn my horse away and head down in the direction of the saloon at a trot.

"Kate." Ted's voice is low. "Do you think—?"

He can't finish the sentence, and I don't blame him.

"We'll see. Maybe." Perhaps it'll be as simple as walking in with the piece of paper.

A body can hope, anyway.

I can spot the Broken Wheel half a block away, just from all the horses tied up on the street outside.

I stop a few buildings down and dismount.

"Are you going in there?" Ted asks, following suit.

"Yes."

He goes to tie up his horse, but I stop him. "No, wait out here with the horses. And don't draw attention to yourself. They don't know me from anyone else. I'm going to see what's going on."

"I need to see if it's Luke."

"Seeing won't help anything. Have them ready in case we need to leave quickly."

"You'll tell me if it's him?"

"Yes. If we're lucky, maybe I'll bring him with me."

Ted flashes a quick, hopeful grin. "All right, I'll wait."

I check my gun to make sure it's fully loaded and stick the letter from Marshal Lacey in the pocket of my jacket. "I'll be back as soon as I can."

I glance back at him and for the first time, I see he's scared.

"What do I do if you don't come back?"

"I'll come back. But—if something goes wrong, you just hold onto that rifle and get yourself out of here."

He nods, and I mount the steps to the saloon.

The saloon is dim compared to the bright sunshine

outside and hazy from cigar smoke. A thick crowd of people lines the walls and sits in chairs that take up most of the room. One man sits at a table, his hands folded judicially, and to one side, facing him, sits a young man flanked by two or three men standing and wearing guns.

No one needs to tell me it is Luke. He has the same expression as Ted. It's like it's stamped on their features: the dark eyebrows that draw in, the thin lips pressed tight, the sharp jaw that looks like it's permanently clenched.

He's shackled, and his clothes are trail-worn and stained, consistent with Ted's story of them being fresh off the trail.

A grating noise outside keeps catching at my ears, like a fly buzzing, and I realize all of a sudden that it's the sound of saws on wood.

They couldn't even wait until sentence was properly passed.

"This young man has committed a heinous crime, a heinous crime in our town." I can't see where the voice is coming from. "Killed good, honest Thomas Durham, who never hurt a soul in his whole life. In cold blood, he did. I ask —no, I demand—that justice be done in this town. Your honor, you see that there is no other possibility. This man here is guilty!"

The judge nods slowly, unmoved by this passionate speech. "Thank you, you may sit down." He clears his throat and looks over at the shackled man. "The defendant will please rise."

With an iron face, he stands.

"Luke Westfall, I hereby find you guilty of the charge of murder. It is therefore my duty to sentence you to hang by the neck until dead. The sentence will be carried out tomorrow at noon."

He bangs his gavel. Luke could almost be a statue, for all that he reacts. He wets his lips, that's it.

The room erupts in low talk. None of it is outrage. It's pleasant, light, expectant.

A man's to die, and they sound like it's a Sunday picnic.

I move through the crowd to the small cluster of men who stand around Luke, talking. One, a strapping fellow with steely dark hair and a heavy mustache and beard, wears a vest with a star pinned to it.

He's smoking a good cigar.

"Are you the sheriff in this town?" I ask, raising my voice only enough to get his attention.

"That's right. Terrence Rojo." He looks me up and down with mild puzzlement.

"I am here on the authority of Raymond Lacey, appointed marshal of this territory by the territorial governor."

"I see. About what?"

"About that man."

"What about him? He's committed murder. He's going hang tomorrow. Ain't no one reversing a judgment from a judge of this territory."

I pull the letter from my pocket. "Read this."

He takes it from me and unfolds it, all business. I watch

his face as he reads and I see he understands. Something slow dawns on his face, something like fear or anger; and then it's gone, like a snuffed match.

"Hm." His laugh is just a grunt around the smoking stub of his cigar. He glances up from the letter to my face, and his gaze lingers too long.

Then slowly, deliberately, he rips the letter in half. He turns it and rips it again, and then again. He drops the shredded pieces on the floor.

"This Marshal Lacey sure is something if you're the only one he could get to bring this up here. And the governor? What a joke."

Laughter fills the room.

My face burns, but it's pure anger. I see exactly the kind of man he is. The kind of man who would use a tin star to steal from a pair of brothers who have no advocate, the kind of man who thinks he can laugh in the face of justice just because it looks smaller and weaker than him.

I glance at Luke, and he's staring at the floor with an expression like someone's just slapped him in the face.

"You think ripping it up changes its contents? If you flaunt the governor's authority, you will lose what little you hold here."

I bend down to pick up the letter and the sheriff steps on it quick-like with his mud-caked boot, nearly catching one of my fingers.

I straighten, look him in the eye. It takes every ounce of my willpower to stay calm. "Very well. If you want it so badly, keep it. But this isn't over. You will release this man into my custody."

The sheriff laughs under his breath, a little too hard. The room joins in.

"Take him out." He jerks his head toward Luke. The deputies standing by the prisoner take him by the arms and lead him towards the door.

I follow the crowd out, searching the street for Ted.

He's waiting by the door, and I see the moment he glimpses Luke. His eyes widen and he takes an involuntary step forward.

And Luke sees him.

"Ted!" He strains against the men holding him. "Ted, I told you to get out of here!"

"I went for help," the boy shouts back. "I couldn't leave you. I got help!"

But his brother's face just goes blank and white and he shakes his head. "Just get out of here, Ted, before it's too late! Get!" He's pulled on by the deputies and lost to us in the crowd.

Ted is standing stricken, staring at the street, numb and distantly horrified.

I reach out and take my horse's reins from his hand.

"Did you—?" He looks up at me and there are tears in his eyes. "Where's the letter?"

"We're going to try a different way," I say, with as much assurance as I can muster. "I swear it, we are not going to leave your brother."

"Did they—what did they—"

"Noon, tomorrow."

Ted's chin trembles suddenly.

"Ted. Ted, listen to me." I come around to look him in the face. "They will not hang your brother. Did you hear what I said a moment ago?"

"They tore up that letter, didn't they?"

"Yes, but that man's just a coward deep down. He thinks if he acts big, he can get away with it. We'll show him."

"How?"

"I'm going to wire Marshal Lacey. If I get a reply through from him to halt the hanging, they have to listen to that."

I glance at the street and the men dispersing. A quarter mile or so down, I see Luke's escort shove him up the stairs and across the porch into the jail.

"We'll go right now, Ted."

"One minute there!"

I look up and see the sheriff standing in the doorway of the saloon, his arms folded. He rolls the cigar around in his mouth and then comes down to us.

"Son, ain't you the accomplice?"

Ted freezes.

I step between them. "I'm a deputy marshal of the Western Territory. I've come to see that justice is carried out, and Ted is with me."

He gives a laugh, and it's not a nice one. Like he's got me beat and is just pondering the most satisfactory way to break it to me.

"If you're a deputy marshal, young lady, why don't you prove it?"

"I'm not drawing on you today," I reply calmly. "Come on, Ted."

I back my horse and start up the street, careful not to let him out of my sight entirely. I think Blue Harding was telling the truth when he said this man wasn't the type you could turn your back on.

"Stop!" he shouts. "I'm sheriff in this town!"

I keep my eye on him, but I do not stop. I hear a curse, but he doesn't come after us.

We pass the same old man, his boots still up on the hitching rail.

"Could you tell me where the telegraph office is?" I ask, my eye still half on the street behind me.

He takes his boots off the rail and sits up to peer at me. "The telegraph office? Now what would you be wanting that for?"

"That's my business. Please be so good as to point me in the right direction."

"One block down, two streets over. Next to the newspaper office."

"Thanks." I don't wait for him to launch into a story. I suddenly have a bad feeling.

THE TELEGRAPH OFFICE is small and tidy and run by a big man with hulking shoulders and a black beard.

"Evening, ma'am. This office is going to close for supper soon."

"I just need to send a quick wire to Glory Mesa."

"Glory Mesa?" He looks at me with respect. "That's where the governor lives, ain't it? Have you met him?"

"He's a friend."

"Gollee." He whistles. "Do you have the message?"

"I need to write it down."

"Well, sure thing." He produces a pencil and a scrap of paper.

My note is quick and short.

The man doesn't even hesitate as he begins to tap it out.

Sheriff tore letter. Hanging tomorrow. Request stay of execution. Please come.

Halfway through, the man stops. "Wire's dead," he says.

"What? Why would it—"

I look out the window, and somehow I knew he was going to be there. Sheriff Rojo stands across the street, staring at the telegraph office. He takes his cigar out of his mouth and blows a long stream of smoke into the air.

"Wires are cut, probably." He looks apologetic. "If you've got a problem with the sheriff, well—"

"He'd cut his own wires?"

"He's done it once before."

"How long until they're up again?"

"Well, now that we have the railroad, maybe a day and a half."

That's too late. And Sheriff Rojo knows it.

"Thank you. If anything changes, we'll be staying at the hotel."

"Of course. Pleasure, ma'am."

I step out onto the street and check my horse over carefully, but the sheriff hasn't touched the horses. I ignore him because I don't want him to see how angry I am. He doesn't deserve that pleasure.

He's thrown down the gauntlet, and I have no choice but to pick it up. But this is a duel I'm determined to win, and I have one distinct advantage.

He underestimates me.

We put our horses up in the livery stable down the road, leaving them in the hands of a couple competent-seeming men and a stubborn, mean sort of proprietor.

I'm glad. I feel better leaving our horses with a man who looks like he'd balk if a bigger man tried to tell him what to do.

The hotel is not far from the stables. It's a bright, newfangled place, but looking at it, I suddenly have doubts.

The gilded letters seem like a warning—like fool's gold. I feel it strong in my stomach that we should not go in there and should not stay the night.

"I don't trust it."

"What do you mean?" Ted's expression darkens.

"Come on, Ted. We're going to get a drink."

"What?"

"Shh. Trust me."

We head back down the street, pass the livery stables,

and go into the Broken Wheel. Tinny piano music and the smell of cheap beer, worse than Carson's, accost me the moment I step in the door.

I walk straight up to the counter.

"Chocolate and a sarsaparilla."

The bartender eyes me slowly, then moves to get the drinks.

"Which one is yours?" asks Ted.

"It doesn't matter." I muster a smile. "Just drink one, and take your time at it."

"I'll take the sarsaparilla."

I can hear Ted's foot drumming nervously against the bar as we wait.

"Your drinks." The bartender pushes them across the counter. A couple of the men at the bar eye us slowly, and one leaves.

We move to a table and sit down. Ted seems comfortable enough in a saloon—they're just about the only feed stops in tiny towns—and he watches the men with as much coldness as they watch him.

I just turn my chocolate in my hands, waiting for it to cool.

All this was a trap. A trap, sure as sunset. But I've taken them all off guard, because it wasn't a trap for me.

The lone gunslinger and Blue Harding were told to expect Archer Scott. If he'd escaped them, he would have come here. And it's this, more than a self-important sheriff, that has me worried.

Where is the trick? Why is this sheriff fighting with me and enjoying it if he was expecting Archer?

I raise the chocolate to my lips and stop. The sharp and distinct scent of *patami* syrup stings my nostrils. It's a poison common to the Red Tree clan, made from the sap of painted thorn trees. It won't kill you in small doses, but it'll make you sick, sure as shooting.

"Stay here. Don't worry," I say briefly and take the chocolate back to the counter, set it down slow and hard.

"Another chocolate. Not spiked this time."

The bartender turns red. "Are you sure?"

"Yes, I'm sure."

"All right, ma'am."

He reaches for the tin cup and I catch him by the wrist.

"It was a nice try, but I'm no stranger to this land, so you may as well not waste the commodities, hmm?"

He sneers.

But this time, he gives me an untouched cup.

WE WAIT. Ted and I order food, and I watch it being cooked. We order another round of chocolate and sarsaparilla, and we switch.

I wait until the sun has gone down and it's truly dark outside. Then I leave my money on the table and we leave.

We walk up a block and wait again, in the shadows, until the curious and suspicious who inevitably thrust their heads out into the street are satisfied.

"Where are we going?" whispers Ted.

"The livery stable. We'll sleep in the loft."

The stable is a little too warm, but it smells honest and comforting, especially after that tin horn saloon.

The hay is soft, and we lay our bedrolls down next to each other in the corner of the loft furthest from the door. If we're quiet—and I know already that Ted does not snore—no one will ever know we slept here.

I pull my gun partway out of its holster and put it by my head, where I can reach it in a split second if needed.

I lie still, watching the moonlight through the cracks in the barn wall opposite us, trying not to think too hard on the day.

Luke's face when he saw Ted. The sheriff's smile. The finality of the gavel, sentencing an innocent man in a room packed with crooked men. Ted's voice, when it cracked.

I sit up. There'll be no rest tonight. Just weary waiting, trying to steel my nerves and brace my courage.

"Kate, aren't you going to sleep?"

"I don't think I can."

He gets up and moves over beside me. I feel him lean against the wall. I can hear his soft breathing next to me, the rest of him as silent as the wood against our backs.

"Kate?"

"Mhm?"

"I want you to know, I'm sorry. Sorry for—doubting you and being rude about it. If it were me, not Luke, I'd tell you to get out of here before tomorrow. But I can't leave him."

"Of course you can't. I wouldn't, in your place."

"And it's not just that he's my brother. If you knew Luke —he's the last man in the world to kill if he doesn't have to. He'll nurse a sick steer back to health out of pure kindness. He'd probably cut off his hand before he'd hit me or a woman or anyone who didn't deserve it."

"He sounds like a fine man."

"I get sick in my stomach at the idea of him dying this way. Murder's the last thing he'd ever do."

"Don't think about it, then. We're not going to let it happen."

"But what if—"

I reach out and lay my hand over his. "Don't think about it, I said."

He pulls his hand out to scratch his ear.

Somewhere out in the pens a steer lows, and below us one of the horses shifts in their sleep. It's just our breathing— mine, Ted's, the horses'.

The moonlight filters gently through the cracks in the wall and lights the edges of everything with silver.

A tear rolls down Ted's cheek, slow and silent. "He thinks he's going to die, Kate. And I left him alone."

"You went for help."

"If we don't save him, I'm never going to be able to forget it. Maybe—maybe I could have tried harder to free him. They had our wrists tied, they didn't have cuffs, and I slipped mine. I tried to get Luke's, but I couldn't in time. I had to run or they would have caught me again. I keep thinking on it."

"Ted, you aren't responsible for the sheriff's bad ways. You tried. Sometimes that's the very best you can do."

Ted swallows, quickly shoves a tear off his face. "I left him."

"And you know what? He was braver knowing you were gone. I could see it on his face. You have helped him, every inch of the way, and you're not going to quit on him. I can tell, Ted."

"I can't get—never mind."

It's silent between us a space. My mind is filled with every worry of Ted's. Determination takes a person beyond what they think they can survive, and it's held me in good stead thus far; but in conflicts, there are winners and there are losers.

I can't lose. I mustn't. But this man, with half a town behind him, has determined to see me do just that.

"Ted?"

"Mhm?" His tone is brighter. He's trying to pull it together.

"All fears grow at night. Sleep, if you can. I'm going to keep watch. I promise you, everything will look brighter at dawn."

"That's all right. I'll stay up." He reaches for my hand and takes hold of it gently. "Whatever's coming, we'll face it the same."

I swear, the boy grew up right there, in front of my eyes.

GABLE

My fingers work automatically on the buttons of my shirt as I gaze out on the growing beauty of the day. The morning light is bright and inviting beyond the curtains of our bedroom window. It slants golden over the rough wood of our neighbor's barn across the street, and I can hear birdsong.

Edith reaches for the necktie on the dresser and pulls it around my neck. "What are you thinking about? You've got stars in your eyes again."

"I do not," I protest gently. "I only get stars in my eyes when I look at you."

"Liar." She smacks my shoulder good-naturedly. "This town puts them in your eyes."

"But I'd give even that up for you."

"Yes, of course, darling, but that's hardly needed. Are you going out to the Bridger place again?"

"No, I've finished that survey. I'm working in the office today. Governor Scott says that he's expecting a few of the railroad folk to come into town this afternoon and they may want access to some of the survey charts."

"Look at you, my husband, doing business with the highest men in society. And you have only been here a matter of months." The stars are in her eyes now. "You are going to be someone in this town, I know it. How is the starch in your collar?"

"The collar stands perfectly, as always. But I'll be careful with it." But I'll be careful with it."

"I know you will. Can't have you embarrassing us now." She reaches up and plants a kiss on my cheek. "Will you be back for lunch?"

"I imagine so. If not, I will send back word. What business will you be about?"

"I'm meeting Maria Pike at the general store. She is choosing a new set of drapes for the front windows, and the new fabrics are in. I don't know why she would choose me to help when there are any number of other women in town more qualified, but I think she's taking a liking to me."

"It's because your taste is impeccable. I am so very happy that you are making friends here."

"Maria is so very refined. I'm always a little afraid that I will say something wrong." She takes a deep breath and then presses on. "She is having the railroad men over for tea today, and she wants me to come."

"Well, go. Don't worry about me."

"I don't have anything suitable to wear."

"Oh. I see." I reach into my pocket and count out a generous number of bills—enough, I think, for one of those newfangled ready-made dresses. "Will that do?"

Her face brightens like sun after snow. "Thank you, Les." She throws her arms around my neck.

"You must tell me all about how it was."

"I will. And I'll show you the dress when I get home."

"I shall look forward to it all day long." I kiss her and she straightens my vest and tie once more. "Remember, don't let that collar fade." She dances from the room, humming under her breath.

I smile. I've brought her to this wild place, and she's followed without a word of complaint. It's the least I can do to give her joy when I can.

It's a hot afternoon. The open windows do little to ease the oppressive heat, and my vest and jacket and tie are all lying over my chair as I work over my chart.

I grimace and undo a button on my shirt.

The door swings open and a man, tall, bearded, and wearing suspenders over a blue-and-white checked shirt, is standing uncertainly in the doorway. "Is this the survey office?"

I reach quickly for my vest and tie. "Yes, it is. Can I help you?"

His face relaxes into a wide smile of relief. "Excellent.

Yes, I am looking for some surveys done by the previous surveyor here, a G. Levine. Oh, don't bother. The heat is terrible." He nods to the jacket I was gritting my teeth to don.

I set it back down with no small measure of relief. "Yes. I still keep his surveys. Nearly anything that's mapped around here is his work."

"So I've heard, and this office is one of the few places they are to be found. I'm—with the railroad."

"Are you? I heard some of you were coming to town today."

"Yes, quite a few of us. Most of them are up at the governor's office, playing a game that Archer Scott doesn't play." He laughs. "They talk themselves blue in the face, but he's having none of it. I'd rather go get the real work done. Which brings me here."

"Are you a surveyor as well?"

"Oh, I'm not nearly clever enough for that. I'm just vice president of the railroad." He winks. "Don't tell anyone."

"They won't hear it from me." I go over to the drawers along the back wall. "Now, what are you looking for?"

"I don't know exactly which region you'll find it under. They're surveys from before there was a trail through the Black Shaft Pass. Local legend says there are hidden perils in that pass, and I'd like to take a look before I clear a path for the railroad through there."

I take two surveys out and bring them over to the table, rolling up my current map. "Take a look at these and see if they suit."

He takes a pair of spectacles out of his pocket and puts them on, leaning over the first survey. "Hm." He taps a spot and continues to search.

The spot is a tall rock formation, standing off to one side of what became the trail.

"Can I see the other?" He glances up at me.

I roll up the first and spread out the second.

"Ah, yes. This is what I was looking for. Look at that."

In old, cramped handwriting on the edge of the map is a note.

Strange odor. Assistant dropped his watch and we heard it fall between rocks some length downwards, possible thirty or forty feet down. Investigation futile, too little daylight.

"What do you think it means?" he asks, looking up at me.

"Sounds like caves. Or maybe a shift in earth once left a crevice of some sort. Are you concerned about the stability of the pass?"

"Rock slides are a concern, and we plan to do some blasting. Caves could make the walls unsteady, especially if the express comes through twice a day."

"True. Who is your surveyor?"

"Fellow named Partridge. Solid. Knows his craft. He voiced these concerns to me."

"And he is probably correct. You can see here, Levine was starting to map a separate trail, a little south of there."

"What do you think of that southern trail?"

"I doubt it's much different."

"I see. Well, thank you for your advice. How long would it take you to produce a copy of this?"

"A couple days, if that's convenient."

"Perfectly. Bring it out yourself and I'll give you the grand tour." He winks. "Good doing business with you, Mr. Gable."

The vice president of the railroad thrusts out his hand and I take it. He has the calluses of a farmer.

Perhaps Archer Scott is right—a common man can truly become anything out here.

34

CARNEGIE

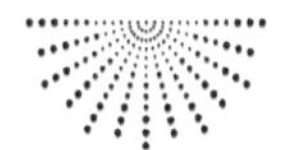

I scramble awake as the livery stable door opens. Warm sunlight floods the center of the stable, and hazy wisps trickle through the cracks in the eastern wall.

I have a horrible knot in my neck.

"Ted," I hiss. He's slumped over his rifle, sound asleep.

He jerks awake, dazed and confused. "What time is it?"

"It's morning yet," I reply. The air is too cool yet for it to be past eight. "Come on, we'll rustle up some food, maybe some coffee."

I buckle my gun belt back on, pick up my saddlebags, and climb down the ladder. There's only one hand here, forking hay to the horses from the lower haymow. He doesn't even look over his shoulder.

The sunlight is blinding. An unearthly grinding and shriek come from down the street where the steam engine is being readied to ship a load of cattle.

"Did you ever get your cattle sold?" I ask.

"No, it was our first night. I figure they confiscated and sold them."

"We'll look into that, straight after breakfast."

"What about Luke?"

"Luke has about four hours. Our business won't take long, I hope."

WE EAT a brief breakfast at a tiny shack of a restaurant and don't see another customer the entire time we are there. The proprietor is a nervous, balding man who thanks us profusely for our patronage.

I leave him an extra twenty-five cents.

Afterward, Ted and I walk down to the corrals near the train tracks where all the stock is penned, waiting to ship out.

Cowhands are riding past, shouting, driving cattle up into the boxcars, separating herds. We wander from corral to corral, Ted peering in at the cattle in each before moving on to the next one.

"There they are, Kate. That's our brand."

I shade my eyes and look at the milling cattle, branded with a bar and a lazy s. They're fat and well-kept.

"They come off the trail looking like this?"

Ted nods and grins proudly. "We camped them out for a week on good grass before we drove them in. Luke—Luke thinks that's when someone in the town saw us."

"Well, they're good stock. I can see why someone would

kill for them." I raise my hand to catch the attention of one of the stockpen bosses.

He comes over and raises his hat. "Howdy, ma'am."

"Excuse me, have these cattle been sold?"

"Yes, ma'am, they ship out tomorrow."

"Who transacted the sale?"

"Sheriff Rojo."

"Ah. Well, these cattle are stolen property and I am here under the jurisdiction of Marshal Lacey of the Western Territory to take possession of them."

I pull the badge out and hold it up.

The man pales. "I didn't have nothing to do with his sale."

"I didn't say you were charged with anything. But I'd like to speak to the buyers and see the bill of sale. How much did they pay?"

"Seven hundred dollars for the lot."

"And where's the money?"

"It'll be wired to the bank here. There's a draft notice. I can get it."

"Do. And bring the buyers. I'd like to settle this to their satisfaction, if possible."

"Of course. I'll get them right away—they're staying in the hotel."

"I'll wait."

I lean back against the slats of the corral. "Have you ever handled trading, Ted?"

"Yeah. I used to get all our supplies for us. Never done

the cattle, Luke did that."

"You can do it today, if you want. I'm going to rip up that bank draft and request one made out to you and Luke. Then you can light out of here if you want, soon as all this is over."

"Really?" His face lights up.

"Sure."

"But what about you?"

"I'll just go home."

"Alone?"

I smile and lean back on my elbows against the rails of the corral. "Why not? I can ride fast and shoot fast. I'll make good time."

"Well, you're gutsy." He squints against the sun and grins.

The man from the stock corrals returns with a couple wiry fellows who look like they've seen a bit of the territory, though they are dressed crisply.

"Which of you is the deputy marshal?" asks the older of the two. He leans on a cane and regards us with keen eyes.

"I am." I take my badge out and show it to them.

"May I?" The second man takes out a pair of spectacles and looks to me for permission. I hand over the badge.

He studies it a moment and nods, handing it back. "Welcome, ma'am. It must be special circumstances that bring you out here with this kind of authority."

"It's a tangled web," I reply. "But your part in it is simple. These cattle have been confiscated as stolen property, but this young man has my sanction to transact a sale with you if you want to keep the stock."

"How much do you want for them, young man?" The older man fixes Ted with a sensible look. This probably isn't his first go at this sort of thing.

"I'll sell them to you for the same price. Then they can go on schedule."

"That's fine with me." He holds out his hand and shakes with Ted.

The three of them move off to one side to sign the bill of sale. And then I see them. Three men lounging against a train car, watching us with interest. One of them I know for a fact I saw with Rojo at the trial, a man in a striped shirt with a heavy mustache. Another is wearing a black suit, and the other is an older man, smoking.

We watch each other slowly for a long minute.

One of them pushes off the train car with his shoulder and starts to saunter over.

"Kate, take a look! This is real, a whole seven hundred."

I take the draft and look at it, crisp and new and promising. "It's something, isn't it?"

There's a shine of pride in his eyes, the first spark I've seen out of him. "That'll show him. He can't fool everyone and he isn't getting away with thievin'."

Someone laughs, right next to us.

"I don't think that's legal, what you done." The one in the striped shirt sticks his thumbs through his suspenders and slouches against the slats of the corral.

Quietly I hand the draft to Ted.

"And you talk big, but that ain't going to help you here." He looks back at his friend, who smiles and casually puts his hands in his pockets, revealing a pair of guns.

"I'm not looking for trouble with you men." I look at the nearest man and then the others. "My business is with Sheriff Rojo and it doesn't have to be with you."

"And what are you going to do, little miss, against all three of us?"

The third man, still smoking, puts his hand to his gun a little late. I think he'd rather have his smoke than get involved. Even better.

"You forget she's not alone." Ted sets his hand on his pistol. "You heard her, get lost."

The one in black starts to laugh and he glances at his friend to share it.

"A boy?" he snorts.

Ted's like stone. I don't know where it came from, this sudden inability to be ruffled, but he is standing firm.

"All right, give us that bank draft."

"It's not made out to you," says Ted. "I figure that wouldn't be legal either."

"Try and stop me."

He lunges for Ted. Calmly, as if it had been rehearsed, Ted swings his gun up out of his belt and it meets the man's jaw with a hard, dull crack.

His black-suited companion whips out his gun and I'm

ready for him. My first bullet lands between his feet and the second in his shoulder.

"Get their guns."

I step past them as Ted bends to collect their pistols. The third man is standing slack-jawed, ready to bolt. His cigar lies in the dirt at his feet.

"You tell that sheriff I'm coming down to the jail and he's going to give me Luke Westfall. Go on, tell him."

He shies away from me and hurries up the street towards the jail.

"Here you are." Ted hands me a pair of pistols. I go over to the hitching rail and stick them in my saddlebag.

"Bring the rifle. We'll probably need it."

Ted slides it out of the sheath and falls in step beside me. It's getting hot; I haven't a precise idea of the time, but I figure we're getting down to the last hour or two. I reach up and loosen my collar with one finger.

"Kate, how come you always win? You're fast, but I've seen quicker draws."

I push a sweaty wisp of hair out of my face and tuck it back into my pinned-up curls. "You breathe steady and you pretend the man in front of you isn't going to shoot a hole in you. When it's just a shooting contest in your mind—you can't really lose."

"That's all?"

"Well, that and practice, so you can't miss if you aim."

"Huh." He spins his pistol. "That's sure different from those cowhands say."

I give a short laugh under my breath. "That's why I win."

There's a crowd gathering outside the jail and I can see Sheriff Rojo on the steps, hands on his hips, waiting for me.

The morning light is streaming over the roof of the jail, shrouding him in golden beams. He's smoking one of those thick cigars, and the smoke mingles with the haze of the sunlight.

"Sheriff Rojo, I have come for Luke Westfall."

"Come and get him," he sneers around his cigar.

"I am a deputy marshal of the Western Territory," I reply, loud enough for the crowd to hear, and hold up my badge. "I have jurisdiction from Marshal Lacey, appointed by Governor Scott himself. Bring him out, then."

He looks around at the crowd with a little smile, nodding slowly. Then he takes a step towards me. His hand rests on his gun, that pearl-hilted sixshooter.

"You impressed by the performance, folks? It's all show." He fixes his eyes on me. "You're nothing, with or without that tin. Luke Westfall committed a crime in my town, and it's my duty to deal with him as the law dictates."

"Does the law dictate pocketing seven hundred dollars of his personal property?"

Something freezes on his face for a moment. Then he laughs, a little louder. "Ridiculous. The man's cattle were confiscated, of course, but—"

"Do you want to see the bill of sale?" I reach into my pocket. "This one was nullified this morning, thankfully— however, if you stood to profit seven hundred dollars, you certainly weren't unbiased in the matter of his innocence. Why, I think a man might even kill for that sum."

A quick murmur runs through the crowd.

"What's more, I met this outlaw out on the road, on the way here. And even he told me not to turn my back on Sheriff Rojo!"

I take a deep breath and start toward him.

He reaches—his last mistake.

My eyes never leave his chest, never once flicker towards the moving gun. The air splits with the noise and my ear gives a high pitched whine.

I cock again. "Anyone else object?"

They are silent, bristling, but none willing to make the first move.

I look down at Rojo, my cocked gun still in my hand. "You disgust me," I whisper. "Those boys didn't do anything. By the law, you could swing."

"Please." A voice comes, finally, from the men. "Please—don't kill him."

It's a young man, tall and boyish-faced. Probably my age.

"We'll go," he begs. "We'll leave town. I swear."

I thin my lips into a hard line, taste the gunpowder and the acrid smoke that's surrounding me. "I have your word, then. Take him to the doctor first, I shot him high."

They come, quick and cowed, to collect him.

"I'm sorry," I say, pausing to look down at his gasping form as they take him away. "I warned you."

I glance back. Ted is still standing there with the rifle cradled in his arms. His eyes are proud.

"Hand me that rifle, Ted. Get Luke out and come straight back out with him."

"Yes'm." He shoves the rifle into my hands.

I stand in the doorway and watch the men leave. Somewhere in the back of my mind the grate and squeak of the jail door registers, but I'm watching the lonely, ramshackle town.

The railroad is good, but it brings all manner of bad with it too.

I push my hair back, out of my face. The breeze feels suddenly so cool, so refreshing.

It's been too long.

"Ted?" I duck into the cool, dark doorway, ready to ask what's wrong, but I'm halted, the words dying on my lips.

The brothers are clasped in each other's arms. Ted is sobbing into his brother's sweat-stained shirt and Luke is smoothing down his hair, talking to him low and steady.

"I'm proud of you, Ted. Proud of you. What you did was a man's work, you hear?" He ruffles his hair comfortingly. "You cry all you like. You earned it."

Luke looks up and sees me standing in the doorway. "Marshal?"

"Deputy marshal," I supply quickly.

I'm suddenly awkward, and all the cool authority I felt a minute ago has gone a little stale.

He lets his brother go and comes over.

"Thank you." He reaches out and clasps my hand. "I

certainly didn't expect help was coming, or that it would come looking like you—no disrespect, ma'am. But I can tell you, I've never seen a stranger I've loved more."

I smile slowly. "I'll take it."

Ted has composed himself and he comes over, giving a quick glance out the door.

"You have the draft?" I ask him.

He pats the breast of his jacket.

"Well, I'm going to send for someone else from Glory Mesa to make sure these men leave, but I want to ride out of here before anyone's got a chance to stir up more trouble, and I suggest you do the same."

WE RIDE out of town together half an hour later, after finding Luke's horse in a selling pen near the tracks. No one seems of a mind to oppose us.

Just outside, at the crossroads where one trail heads south and the other west, we stop.

"Where you boys off to?" I ask.

"Up north, probably further west, out past the territory lines," says Luke.

"What's out there?"

He grins. "I don't know."

"How come you're going then?"

He glances out that direction, toying with the end of his reins. "That's why I want to go. To go westward, on and on, into the setting sun—I can't think of a more glorious thing."

A sudden surge of longing overtakes me. I wish I could go with them, just pick up and discover something unknown. Just because I could.

Perhaps he sees it on my face. He smiles shyly. "You're welcome to come along. We sure could use a third gun, and you can split off whenever you want."

I hesitate.

"I'd love to, but I have to return to Glory Mesa with my report, and—and there's work to be done there. I'm not free yet."

"Well." He nods, understanding. "If you ever want to, just head west and I reckon you'll find us. You'll always be welcome."

He tips his hat and turns his horse north, off the path.

Ted tips his hat to me as he follows, his manner the same. "Bye, Kate."

I raise my hand in farewell as they spur their horses north. I watch until the dust and shimmering sun swallow them from view.

35

NEWTON

THE RISING SUN IS FIRE LACING THE EDGES OF THE
eastern range. The horses, breathing steam in the early
morning chill of the yard, champing the bits slowly, moving
with the thick creak of leather, are just black silhouettes in
the red and gold of the dawn.

It's on mornings like these that even the hands speak in
softer voices; it seems wrong to act as if nothing is remarkable
with the sight of fire and molten gold spilling over the
surrounding land.

Britt is tightening his cinch with an iron face. When he is
not displeased, he seems only to have one expression.

Buck is laughing with the hands, chuckling softly, a
broad grin on his face. He gestures to one of the horses in the
corral and then another. Like any good horsebreaker, he
knows and talks the business.

I cannot wait to see what these boys do with the herd out north of my place. It's the finest band I've ever seen.

My horse is ready; I had him out and groomed before first light. It feels good to walk more than a room's length without being weary, to prepare my own horse without having to stop to breathe through burning pain.

I suppose when a man's lost what he took for granted, he gets to value it.

On the porch, arms folded, tired eyes hooded, Harrison Terhune watches the preparations.

"Chris." He catches my eye, motions for me to come close.

I stride back across the yard and mount the steps with an ease I didn't have a week ago.

"Here, take this. I have its twin." He holds out one of the *darani* claws taken off the beast before the body was dumped for scavengers. "We will talk about the water by and by, when you've had time to settle, but in the meantime, if ever you need something from me, you just send this along and I'll know it's you."

"And you?"

"I'll do the same." He opens his hand and inside is a hooked claw, just like mine.

I thrust the thing into my pocket.

"He's bound to be out there," Harrison Terhune says quietly. "Watch your back."

"Yours too." I mount my horse and shoot Harrison a wry

smile. I gather my reins and my horse sidesteps and shifts under me. "You boys ready?"

They let out a whoop and we tear out of that yard like cowhands at the trail's end.

36

ALAN

"WHAT ARE YOU BOYS DOING IN TOWN? I THOUGHT THE herds were driving north." Archer Scott eyes us with concern. "And Tagweiah, it is always good to see you."

Tagweiah gives him a silent, pleasant nod. My cousin is very fond of the governor.

I am painfully aware of the thick smell of horse and sweat and trail dust that is filling the small territorial governor's office with the four of us towering like pines in front of his desk.

"They are," says Jem, always our spokesman. "But our cousin here had word for us, something we think you should know."

"Well, go ahead. Please, have a seat." He gestures to us to pull out chairs, and when we come up one short, he goes into the back room and brings back a fourth for Max.

272

"Are you going to tell him what they say about our father?" whispers Max.

"He has a right to know that too, I think."

Max glances to me, hoping I'll protest.

"If it's needful, Jem," I reply. "Don't drag it out if it doesn't need to be."

"All right."

Archer Scott returns with a chair and Max sits down in it with a conspicuous scrape across the freshly scrubbed boards.

"You were raised by an Auki woman," begins Jem. "Did she share her knowledge of the stars with you?"

"She did." Archer's face softens. He has never talked to me about her, but I see in his eyes that whatever kind of man Hector Muley was, his wife was kind. "She told me of the stories and of the signs and the things they meant, the harvests they predicted."

"Do you know what the meeting of the sign of the white stag with the lone mountain and serpent is?"

Archer's face goes rigid and blank. He knows.

"What about it?"

"They have met in the heavens."

The back door opens and Rosamund steps in, a basket in her hand. She stops short. "Oh, I didn't know you had guests, Archer. I'll come back later."

"Thank you, Rose. Love you, dearest."

She smiles to her husband, then turns her beautiful, broad smile on me. "You're looking well, Alan."

I could say the same about her. She's glowing; even the gutsy girl I traveled a desert with hardly compares to the strength and confidence she exudes today, over a year later.

I am glad, very glad to see she is thriving in this place.

She shuts the door.

A long, deep silence follows Rosamund Scott's departure.

Jem reaches up and scratches his jaw. Max is fiddling with his jackknife, flipping it open and shut.

"So you have seen it," Archer says at last. "In the skies."

"Yes."

He sighs softly. "Tell the Auki nation if they desire anything of me, I am happy to give it, if I can."

"The Auki nation fears for you," says Tagweiah, leaning forward. "We can take care of ourselves, but we want to protect also those who are our friends, kin, and fosterlings."

Archer looks to us—Jem first, then myself, and then Max. Max squirms a little under his gaze.

"This may have nothing to do with your parents," he says. "Matching people to legends isn't like doing figures. Things rarely pan out the way you expect."

"And yet we could be the ones," Jem says dutifully. Max groans under his breath.

"There is no way to be sure," Archer insists, almost gentle. "Really."

He looks to Tagweiah, who nods.

"So until such time as we know without a doubt, we will refrain from speculation. Understood?"

Jem nods for all of us. Max ought to be relieved, but he's still irritated.

I think he's always minded the accusations more than the rest of us. When our half-Auki mother and our father, Ian Swift, went to settle on a piece of cursed land, the Auki nation told them that they might bring death on us all, and that we, their sons, might pay the penalty one day. But neither of our parents ever gave an inch.

They loved our ranch with all their hearts, as we do after them.

"I am glad you told me," says Archer. "If it is our fate to go up in flames in the end, we will make it a good end." He smiles with that strange, boyish light in his eyes that only manages to make him more the man, not less. "And for now, we wait, and live our lives, as we always have, the best we can."

He speaks lightly, but his words reach the deeps in me.

Many men could say those words. Few could mean them the way he does.

"What about—" begins Jem, but a sudden sound stops him short.

The street outside is suddenly, from nowhere, filled with the thunder of galloping hooves, rolling like a flash flood from the road outside of town, streaming into the town, seemingly unending. They mill, flow black, settle, and come to a halt before the governor's office.

They're mounted men, wearing pale blue handkerchiefs on their arms.

We scramble to our feet so fast that Max's chair crashes to the ground.

Archer is transformed. His quiet, easy demeanor snaps into the sharp, hard air of command. He strides to the door and throws it open, standing framed in the doorway.

A single rider on a lanky gray colt waits in front of the rest: strong-shouldered, with tight-pressed lips, sandy blond hair, and shocking blue eyes.

Archer gives a short, dry laugh. "Blue Harding."

37

CARNEGIE

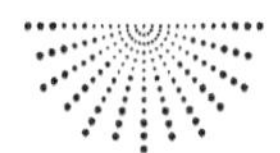

I NEVER THOUGHT IN ALL MY LIFE I'D BE THIS GLAD TO see Glory Mesa in front of me and the wide, dusty unknown at my back.

The morning sun hits the fronts of the buildings with the clarity of golden wine, and even from this distance, I can see the early morning folk sweeping steps, driving their teams up the street, throwing curtains wide on the new day.

I whistle to my pinto and urge her into a canter. She can feel it; we're almost home.

"KATE, YOU'RE BACK!" Peter comes running up the street, waving his hat in the air. His broom is leaned up against one the posts of the porch instead of thrown forgotten in the dust. I swear, he must have grown whole inches in the week and a half I've been gone.

I rein in the pinto and throw my leg over, dropping to the ground. Peter throws one arm over my shoulder and thumps me heartily on the back. He has definitely grown.

"Did you miss me?" he asks.

"Sure, I did. Missed you every day. How's Glory Mesa?"

Peter shrugs.

"Is that good or bad?"

"Good," he admits finally. "But I missed you more than you did me. Doctor Sikes came home and Carson made me go with him into the hills to pick herbs. I wished you were here because you wouldn't have forced me."

"Doctor Sikes isn't that bad, is he?"

Peter shrugs. "He's strange. He tells me that I will remember everything."

"What's wrong with that?"

"I do remember everything," he says with a touch of stubbornness. "But he talks like he thought of it first."

"Well, ignore him, then."

Peter shrugs again.

"Did anything else happen?"

"I saw Tora-Teth in town." He brightens. "But no one believes me."

"What was he doing?"

"Eating."

I cock my head and wrinkle my nose at him. "Are you sure you saw that?"

"I can tell you what he was eating."

"Hm."

"Do you believe me, Kate?"

I consider this. Tora-Teth hasn't been seen in these parts for a while, but the kid saw Mortimer last year.

"Sure, I believe you."

He grins at me.

"Is Governor Scott in his office?" I nod towards the territorial governor's office, with its blue and white flag fluttering proudly in the rich morning light.

"I reckon. I saw him ride thataway an hour ago."

"Thank you, Peter. I have business with him."

"With him? What about with Marshal Lacey? He's got a surprise for you!"

"He'll be next!" I call back over my shoulder.

I TIE the pinto up outside and take my saddlebags down, hauling them over my shoulder. I trudge up the steps with my load and knock on the door.

"Come."

I turn the handle and push my way in. Archer Scott is the only one in his office, and I'm glad of it. He's had more and more men in these days, and I want him to hear this first, by himself.

"Kate!" He gets up and comes over to shake my hand. "How did it go? I see you're looking well, regardless."

"I finished the job," I reply. "I want to thank you for giving me this opportunity."

"Of course. I owed it to you, remember."

I sling the bag off my shoulder and drop it, heavy, on the table. I unpin the star and set it down with a clink.

"There's a problem, Governor."

He sits down and waits, quiet.

"I kept meeting men out there. Gunmen. Looking to collect." I open the bag and give the bottom seam a tug, spilling the guns out.

There's the pearl-hilted one, Blue's Croix-Savannah .45 commission, the one with the bullet scar on the barrel...five in total.

He looks up at me, not understanding. "You outgunned them."

"Yep. Most of them." I give the nearest one a push, away from the edge of the table. "Problem was, they were all expecting to collect on you."

"On me?" His eyebrows shoot up. "Are you sure?"

"Yes. Someone's paying them."

"And they thought I would go?"

"I reckon."

His eyes meet mine, sincere and concerned. "I'm sorry you had to deal with something meant for me."

"But I dealt with it. And for what it's worth, I'm glad it was me and not you."

"Well, I'm glad you feel that way." He opens his drawer and pulls out a sheet of paper. "You plan to stay back of the saloon?"

"I reckon, if Carson lets me."

"He will." Archer writes a sentence or two in his bold,

sprawling handwriting. He folds the paper and seals it in an envelope. "Give this to him. He won't bother you."

"What's in it?"

"Just a message from me to him."

"Do you want to look at any of these guns? You might see something I don't. I can't possibly use them all anyway."

"Probably wouldn't hurt." He starts to go examine them slowly.

I reach out for Blue's .45 and stick it in my belt. "Keep the others for now. I'll be back for them someday."

"Kate?"

I pause and look down at him. There's a gleam in his eye.

"Go drop in on Raymond. I think he'd like to talk to you."

I sling the light saddlebags over my shoulder with a slap. "All right."

THE MARSHAL'S SMILING JUST a tad when I walk in, as if he's expecting me.

"Miss Carnegie." Raymond's voice is the same slow rumble, but it's amused. "What in tarnation did you do out there?"

"It's a long story." I set the sheathed rifle and the spare guns he loaned me on the table in front of him.

"I reckon." He folds his hands.

"I tried to send word, but the sheriff cut the telegraph lines. I promise, I tried."

"I'd like to know what you said to Blue Harding that made him come turn himself and fifty of his men in."

"Blue turned himself in?"

"Don't look so stricken. They're helping me clean up the territory in exchange for amnesty. With Blue on our side— why, we'll have the Western Territory cleaned up and safe in no time."

"I don't think I said much of anything."

"That's not how he put it."

"I told him you were a man of your word and that you'd listen if he mentioned I'd told him. Just to—avoid suspicion, you know. I don't remember that I said much else."

"Well, you've done me a service bigger'n I can pay back. I wouldn't have won Blue over if you gave me five years to do it. So, if you want to keep that badge and ride patrol down the southern trail—I reckon I could afford to pay you to do it."

It takes a moment for the words to sink in.

"You mean it?" Tears threaten to well up in my eyes. I fight them hard.

"'Course I mean it."

I want nothing more to throw my arms around him. Instead I straighten, smile, and hold out my hand. "Deal."

3 8

IRENE

I HEAVE THE HEAVY BASKET OF LAUNDRY ONTO MY HIP and trudge out to the line. It's a warm day, and the wind is dry and brisk.

I set the basket down in the dirt and pull a couple pins out of my apron pocket. I shake out a sheet and pin it up, then a dress, then a tablecloth.

The wind catches at the linen and calico and pulls it, flapping wistfully, towards the horizon. It's been a dry summer and a warm autumn, and there's talk of feuding between some of the smaller ranches over water.

But it's just talk, from what I can tell.

A loud wagon rattles up the road, approaching my house. It slows as it comes near, then turns into my yard.

I set the laundry basket down and shade my eyes to see.

It's a wagon filled with building lumber.

283

"Excuse me, ma'am, do you mind if we water the horses here?" One of them jumps down and whips off his hat.

"Of course not, go ahead." I gesture to the trough. Peter, Carson's errand boy, keeps it full for passersby.

"Where are you hauling to?"

"Up north of here a little ways. Marshal Lacey's been building a house out on his land. These are for the inner walls. Next comes roof and plaster. Though it's been so dry you could probably plaster without a roof." He laughs.

"I'm glad to hear he is building a place of his own."

"It's going to be a right fine one from the looks of it, ma'am," he says with cheerful conviction. He pulls the horses back from the water and climbs back up onto the seat.

"Well, good day, ma'am. Thank you."

I smile in acknowledgment, but as he drives away, my heart aches.

"He's been at it since the end of summer," says Maria, as she measures out three yards of muslin. "Decided it all of a sudden."

I count out another length of ribbon before I reply. "It's not really a topic for gossip, but still, I'm surprised I didn't hear of it."

"That is where he goes when he leaves town these days, more often than not. Not outlaw hunting." Maria smiles serenely. "He's asked my advice on furnishings. I help him go through the catalogs."

My fingers stop winding the ribbon.

"It doesn't do to talk like anything is settled...." Maria glances at Rosamund Scott across the store and thumbs through the stack of calico and linen, peering closely. It is late afternoon, and the light is going. "Four yards of this," she says to Trasker, pointing out the fabric of her choice.

"But you have to imagine," she continues, "that something has made him suddenly interested in building a house—and quickly—when he seemed perfectly content in town over the last year."

I wrap the ribbon around my fingers and start counting again. "He's was busy, I expect. After all, Mortimer was ravaging the land."

"Abernathy was ravaging the land. Mortimer just invited him to do it," Maria corrects. "It is far more civilized now, but I do worry that the marshal is not keeping his mind on his work." She stares out the window and gives a sigh. "If you want my advice, Mrs. Sandler, you'll keep your distance from him. He—"

"Irene?" Rosamund beckons me over.

"Excuse me," I say, and cross the room to join her. The color is high in her cheeks and she gives Maria Pike's silken back a stern look before turning to me.

"Do you think that you could you do me a great favor?"

"Of course."

"I am not feeling entirely myself, and I was getting these things for Raymond. Would you drop by his place on your way home? If it isn't too much trouble?"

"It's no trouble. I hope you're not unwell."

"No, it's nothing serious, and do tell him that. Just tired."

"To be sure." I take the basket and make my escape with gratitude. I'll come back for the ribbon tomorrow.

He's sitting outside on the porch, repairing a bridle strap in the gentle dusk, a lantern next to him for better light.

"Evening, Mrs. Sandler," he greets, with a rare smile. "To what do I owe this pleasure?"

"I'm bringing a couple things from your sister. I saw her in Trasker's mercantile and she is feeling a little poorly today, so she sent them with me."

His eyes go sharp. "Poorly?"

"Nothing serious," I reassure him. "She told me to tell you that."

He chuckles wryly. "She would, wouldn't she?"

"It's just here in the basket. Is it all right if I just set it here?"

"Of course."

I set it on the edge of the porch and hesitate. "Well—good evening." I give him the slightest curtsey and turn to leave.

"It's lovely on the porch tonight," he says quietly. "If you're not in a hurry, you can have a seat."

"No—no, I am not in a hurry. Thank you." I climb up the steps to the porch and sit carefully on the edge of the offered chair. My heart is beating a little faster than it ought.

"I haven't seen you around town much." He spares me a glance before returning his eyes to his work.

"We must be missing each other in public. I haven't kept to my house any more than usual."

"Hm. No trouble from Carson?"

"None."

"Good. He's feeling cantankerous right now, by all reports."

"I don't doubt it," I smile. "But he's always civil to me."

"I'd have words with him if he wasn't. I think he's sore that I stole Kate Carnegie from him. Not that handling an evening of his customers is any less dangerous than riding a little line for me. It's not even outlaw territory."

"What is it that she sees in the land that she wants so badly to be out in it?"

"Beats me." Raymond chuckles. "No, it's a powerful good land. And it's beautiful. I think she just loves it a mite more than some of the rest of us."

He gives a contented sigh and his hands stop their work as he admires the evening.

"The still of twilight is one of my favorite times," he says, softly.

"Why is that?"

"Well, I always thought it was one of the most beautiful things the sky does. But back in the war, we got trapped once. Out on the field under enemy fire for three days. Every time dusk came, I knew that we'd have a reprieve and my boys would have a few hours to recover. It was like hope, reaching out to us."

"I've never thought of twilight like that, as the coming of hope."

He sighs again, and I can hear the smile in it. "And the stars, too. I'd lie there and think about every man and woman who'd stared at the stars with their troubles over the course of all time, and how small ours must be against the weight of that."

"I love the stars."

"Mhm?" He glances at me as if hoping I'll go on.

"I was trapped too, for two years after my husband died. But I heard a man say once that the stars were brighter in the Western Territory, a man who had spent time out here. And in the middle of that party, surrounded by champagne and diamonds and starved for kindness, it sounded like the most wonderful thing in the world to me."

"Seems to me I heard you say once that you came from rich folks out East."

"My aunt and uncle. They didn't approve of James, and more so after he died. They'd be scandalized if they knew where I was."

Raymond's eyes are twinkling. I like that he finds them and their consternation amusing.

I find myself less afraid of them, somehow.

"Well, they're missing out," he says slowly. "There are few things prettier than an evening like this."

I'd never thought of it that way. This, here, is a good

thing, and their disapproval doesn't make it any less so. They are missing out on beauty.

Then it hits me that it's dark and we're talking about the stars. Night has fallen while we sat here. I should have paid better attention.

I stand up."I should be on my way."

Raymond looks up at me. "I'll see you home."

"That's all right, it's not far."

"No, I should have kept better track of the time. Can't let you walk alone in the dark, now can I?" He smiles wryly under his heavy mustache.

"Really, it's not—"

He stands up and holds out his arm. "I'm the marshal. It's my job."

It's different walking home with Raymond Lacey.

Despite my protests, I do watch the shadows at night, and I listen for sounds, not stopping or slowing until I'm inside my door. But with him beside me, I enjoy the night air without fear. It's sweet and cool, and the moon casts beautiful shadows that paint the town across the flat streets in silver and black.

It's a unique beauty, and a new one for me.

We pass Maria's house, and I think I see, for a moment, the golden glow of light within and a curtain moving. But not even Maria's opinions—and she will have plenty if she sees me walking at night with the marshal—can ruin this evening.

We don't talk, but our silence is perfectly amicable. In fact, I think it is more comfortable this way, just walking down the quiet road in silence together, than if we were having a lively conversation.

I used to love those. Now there's nothing I love more than the quiet.

"Here's where I leave you," Raymond says as we reach my gate. "But I'll wait until you're in the house."

I turn to him. "Thank you."

"My pleasure, ma'am." He kisses my hand.

I walk straight to the door and go in so he isn't left waiting. But I wish I could linger, take this moment and stretch it out forever.

3 9

NEWTON

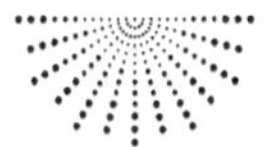

"THERE IT IS." I REIN IN MY HORSE AND POINT OUT A distant cluster of bluish hills. "That's where the band's been ranging."

Britt squints hard and shades his eyes with his hand. "And how far from the ranch house is it?"

"Few days' ride, perhaps. That is, if you want to set up good traps and corrals."

Britt chuckles grimly. "Sure do."

"Beautiful land," comments Buck, taking off his hat to wipe the sweat from his forehead. "Just beautiful."

"It's home."

Britt looks at me keenly. "I hope this herd is as good as you say it is."

"I'll let you judge that," I reply. "But it's the finest I've seen in these parts in many a year. There are plenty of hills

291

and gullies out thataway, a lot of hideouts, so we'll have to give ourselves time to beat them out."

"That ain't going to be a concern," Britt grunts. "If they're there, we'll have them out. Won't we, Buck?"

Buck nods.

"Well, I've done enough staring, begging your pardon," says Britt. "Let's get to that house of yours and get ready to catch us some horseflesh."

He slaps his horse with the end of his reins and takes off.

THE YARD of the ranch house is neat and tidy. The hitching rails are new, and I see the corral has been expanded to fit another ten head or so.

"They're here! Pa, they're here!" A long-legged boy runs out of the barn and catches my bridle.

"Sir, welcome home! We weren't expecting you today, sir."

"And who are you, son?" I dismount and tie my horse at the new hitching rail.

"I'm John Ramsey."

"Ah—you're so tall I didn't recognize you. Your father's done a good job with this place while I've been gone."

"Yes, sir, he has!"

"No need for the sir. Mr. Newton's just fine. You can call me Chris when you're older."

He grins. "Well, Mr. Newton, sorry it ain't all gotten-up. We hadn't heard from you."

"Well, I couldn't wait." I pull the saddle off my horse and heft it over the hitching rail. "I missed this place."

"Yes sir!"

I chuckle under my breath and lead my horse into the near corral. "John?"

"Yes sir—Mr. Newton?"

"Show these two men a place in the bunkhouse. They're new horsebreakers."

The boy looks at them with new interest. "Sure."

"Is your father in the barn?"

"Yes. He's shoeing one of the heavy drafts."

"Thank you, son."

I step into the vast barn, smelling of sweet hay and hot hooves. There's a large brown and cream horse standing in ties, with a man bent over a rear hoof.

"Nathan?"

"Over here," grunts a low voice. "Sorry, you've caught me at work."

"That's hardly a thing to apologize for. I can wait."

"Thank you." The hard tap of a hammer follows, crisp and sure. The man sets the hoof down, patting the horse's flank as he straightens.

Nathan Ramsey is a big man, built like an ox. He smiles and rubs his beard with dirt and soot-stained fingers.

"Well, Chris. Aren't you looking well?"

"Me, well?" I laugh. "I feel like I'm still half a man."

"Perhaps you're just a sight for sore eyes." He slaps me

on the back. "There can't be many *darani* left in this part of the territory, and you had the luck to find one."

"He found me," I say ruefully. "And caused me a great deal of trouble."

"I wish I could have seen it."

"Why don't you come inside and we'll have a drink and you can tell me how things have been?"

"I'm afraid your stores aren't what they usually are," says Nathan. "But we have coffee and whiskey and anything your father put down in the cellar."

"Any of that suits. You know me."

"Good." Nathan goes over and unties the draft horse, leading it by its halter out to the corral.

"Go on." He waves it off and it trots over to the new horses with interest. Buck and Britt are hauling their saddles into the bunkhouse.

"Who are they?"

"Horsebreakers. A pair of brothers I found out in Glory Mesa."

"Brothers?" Nathan raises his eyebrows.

"Yep. Britt and Buck April."

"The Aprils? By gur man, they're notorious."

"Well, they're going to help me with that herd up north. Are they still ranging there?"

"More or less. I've seen some down in the flats too." He rubs his nose and hesitates. "The boys, they saw Tora-Teth out there a couple days ago."

"Tora-Teth? They're sure?"

"They are. He was just slinking around on a scrub pony, weren't doing nothing. But he's on your land."

"Well, we'll keep an eye out for him and you make sure the boys don't go anywhere without guns, right?"

"I already told them."

"Good. Mind you tell them not to tangle with him either, unless he's after them or the cattle. He's a dangerous fellow."

"I'll do that. After you."

We duck into the ranch house together. I take a deep breath of the smell of wood and ink and a hint of old tobacco. It's good to be home.

It's dark and I am weary, but I cannot sleep. Nathan and I talked until it was far too late for sensible men, and when he left, I simply couldn't move.

I drag my feet off the low table and sit up. Too many nights spent inside. I need the stars.

I thrust my arms into my jacket and head out into the night air. Over me hangs a silver canopy of stars, like the diamonds set in chandeliers out East.

But I'd take these stars and the pines stretching tall enough to rake them out of the dark sky over those diamonds any day.

The beautiful stillness of the night overtakes me and my eyes well with tears. There is nothing more beautiful than one's home, one's stars, and the smell of the trees standing like sentinels around the land you love.

"Can't sleep?" A brief flame lights in the thin darkness, illuminating Buck April's face for a moment.

He shakes it out and the end of his cigarette glows as he takes a draw.

"I guess I just missed this."

"Ain't nothing like home, I hear." Buck leans back against the bunkhouse wall and blows a slow stream of smoke.

"That's right."

"Must feel mighty good to belong someplace. I never had that."

"Really? I'm sorry to hear that."

Buck shrugs and comes over, slow and lazy on his long legs. "I'd say I don't mind, but I'm a firm believer that a man's got a longing for home built right into him, same way's a mustang knows how to find water in the wilderness."

"That so?" I smile, but it's probably lost in the darkness.

I don't think any philosopher could put it clearer or better than this horsebreaker just did.

"I reckon. I've always felt it. But my brother was more important than settling." He raises the cigarette to his lips and takes another draw.

"He's quite a man, your brother."

"He is." Buck gives a soft laugh. "He ain't perfect. Sometimes he's downright mean. But I love him, and I reckon he's the only thing I've ever really loved."

"May I ask you something—something you do not have to answer, if you wish."

"Sure."

"Have you ever wanted anything? Just you, not connected to Britt in any way?"

Buck grins and drops the stub of his cigarette, grinding it out with his heel. "Chris, if I had, I don't remember it. I was three when my parents died, were killed, I don't know. Britt never told me. My life's been following my brother and I never knew different. If I had an idea he didn't like, I learned to forget it. But you know the funny thing? He needs me. More than I need him. He don't admit it, but I think he knows, deep down. And that's why I don't care."

He looks at me, quiet and deep.

"I believe that things are meant to be. And I'm meant to be with Britt, long as we're both breathing."

He smiles and sticks his hands in his pockets. "But I've liked the stars, always. And Britt never gave a hang for the stars."

40

CARNEGIE

I T'S STRANGE TO WALK INTO CARSON'S SALOON, SAME steps, same boots on my feet, and yet feel so different. Like a lifetime has passed in between.

"Ma'am, we're not—" Carson stops short.

I think at first glance he didn't recognize me in a blouse and skirt. First money I got from Marshal Lacey, I bought new ones. Even the sight of my worn-out dresses, stained with coffee and beer and grease, turns my stomach.

"Kate." His greeting is brief but respectful.

"I know you're not open yet," I tease. "Raymond Lacey wants to know if you are coming."

He looks me up and down with a slight scowl on his face. "Comin' where?"

"The railroad is starting work on the pass in the next couple weeks, and they are concerned about being ambushed for the payroll, seeing as the Black Shaft is notorious for that sort of thing."

"They should beg help off the army. Why do they think just because we have the governor here that we need to fight all their battles? We're not getting their money."

"Well, Governor Scott's been invited out to view the work, and our new surveyor's been back and forth a little. We have stake in it."

"A stake," he grumbles.

"And Blue Harding has it, reliably, that a bunch of Abernathy's men and some others who used to follow Mortimer are gathering to watch the pass."

Carson mutters something I can't hear.

"Marshal Lacey wants to take them out while they're together."

"Marshal Lacey is putting his head in a noose. And why's he trusting the word of that scoundrel? Blue owes me almost two hundred dollars in damages, you know."

"How old's the debt?"

"That don't matter," he snorts. "You know that."

"Well, either way, the railroad and our governor need protecting."

"I remember the days when Archer Scott rode line alone for months on end. And look what that government out East has done to him—turned him into a china doll!"

"They've done nothing of the sort." I feel my face flushing with annoyance.

"He's worried about laws now, about keeping people

safe, he's itchy as a tied bronc to break loose, but he don't. What kind of life is that?"

"He's happy here. His wife has done him a lot of good."

"He's chained to a desk. And that brother-in-law of his is so keen on bringing peace fast that he's lettin' outlaws back into society helter-skelter. I wouldn't be surprised if some of them start gunnin' for some of us, for those times we had to use force back in the wild times. And he'd let 'em all because of amnesty!"

"Do you have a problem with peace and quiet and happy folks?"

"No."

"Then don't stir the pot."

"I'll stir what I want to stir. Don't think just because you got yourself a piece of tin, it lets you go all sorts of places that are supposed to be closed to the public." He thunks the coffee pot down on the bar harder than strictly necessary.

I should have known better than to get into this with him.

"Well, are you coming?" I ask.

"No," he snaps. "I am not. I've got it bad enough here short on hands without hurting my back with days in the saddle, sleeping in the dust, and asking for lead in my guts. Besides, the marshal's got fifty scrappy outlaws now, what does he need with me?"

"Nothing, I guess." I shrug and tap my finger on the bar.

"Well, good," Carson snorts. "That's that."

"Good day." I push myself back from the bar. It feels good to be on this side of it.

"Kate, wait."

He comes to the end of the bar, motioning for me to come back.

"Look, we parted on bad terms a few weeks ago. I'm sorry. There ain't no bad feelings from me." He scratches his neck and frowns. "That don't mean I'll go riding with the marshal, it don't mean I'll agree with you about the way this territory is being run, it don't mean none of that. But you've got spunk, Kate, and I hope it takes you far."

He holds out his hand, and I take it gladly.

PETER IS STANDING outside the doorway, leaning against the wall, cleaning his knife.

"Are you riding out with Marshal Lacey?"

"Sure am."

He squints at me and smiles. "I'll go someday. Someday before these are over."

"That might not be in your lifetime."

"It will." He glances out at the distant hills. "Sam says he's going."

"Sam?"

"They cut his stage line running north, says the railroad is taking it over. He and Barnes are waiting on a transfer to a different line."

"Whereabouts, do they know?"

"South, I think." Peter gives a sigh. "Do you think it's true that if you get these outlaws, the problems with them will be mostly over?"

"I reckon. But we'll need more marshals all over the territory to keep the peace, so more don't spring up."

"I'm riding with you," he announces with sudden determination. "Carson's not coming, so I'll make the coffee and watch the horses. Someone would have had to do that anyway."

"But what about Carson? What's he going to say?"

Peter gives a chuckle under his breath, rare from him, and shoves off the wall with his shoulder.

I guess I'm one to talk.

41

ALAN

"You know, I think pa would've been proud to see the way we boys clean up."

Jem is leaning into the tiny boarding-house mirror, shaving his jaw with utmost care.

"You mean the way you clean up," says Max, craning his neck to look at Jem, pulling out what little of his tie I've tied.

"Easy, I can't do this if you keep moving," I mutter.

"Sorry." Max takes a deep breath and goes stiff.

"It's not an execution, Max. You can let your breath out," laughs Jem, looking at us through the mirror.

Max shoots him a look our mother would have disapproved of, were she still with us.

"It's been a long time since we've been to any sort of dinner party." Jem gives the mirror a teasing look. "You figure you still know how to tell your forks apart?"

"Sure I can," Max shoots back, figuring the comment was for him.

"I don't know." I pull Max's tie tight. "Do we really need to go to this? It's not really, well—you know, necessary." I'd honestly rather spend an evening in the company of my horse than Maria Pike.

I turn Max loose with a slap to his shoulder.

"Maria Pike is a prominent figure in Glory Mesa, in the territory," says Jem patiently, as if reciting from an invisible book of etiquette he was born knowing. "One could argue it's polite to accept. She's invited the governor and his wife, most of the larger ranch owners, the railroad men, the marshal, anyone of note. To bow out for no reason—"

"I suppose." I reach into my collar to let a little air in. "I thought Tagweiah not being invited might be reason enough."

"Tagweiah wouldn't come to a party like this if you paid him ten thousand dollars, you know that. It's just a couple hours. We wouldn't have been doing much anyway. And this way you won't be wasting money in the saloon." Jem throws his shaving towel at Max.

Max catches it midair and throws it on the ground. "Who says I'd be in the saloon? Now that Carson can afford good spirits, he won't put them on the house."

"Well, mind you behave yourself," says Jem, shoving his arms into his fresh shirt. "Else all the cleaning up in the world won't make a lick of difference."

. . .

THE LIGHTS ARE on in the new house down on the third block of main street. It's a sprawling, white affair with flowers lining the walk to the door.

"Where'd she get the money for this?" whistles Max.

The door opens and Maria is framed in the doorway. She's wearing a dark color—red, I think—and the velvet of the dress clings and winds around her arms and neck in a rush of opulence.

"Welcome, gentlemen!" She stands aside, ushering us in. "Your coats?"

There's a girl, some shy pioneer sort, who takes our jackets without a word, and Maria leads us down the front hall. The room she leads us to is wide, richly furnished, and well-lit. Jem hasn't told me much about what it's like in the fine circles back East, but I figure this is probably a taste of it.

If this is all it is, I can do without it.

Across the room I spot Archer talking with the vice president of the railroad, one Christopher Bracken. Rosamund stands with her husband, her arm through his.

She turns a little and smiles at us.

Raymond Lacey and Jesse Thatcher are deep in conversation, nearly unrecognizable in their starched shirts and suit coats.

Thatcher sees me and excuses himself, coming over.

"Alan! You are looking well." He holds out his hand and clasps mine firmly. Then he grins. "Have I seen you in a suit before?"

"Probably not since my father's funeral," I admit. "We were both far younger."

He takes a sip of the champagne in his glass. Only I catch the slightly wrinkled nose and the sour face he quickly hides.

"Truth is, Alan, I've not been well. Not sick, but—" He lowers his voice. "It's like an itch I can't scratch. There's something wrong and I can't put my finger on it, but I can't ignore it either."

"Like what?"

"It's too peaceful, too happy. Someone here has secrets they're not telling and I don't know who. There have been multiple attempts to lure Archer out of Glory Mesa. I just don't like it."

I raise my eyebrows. "I hadn't heard that."

"Kate Carnegie was on her way to Saguaro City and ran into a gunslinger and an outlaw, both paid to stop the governor. And I've got a note from someone in Glory Mesa promising payment to a bounty hunter once Archer's dead."

"That's hardly comforting."

Thatcher shakes his head, agreeing. "I just can't seem to settle. And I've only got one lead." He pulls out a silver locket engraved with a lone mountain peak. "This belonged, at one time, to whoever tried to hire that gunman."

I take it in my fingers and turn it in the light.

"It's certainly unique. But I think I'd remember if I'd seen it before." I hand it back.

Maria steps into the room with an audible rustle and

clasps her ivory hands together. Thatcher's hand closes over the locket sharply and he thrusts it into his pocket.

"Gentlemen, ladies, esteemed guests," she calls out in her low, rich voice, "dinner is served."

AFTER DINNER, we stand around and talk in the parlor. Some of the mining and railroad men are smoking good cigars in the next room; I can smell them.

Raymond Lacey stands with a fine, fair-haired lady I have never seen before. He seems gentler, somehow, in her presence. Max is talking animatedly with Rosamund Scott, and when she says something complimentary, he blushes to his ears.

Thatcher comes up to me, his hands practically twitching.

"I can't take a moment more of this," he mutters. "I'm heading out. I'm going to talk to Harrison Terhune."

"Terhune?"

"He was involved last year. He might recognize it. Or he might at least be able to tell me who's still got an interest in my cousin's downfall with Mortimer gone. It's like—it's like there's eyes on my back and I can't get rid of the feeling."

I hold my hand out.

"Thanks." He clasps it briefly. "See you around." And just like that, with no other goodbyes, he leaves.

"Where is Jesse going?" Maria is approaching with concern on her face.

"He has business that won't keep." I smile despite the feeling of unease Thatcher has brought on the night. "The party has been lovely. Thank you."

"It isn't over," she says warmly, her fingers cradling her glass of champagne.

"Oh?"

"You haven't had anything to drink. And there is cake and raspberry fool."

"I'll have to sample it all, then."

"I will see to it." Her voice is almost motherly. "After all, it's the least I can do, with you men riding out before too long. Protecting us and the governor from those outlaws. I long for the day when they are no longer a concern."

"Is that common knowledge?" I ask, unable to mask my surprise. I'd only heard about it myself this morning.

"Oh, it's around town." She sips her drink delicately. "You men are all our heroes."

4 2

NEWTON

"Just look at the grullo in the back there." Britt points with a long arm to a lanky stallion. "He's going to be a real horse."

Some thirty or forty mustangs are milling in the pens before us, separated, more or less, by their bands. Their coats seem to almost to reflect the wild landscape of their range: the mixed pebbles of a mountain stream in the roans, the red rock dust in the chestnuts, the night sky caught in the blacks.

And they are as fierce as the desert storms, proud as the mountains ranges.

"Is he going to grow out of being so leggy, do you think?" I ask, shading my eyes to get a good look at him.

"Sure, he's probably only about two." Britt turns his head and spits in the dirt. "But his daddy was probably that dun stallion we left loose out there. And that stallion had bone

309

and shoulder that would make those racing men out East weep."

"You can see a little bit of it—there, when he turns." Buck shoves his hat back on his head and points, quick. "Look at the thickness of the bone. Not too heavy, but not fragile. Developed on those rocky hills and hard, fast flats."

"I like the look of that mare," I comment, leaning my arms on the rough top bar of the corral. "She's got sense."

"I noticed her too." Buck's voice is warm. "Breed her with a good cowpony and you'd get yourself a horse with sense and stamina and quick as a mountain cat."

"How many of these do you figure on keeping?" asks Britt.

"Fifteen or so. We'll keep some of the younger ones, turn the older ones back out. That mare there, with the buckskin filly—we'll keep her, and maybe that gray."

"We should pull a couple for Terhune," says Buck.

"That's right." I take my boot off the rail and step around to the side of the pen. "Maybe we should send for him before we turn them back out, give him the pick of the rest."

Britt seizes the top rail and swings himself up on top of it. "Let's get a move on some of these first."

Buck goes for his horse.

"Got one you want started?" asks Britt, scanning the herd.

"I'll let you choose your first, for luck."

"Right."

Buck goes into the herd and moves alongside them carefully. Occasionally one of them charges out at him, and he shakes the rope in their direction. Most only jerk their heads away, ruffled, and then retreat.

He's as calm as a still summer day, and I think it makes a difference. The horses can feel it.

Britt is still scanning the herd, watching as the horses move and mill away from Buck and his pony. Then he shoots out a hand, pointing to a dark bay.

"Bring that one out, will you?"

Buck swings the rope and throws. The bay comes protesting at first, but with the calm pony beside him, he settles and follows easy enough.

Buck turns him loose in the breaking pen, then ties up his own horse outside and walks in with just a rope coiled in his hand.

The bay colt tosses its head, makes a try at a challenge, and immediately backs off when Buck hisses.

It bolts. Picks up its head and runs circles clear around the pen. Buck stands in the center and watches until the colt stops, bored, and takes a step in his direction.

Buck raises his face to the colt and they both stand, proud, cautious, unafraid, watching each other.

Perhaps this is why these April boys are such good horse-breakers. They don't just work the horses; they are of the same spirit.

Wild and clannish and mistrustful.

The horse takes another step, and another, until he and Buck nearly touch.

"Easy," says Buck, soothingly. He reaches up and touches its neck. The horse jerks its head in surprise, but Buck doesn't flinch. He keeps talking and tries again. This time the horse stands.

"Good boy," Buck whispers. He's talking the whole time, quiet earnest words.

Then he turns and walks away, back to the fence.

"He's got sense. A little more of this and he'll be ready for you."

I watch the brothers work the colt over the afternoon, talking, reaching out, walking away, touching his neck, then his shoulders, then his head and his back.

And finally, Buck gets tack on him.

Britt puts on his chaps and goes into the pen where Buck holds the horse.

"Easy now, easy," Britt is saying, low and drawn out as if it's all one word. "Just face him that way and get ready. He's going to want to run."

Buck gets the horse standing, talking to it softly, running his hand on its neck.

"Ready?" Britt asks.

"Ready."

Britt swings into the saddle and the horse tenses.

"There, now," says Britt, reaching down to touch its neck. He straightens and gives his brother a nod. Buck lets the horse go and shoots out of the way.

The colt breaks away, popping a couple bucks, sidewinding, then tears into a dead gallop, round and round the pen.

Britt's face is like iron as he hangs on, his legs almost unmoving, his spurs never touching the animal.

After a while of this, Britt's seat never shifting, the horse gets tired and settles.

They walk, quietly, around the pen.

"That's some riding," I say, shading my eyes to see his face.

Britt smiles. Just a small one, but it's something real, something beyond the stony face he always wears.

AFTERNOON WEARS TO EVENING, and the Aprils are in a good mood. Our meal of beans and bacon is cooking over a smoky fire, and they are talking together about the horses, shoving each other a little as brothers do, hand-rolling cigarettes to smoke.

"What are you boys going to do once you're through here?" I ask, adding more pine cones to the fire.

Britt picks up a stone and tosses it into the air. "Figured I might pick out a couple of those mustangs for myself and Britt after you ranchers have had your pick, and we might—I don't know—drift."

"You're welcome to your pick before I'm through. I won't tell Harrison."

Britt laughs. "I've a mind towards that grullo stallion. He's got a lot of good in him, even though he's stubborn. And

I'd be gentle with his spirit. He's one best changed gently or let go. I'd rather he go free than have the wrong man in the saddle."

"He's yours." I turn to Britt. "If you can talk about a horse that way, I reckon you're the man for him."

Britt's thank you is just a nod, but that's enough.

"What about you, Buck?"

Buck gets up and peers at the herd through the shards of bright sunlight. "You see that light roan mare? The one with the dark, narrow face?"

Britt grunts.

I see her; she's slim and delicate, nothing remarkable save that she follows the grullo close.

"She's bonded with that young grullo. I'd take her."

Britt chuckles under his breath like he could have guessed.

"Again, she's yours."

"Thanks." Buck holds out his hand for me to shake. I clasp it.

I'm sure going to hate losing these boys to the wilds, but I reckon I have as much chance of keeping the April brothers in one place as I do a band of mustangs.

THE *DARANI* ATTACK has left me with lingering pain that increases at night, more so if the day has been long. It makes sleep hard, and when I do sleep, it's as one completely exhausted.

Tonight is one of the worse nights.

I thrust my hands under my head and stare up at the stars. There is no need for me to keep watch at the moment, as the Aprils and our horses are as quick and touchy as wildcats, but I pray I won't be like this for the rest of my life. It would make it hard to travel safely alone.

One of the horses in the pen moves restlessly; another gives a long blow through his nose. It's Buck's watch, and the firelight dances off the side of his face as he reads by the light of the flames, making him look stark and dangerous.

Both brothers are younger than I am, and I am not much over thirty, but their faces are like those of the aged clansmen who tell tales of the old times.

They have seen too much, lived too much, in the short span of their years.

"You should sleep, Britt," Buck says, glancing over from his book. "I can watch just fine, book or no."

"What good is a book to you?"

"Plenty of good. Now sleep or it'll be your turn before you know it." Buck goes back to reading calmly.

My arm burns and I lean into the the cool sand beside my bedroll, trying to find relief. Britt turns over with a groan; he can't seem to get comfortable either.

Somehow—a long while later, by the night sounds—I rest.

. . .

Gunshots split the air, two of them. I am awake and sitting up, my hand reaching for my gun in the same movement.

Britt is staring off into the night with the tense focus of a mountain stallion, a smoking gun in his hand. Buck is stirring up the fire, adding fuel fast.

"What was it?" I ask.

"Tora-Teth. He was just inside the light of the fire. I could see his face."

"Did you get him?"

"I think I missed." Britt spins his pistol and thrusts it back in its holster.

Buck comes over and pulls his rifle out of its sheath. "I'll watch a while, Britt."

"You had your turn."

"I'm not sleeping."

"Very well, suit yourself." Britt checks his gun and reloads, then lies back down, the gun still in his hand.

"Sleep, Chris." Buck gives me a little smile. "I'll keep a sharp eye out, don't you worry. If he's out there, I'll be sure to get him."

43

IRENE

I SMOOTH DOWN THE SKIRT OF MY BLUE MUSLIN DRESS and fold my hands to keep them from straying. It is very kind of Maria Pike to invite some of the women from Glory Mesa to a tea, but it is nearly—and I say nearly, not quite—too much like home.

One of the women, a widow who lives with her bachelor son, reaches over and puts her hand sympathetically over Edith's.

"My dear, you must be so worried for your husband. I hear that he is going with the marshal."

But Edith only smiles serenely. "Hardly. Lesley is very capable. After all, he faced outlaws alone with the marshal much earlier this year. The marshal asked him particularly to come."

"What an honor!"

"I thought so." She takes a sip of her tea, her eyes glowing.

"But—what if he is killed?" asks one of the younger women, leaning forward with interest.

"Then I will go on alone," Edith says, as if repeating words heard often. "As he would want me to. Life out here is not for the fainthearted, man or woman. You must learn to take your opportunities, regardless of what misfortunes life out here brings you."

"Well, I would have found it difficult, I think," speaks up the widow, "if I hadn't had a grown son."

"Maria did it," says Edith.

Maria smiles graciously. "That I did. But there is little to be gained in speculating about disaster. Why, I would be surprised if your husband didn't come back with some tale of his heroics. That's the trade we make out here. It is dangerous, but we write the history of this territory with our actions."

"It is a dangerous task these men have," Mrs. Miller, the banker's wife, agrees sagely. "Protecting our railroad, our governor, our interests. I hear these outlaws they're going after are the worst sort."

"And the marshal has joined with some for their assistance!" This is one of the railroad executive's wives. "Disgraceful. To be thieves and killers and get away with it just because you betray other thieves and killers?"

"Yes," says Mrs. Miller. "They're like to turn on them

halfway, mark my words. Raymond Lacey has gone too far this time."

"And that Kate Carnegie, good heavens—she's going to get herself murdered going with them!"

"She's just going to watch and run messages," says Edith, glad to have news of interest. "He wants her because she's light and knows the roads there. She'd get through faster than any man, my husband says."

"I still say it's the last thing she'll do," says the railroad executive's wife, shaking her head. "And probably the last thing any of them will do. Mark my words, they should have hung Blue Harding and his men while they had the chance."

Maria clears her throat and takes a serene sip of her tea, as if reminding her guests that hanging is hardly a subject to be discussed in a civilized parlor.

I SEE Raymond at the livery stable, on my way home.

I hadn't planned to see him before he left; part of me was hoping not to. I am afraid of loving someone just to lose them again.

But he's there, and so I go to him.

He is looking over the horses, feeling down their legs, checking their mouths and backs for sores.

I watch him for a full three minutes at the least, debating whether to stay or go, when he turns around and gives a little start.

"Mrs. Sandler." He fingers the brim of his hat in greeting. "Forgive me, I'm just going over the rented hacks. It's the marshal's job to fit his posse if they don't come mounted."

"Oh, I see."

He unties the horse he's been inspecting and puts it back. Then he turns to me, leaning his hand on the half-door of the stall. "Can I help you with anything?"

"Is it true that you're working with an outlaw to protect the governor?"

"Blue isn't a concern, if that's what you are worried about."

"I've just heard that it's particularly dangerous, this ride you're heading out on."

"It is dangerous, but there is a lot of gossip that gets passed around about things like this," says Raymond quietly.

"Some of the women fear it is a trap."

"It might be."

"Isn't that—a concern?"

"You shouldn't worry about me." His eyes have a kind gleam as he studies my face. "An old piece of rawhide like me is hardly worth the worry, don't you think?"

"I think you are." My voice is light and careless, but I can't look him in the eye when I say it. Curse my sorry heart.

He chuckles and scratches the back of his head ruefully. "Awfully kind. Tell you what you can do...."

He goes across the aisle and picks up a saddle off the door of an empty stall and slings it over his shoulder.

"Go visit Rosamund while we're gone. She's going to be pining for Archer, as she does, and you'll be busy enough with her that you'll forget about me and Blue and the whole situation. A good distraction is the best medicine, and it sounds like you'll both need it."

"Naturally." I force a smile. "I'd be happy to."

"Well, then." He smiles and gives me a nod. "See you around, Mrs. Sandler."

I stand in the doorway and watch him go.

44

ROSAMUND

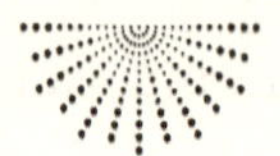

Archer comes back late, well after dark. His shoulders are heavy as he hangs his coat and hat up beside the door and pulls his boots off.

"It's late," he says, apologetic. "The railroad committee had a lot to say tonight about rights of way and how close tracks should be laid to the edge of town and—well, all the other details I'd rather not drag into what little of our evening we have left." He sinks down in a chair with a long sigh.

"That's all right." I get up and come over, putting my arms around him, leaning my head against his shoulder. "Any time with you, however short, is time well used."

"I'm glad you think so." He takes my hand and kisses it contentedly, pressing it between both his hands.

"Do you want anything to drink?"

"No!" He chuckles and pulls back to look at my face.

"Those railroad men had about four different kinds of rot-gut in fancy bottles. I've had my fill of anything wet."

"Poor dear," I laugh.

I bring the lamp from the kitchen and set it on a stand in the front parlor. All day we spend our time fulfilling the duties of the territory, him with the lawmen and the businessmen and I with the social duties; but in the evenings, we sit together in the parlor, enjoying the stillness and the low light. Sometimes we talk, sometimes we read, sometimes we just sit together and watch the flame in the lamp flicker.

But tonight, I have something to say.

His arms are around me, warm and strong, and he smells of leather and ink and someone's cigar. I should ask him to wash tonight, but I'm too content with him at my side.

"Archer?" I lean my head against his shoulder.

"Mhm?" His eyes are closed, his fingers gently rubbing my arm.

"Are you awake?"

"Yes, darling." His eyes don't open, he's slipping into a contented doze.

"I have something to tell you."

"Go ahead." His tracing fingers find mine and he entwines them.

"It's important."

"That's all right. I am listening." He leans his head against mine.

"We're having a baby."

His eyes snap open. He couldn't have been more

surprised if I had suddenly slapped him.

"What did you say?"

"I said we're having a baby, dear." I laugh.

"You mean it?" His eyes light with so much hope—I'd be heartbroken if I ever had to disappoint that face.

"Yes, I mean it."

"When is it coming?" He seems in awe.

I'm not far enough along to feel anything, but I still take his hand and set it on my stomach. "Springtime."

He leans over and kisses me, slow and gentle.

"I'll tell Raymond soon," I say, when he's done. "You can tell Jesse."

"Jesse lit out. Back to the ranch, I think." He reaches out and cups my face in his hand like he's never seen anything more beautiful. "I'm sorry I have to go out to the pass. I won't be more than a day."

"I wish that you didn't have to go at all."

"I will think of you and this little one the entire time."

"Do more than that." I shift around to look him straight in the face. "Be careful. I cannot bear the thought of anything happening to you now."

"Haven't I promised you a dozen times?" He smiles gently. "I will be surrounded by friends, and your brother is handling the outlaws miles away. Nothing will happen."

"Promise me again?"

He reaches out and tucks my hair back, kisses my forehead.

"I promise."

45

NEWTON

Morning comes pale and still. I can hear the rustle of the horses grazing quietly and hear birds singing. A trickle of bluish smoke rises from the cooling remnants of the fire, clinging near to the ground.

The Aprils are gone. The place where their bedrolls were spread is bare and flat, and their horses are nowhere to be seen.

I find the reason written in the dirt beside the fire.

Gone after Tora-Teth. Back soon.

The April brothers are two of the toughest boys I know, but I know better than to stay here and wait for them to come back.

If they corner Tora-Teth, it's going to be the meanest fight of their lives. They'll need all the help they can get.

. . .

I cook breakfast, check over the horses, and saddle my horse up. Nathan and his son ride into camp mid-morning with four other hands and a couple horses loaded with supplies.

"Nathan, you're here none too soon." I head straight for the pack horses and begin replenishing my grub bag.

"Did something go wrong? I thought you had those horsebreakers with you." He's scratching his beard, looking over the camp and corral with a mild scowl.

"I did. Get these horses taken care of, Nathan. I want about twenty. Pick out the best, and keep that roan mare with the neck rope and the two-year-old grullo."

"Where are you going?"

"After the hands. It's all right, there's no bad blood. But I'm going after them."

"Go on, then. Don't worry about a thing."

"I wouldn't leave if I couldn't trust you, Nathan."

He clasps my hand in warm farewell and I mount up. "When should I expect you back?" he asks.

"Hopefully before those horses have to be moved. A day, maybe a week."

"That's a big difference, Chris."

I smile ironically and clap spurs to my horse.

THATCHER

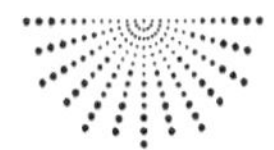

I NEVER THOUGHT, AFTER LAST YEAR, THAT I'D RIDE INTO the wide yard of Harrison Terhune's ranch of my own will.

How quickly enemies can become allies in a land like this.

"Jesse Thatcher!" calls one of the ranch hands, coming out to meet me. "What in tarnation are you doing all the way out here?"

I think they're uneasy at my presence.

"Is Terhune in?"

"He rode north yesterday. He's going to look at some mustangs Chris Newton is breaking up in the hills."

"Which trail did he take?" .

"The Red Fork."

"Thanks." I turn my horse around, but the ranch hand seizes my bridle.

"If you're going after him with bad intent, I can't let you."

I laugh, not sure whether to be annoyed or simply impressed by the man's loyalty. "I'm not the marshal. I need to talk is all."

"All right." He lets go of my horse and steps back. "Good luck, then."

I give him a nod, pull my hat low, and cluck to the horse. We shoot out of that yard like we've got a dozen *isarks* on our tail.

I RIDE THROUGH HALF the night and most of the next day before I catch up with Harrison and his four hands at the Half Springs watering hole.

They regard me cautiously, shading their eyes and murmuring with one another as they watch my approach.

I pull up and let my horse drop its head to drink. "Harrison Terhune?"

Harrison is across the springs from me, dismounted and adjusting his cinch. He gives me a quiet look, and his eyes are hard to read. The men whisper among themselves and give me long, silent stares.

Harrison ties his horse to a dead sapling and comes forward, all business, pulling his gloves off slowly and deliberately.

"What do you want with me, Jesse Thatcher?"

"I need to talk with you. Alone."

Harrison snaps his fingers to the men around the spring

and thrusts a thumb over his shoulder. They mount their horses, no argument, and leave.

"Well?" His voice breaks the silence left between us after the men have gone.

"Harrison, I think you know there's little reason for there to be any mutual trust or decent feelings between us, but I have no one else to turn to."

A look of bitter amusement enters his eyes. "Now this is something I must hear." He folds his arms.

"Someone has been trying to lure my cousin, Archer Scott, out of Glory Mesa."

Harrison raises his eyebrows, unconvinced.

"He's paying people gold to lure him out and waylay him. There was a bounty hunter offered a price to take him out. There was a boy who came for Archer's help, and when Kate Carnegie went instead, she was stopped twice by people expecting the governor. Tell me that's not a coincidence."

"Kate Carnegie?" He seems to find this humorous.

"Yes. That doesn't matter right now."

"What a girl." He chuckles under his breath.

"Come on, Harrison. You know it's not a coincidence. You were with these people last year. You know what they wanted."

"And I don't know them anymore. What you expect me to do about it?"

"I want to know what you think. If you know who it

could be, or why they're so set against the governor—at least one of them's in Glory Mesa."

"Biggest town in the surrounding hundred miles, and you expect there to be no enemies? Last year there were quite a few, I recall."

"But none that you know are there now?"

He shrugs and shakes his head. "I haven't been to town in months. Look, Jesse, I'm just trying to go straight and keep my head down. Someone's tried to kill me twice already."

"Well, I'm sorry."

"Don't be," he laughs humorlessly. "They haven't done it yet."

I shove my hat back on my head. I've gone and wasted my time.

"I guess I just have one more question." I pull the locket out of my pocket and hold it out. "Have you seen this before? It was meant to go to the bounty hunter. Payment for Archer's death."

Harrison takes it out of my hand and holds it up. His face goes strangely blank. "This is from the one who hired him?"

"Yes."

"You're sure?"

"Yes, sure."

His hand closes into a fist over the locket.

"That's it, come on." He shoves his boot into his stirrup and lands in the saddle, collecting the reins as the horse side-steps and tries to rush under him.

"What do you mean?"

"Get on the horse. We're going back to Glory Mesa."

"Well, what do you know about that?" I nod to the locket.

"It was mine. I gave it to someone, last year."

I swing up into the saddle, pull my hat tighter onto my head. "You going to tell me who?"

Harrison's face is like grim death as he turns his horse southward.

"Maria Pike."

47

PIKE

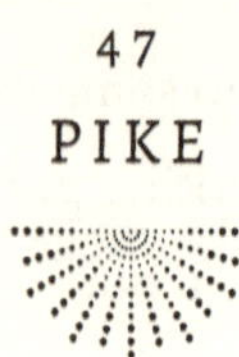

IT'S A CLOUDY, FRETFULLY STORMY DAY. EVER SINCE I moved west and threw my lot in with Glory Mesa, I have hated such days.

But the streets of Glory Mesa are quiet for once. As I step off the low porch of the restaurant, step into the dusty streets, every footfall feels as strong as a thunderclap.

I pass Carson's saloon on the opposite side of the street. The lights linger, but the customers are few. The fool has been wise for once; he will not ride out with Marshal Raymond Lacey. He will live, for now.

I pass the stage office where the men are loading the mail onto the stage. The wind tears at their long dusters; Sam has his collar up against it.

The horses close their eyes and shift patiently at the dust thrown up into their faces. Even the mighty stage will become nearly obsolete once the railroad comes into town.

332

Your days are numbered.

I almost pause outside the Territorial Governor's office. The flag of the territory is fighting in the wind, and a single lamp burns in the window.

He must be alone, the poor man. It's almost a pity, what I must do.

But I tried the gentle way, my boy, and you turned it down.

Enjoy what you have before you're gone for good.

I pass the General Mercantile and Trasker raises his hand in greeting to me. I return the gesture. He's bringing in the front-porch goods in anticipation of the storm.

Stay polite, Mr. Trasker, and I will try to forget that you took the mercantile from me.

The boarding house is full, as it has been for the last six months. The Swifts' matching roans are out front with Tagweiah's bay.

They spill out, laughing, enjoying whatever joke or game brothers share. None of them notice me standing across the street, and I am happier that way.

I pause, watching their bright faces, the way laughter transforms them completely.

You beautiful boys—what plans I have for you.

The governor's house is smaller than mine—that's the government's provision for you—but beautifully, immaculately kept.

Rosamund has poured all her heart into making it so.

Keep your beautiful house, your whitewashed fence,

your man whom everyone can see how you love, Mrs. Rosamund Scott.

Keep them if you can.

On main street also is the marshal's office. Raymond Lacey, the war hero, the beloved soldier, the man who can do no wrong.

But I have found his weakness. She's tall and fair-haired and refined.

Fall hard, my boy. Fall and I will have your downfall in my fingers.

The last building on the street before I turn is the doctor's.

I stop and regard that small, modest place. A place of more power than any other living soul here dreams.

They walk by it as if it is no more than slat boards and a few windows.

The irony is as strong as the tight, charged air that hangs over his house. You thought you could shelter them like you were God. You thought you could play them, and you thought you could do the same to me. You thought you knew me. But you never knew me, Doctor Sikes.

See if you can protect them from me now.

I close my eyes and breathe in the wild, wild air. Civilization comes like a rolling tide, unstoppable, but it will never tame the power of this land. They are two things, entirely separate, and in the right hands, they will move together as a harnessed team.

I turn my back on the doctor's office and stride down the street for home.

Rage on, dark clouds. I'm coming for you.

I clench my fists in defiance and lift my eyes, smiling as the storm rolls in.

48

CARNEGIE

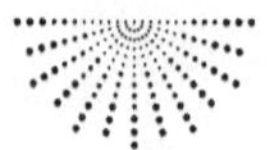

WE RIDE OUT TO THE LOW HILLS SOUTHEAST OF GLORY Mesa, where the Rio Jefe runs strong and wide down toward Auki land.

The hills are still dusty in places, but there is grass and growing things, and the smell alone makes me so glad I came.

Blue meets us just outside of his camp.

"Marshal, there's about ninety outlaws camped over yonder, mostly Red Arms and Mortimer's dregs."

"Any trouble?" asks Raymond.

"None yet. We haven't poked them, and they probably don't know we're here."

"Good, let's keep it that way for now."

Blue glances over our company—there's about twenty or thirty of us—and his eyes light on me.

"Miss Carnegie." He tips his brim. "Pleased, as always."

"I'm glad to see you took my advice," I reply. "How's the leg?"

"Hardly feel it." He gives it a slap.

Raymond looks at me slowly.

"She didn't tell you she shot me in the leg, did she?" Blue laughs. "Figures."

PETER MAKES himself at home in Blue's camp, setting up for supper at one of the fires. Our men settle uneasily, talking and cleaning their guns.

I'm just happy to not be the one doing the coffee and grub for once. I settle down on the ground and pull my father's army coat tight around me.

I watch in contented silence as Peter grinds the coffee, pours it into the pot of water, and stirs it.

It's a comforting thing to sit in front of a fire as the chill of evening creeps in and watch him work. He's so quiet and focused. I'm glad he came, and I hope I don't regret it.

It's impossible not to wonder, somewhere in your mind, how many of these men will still be here this time tomorrow.

Peter stirs the pot now and again and finally sets it down next to the fire.

"You should come get it now, Kate," he says. "Looks like there are more coming." He nods toward Blue and a group of his men coming our way.

Blue comes over to the fire, peeling off his gloves and shoving them into his belt. "Coffee smells good."

The rest of our men around the fire seem to stiffen a little, but Peter just smiles, no different from his usual tranquil self.

"Help yourself," he says, holding out a tin mug.

Blue takes it and reaches for the pot.

"According to my boys, the camp is just over those hills there. You know anything about those hills, Tagweiah?"

"I've hunted them before, with Archer."

"With Archer." He shakes his head and pours out a thick, black cupful. "Are they hard to get over unseen?"

"They will have scouts posted. But we can get a little closer."

"That's good," he reaches up and scratches his stiff hair. "We're going to need all the help we can get. Those are a mean set down yonder."

"Meaner than you?" Max Swift tosses a coin absently into the air and catches it. He winks to Peter and tosses it over the fire to him.

"What do you mean, meaner than—" Blue takes a sip of his coffee and clucks his tongue admiringly. "Wheew, who made the coffee?"

He tips it up and swallows down the rest of it, reaching for the pot again. "Best cup I've ever tasted."

I look at Peter in surprise. He's turning red at the ears, gives Blue a nod.

Blue takes a slow sip of his fresh cup and sighs with conviction. "Kid, you ever thought about turning outlaw?"

Raymond, across the fire, clears his throat.

"That's right, I stand corrected." Blue raises his hands in a placating gesture. "We ain't outlaw anymore."

Peter's watching Blue with almost a smile on his face. He's in the middle of cutting onions for supper—some sort of thick stew with meat that is already smelling wonderful. Probably something he's picked up from Carson since my departure.

"Kid, you know how to cook too?" Blue nods to his preparation. "Anytime you want to ride with me, I'll send my trail cook packing, you hear? Say the word." He snaps his fingers.

There's a general laugh around the fire. Peter turns red at the ears again. I don't think he knows what to do with the attention.

"Here, Peter." Alan gets up and goes over to sit next to him, pulling a sack of potatoes between his legs. "Looks like you could use some help."

He draws his penknife and starts to peel.

It's dark by the time we eat, but we hardly care. Our men loosen up as Blue tells stories of his wartime days, and the tale-swapping grows louder and merrier.

Peter sits beside Max, drinking it in. He's got the face of a boy right now, all glowing eyes. He's had so little of this, I'm happy just watching him.

"Miss Carnegie." Raymond's voice comes beside me, quiet and gentle. "I wonder if you'd mind my putting Lesley

Gable up on the rocks with you for lookout tomorrow. You both have keen eyes and—" He lowers his voice. "You can keep an eye out for each other, especially you for him."

I smile. "Sure thing, Marshal."

"Do you have field glasses?"

"I don't. I think Mr. Gable might."

"I'll get you a pair."

He stands up and I glance back to ask him where I am to sleep, but he's already gone.

49

THATCHER

WE STOP FOR THE NIGHT ALONG A STRETCH OF DESERT ground to eat and sleep. We've ridden hard, as late as we could manage, and I'm pretty tuckered out.

"One day, there'll be telegraph wires stretching out westward too," sighs Harrison, gesturing at the stars. "All this hard riding will be reduced to a signal flying across the sky."

"That'll be the day." I reach out and flip the pan bread, scorching my fingers.

"I figure we're a day and half's ride outside of Glory Mesa, still." Harrison tilts his neck and rubs it. "Once we eat, you sleep. You look dead."

"So do you."

I say it out of obligation, but I do feel dead.

"Nonsense, you sleep."

I find, blessedly, that I haven't any more strength to argue with him.

"I just—I can't believe it's her," I murmur, rubbing my face. "She tried to get her hooks into Archer back before he was married. And now to try to kill him?"

"She's jealous."

"Of who?" The moment the words were out of my mouth, I knew the answer. It's not just Rosamund. It's the territory.

"She loves the land. She wants it. She has grit and ambition, and that's something I liked about her."

"Was she the one who—put you up to that last year?"

He nods, barely.

"Why in the name of all good sense did you listen to her?"

"She led me to believe our lives were in danger. That someone had leverage over her, over us, and that it was Rosamund or certain death. I was trying to protect her."

"Oh." I let my breath out slowly.

"She promised me so many things. She tried to make me marshal, though that failed. I wonder if that's when she stopped loving me." He laughs without humor. "When I was no longer a ticket up."

"She tried to do that?"

"Yes. She was angry at Alan Swift, because she was sure he was the one who turned the tide against me. Why him, I don't know, but she was convinced."

He reaches for the pot of coffee and shakes his head.

"When I was in jail, she didn't lift a finger to help me. I thought her life was still in danger, so I kept my mouth shut.

I would have died taking the blame to protect her. I told her, when she visited me, that I wanted her to have my ranch if I hung, and the very next day, she testified against me at the trial. Nothing like that to throw cold water on a man's head. I knew then that if she had loved me once, she didn't anymore."

"But if someone else was behind it—"

"No." Harrison cuts me off with a bitter laugh. "We have all been had. Do you know what she said to me? I was in jail, the opinion was that I would hang, and she came to see me, just once. And she told me that she couldn't say anything for her own safety, but that she was through. She'd go into hiding if she had to. I asked her to talk to the judge and name the man who was forcing her to these measures. I said the law would protect her. She refused."

He shakes his head.

"She couldn't name him because it was just her. Just her, the whole time."

"But all that gold?"

"Oh, she's rich as sin. She said something about a mine of her husband's, but was never too clear about the details. I wonder now if there wasn't something ill-gotten about it, as she never talked about the extent of her resources anywhere but with me. But I was blinded. I loved her."

I give a laugh of disbelief as I hand him one of the pan breads.

"Don't laugh at it until you've been in love, Thatcher. It's a beautiful think, but it can make a man go insane. You lose

your head and you'd do anything—anything, for that person."
He gives a quiet laugh through his nose. "I haven't spoken to
her since."

He tears a piece of the bread off and eats it. He's staring
off into the fire, and I can tell his mind is running on.

"What are you going to do when we get back?"

"I'm going straight to the marshal to ask for her arrest.
That woman's caused more tears and pain than I care to
think of, and I could've said something, stopped it—if I'd just
—put it together."

"The marshal is out of town, cleaning up some outlaws
that threatened the railroad."

"Then I'll go to the governor. He's got authority."

"He'll be at the railhead the next couple days, by Black
Shaft Pass. He's visiting the vice president of the railroad
and inspecting the progress. I was supposed to go with him,
but—"

"So you're saying he's outside Glory Mesa?"

"Yes." The significance hits me as I say it.

Harrison Terhune gets to his feet and kicks dirt on the
fire. "We didn't need to sleep tonight, now, did we?"

CARNEGIE

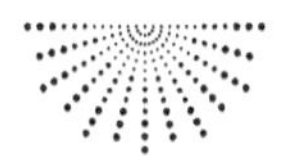

I WAKE TO DARKNESS AND THE GENTLE FLICKERING light of a campfire through the canvas of the tent. Even in the pitch black, the air has a different feel to it. It's morning.

I stand up and unbraid my hair, rebraiding it and winding it up behind my head. It'll have to do for today.

As I step out into the dark morning, I see Peter at the fire making coffee again and frying bacon and bread.

Blue and the Swifts are there, talking friendly-like. Jem notices that I'm up and stands to give me his seat.

I thank him softly and sit down. Without a word, Peter gets another tin cup and fills it with coffee for me.

"Accommodations comfortable enough?" asks Blue, raising his cup to me.

"Yes, they were."

"Don't get too comfortable." He winks.

I don't get Blue, exactly. I shoot him in the leg and

suddenly he's on the right side of the law and letting me have his tent for a night and talking like we're old friends.

I certainly wouldn't want to be friends with someone who shot me. But, then again, I've never been an outlaw.

"You have to eat quick, Kate," says Peter. "Marshal Lacey says you'll need to get out to the heights within the hour. The first set of men are getting into place to jump the outlaws."

"Have you seen Lesley Gable?"

Peter shrugs and hands me a plateful of food. "Nope. Eat up."

Lesley Gable is up on the heights by the time I make it up there on my pinto. He's a tall, thin man with shy, hound-dog eyes.

"You're Miss Carnegie. I think we met some time ago...."

"In the saloon, most likely," I reply. "Just Kate, Mr. Gable."

"Lesley. Call me Lesley." He smiles and holds out his hand.

I shake it. His palm is sweaty.

"Have you ever done this before?" he asks, nodding to the valley below us.

"No."

"Neither have I. Are you nervous?"

I smile and shake my head. I am many other things right

now—in haste, worried for the men below us, thinking through every scenario—but I am not nervous.

"Well, I am." He laughs. "We'd better get into place."

He hands me a pair of field glasses. I settle on the ground behind a scattered pile of boulders and look down below us at the men moving around the twists of the hills, quick and quiet.

I can see it a split moment before it happens; the two forces sight each other.

Below us comes the swift staccato of guns.

I WATCH the smoke rising and billowing from the camp, burning tents and rifle fire. There are men running between the tents, men falling on both sides. But I can see, even with my untrained eye, our men—most of them Blue's, by the handkerchiefs on their arms—are pushing forward and not back. There's a distant roll like drums, and I see the horses running free off the lines, tearing away over the desert.

That's it, then. The outlaws might turn and put up a good fight, might take some of us with them, but they're not getting away today.

The gunfire intensifies and the smoke grows so that I can hardly see what is happening.

"Can you see anything?" Gable asks.

"Not really."

I see a figure down in the fight that looks like Raymond,

on the back of a dun. I hold my breath, almost afraid to watch lest I see him get shot.

I pull in a slow breath and let it out.

Easy there, Kate.

The gunfire is lessening and lessening and then it stops almost entirely.

All I can hear is the distant rush of flames and the river over the hills, the birds singing behind us.

I think Gable and I are both holding our breath.

A flash of light from a pocket mirror cuts through the smoke, followed by a blue piece of cloth waved in the air.

"We got them!" I start up, shading my eyes staring intently down into the valley. "That's us, we got them!"

"Where?" Gable takes his field glasses down and I point. He whips them up again and holds his breath as he looks.

"It's our signal."

I pull out a pocket mirror and catch the sun with it in reply.

I stand, panting, watching for a further signal, but none comes. I was hoping they might have me ride back and take word to Glory Mesa, but no such luck.

I don't see the mirror flash again.

Gable is grinning like a man who's struck it rich, pure relief on his face.

"We did it!" I shout. "We got them!"

His grin suddenly fades and he wipes the sweat from his face. He goes back to where he was watching and starts to pack up his field glasses.

"Is something wrong?"

"No," he answers lightly.

I do not know him well, but I know when a man's not telling everything. "Lesley?"

"I hardly felt I was any service," he says, and I can tell by his face that admitting it is hard for him.

"Just because we weren't needed after all doesn't mean it wasn't important. Besides, somebody dies today, the man who doesn't, dies tomorrow. It's a saying," I add, when he starts to make a strange face. "You'll get your chance."

A swift thunder of hooves comes pounding up the hill behind us.

It's Jem Swift, covered in sweat, his face streaked with blood and dirt.

"Kate—" Jem reins in, dismounting in the same movement. "I need you to ride out to the railhead at Black Shaft Pass, fast."

"What is it? You got them, right?"

"There were fifteen or twenty men missing. Could be nothing, but one of the men we captured was talking about the pass and a secret under the earth—he said they'd finally succeeded in luring Archer out of town."

A chill hits my back and arms. Archer is at the pass.

"Right." I head for my horse.

"We think it's a trap," Jem is saying. "Just get to the railhead as fast as you can. We don't know what they've got planned, but you need to get Archer out of there."

"Get Archer out," I echo.

"Do you need anything?"

"Water?"

"Tagweiah!" Jem turns and shouts. His cousin comes riding up the hill. "Got a canteen?"

"One or two?"

"One. We'll be following the Rio Jefe."

Tagweiah unties one of his canteens and tosses it over. "It's full and fresh. I haven't drunk out of it."

"What about that old superstition that says it's good luck to drink where an Auki's drunk?"

He chuckles and dismounts, coming over and taking a swig out of my canteen. "For luck."

"Do you need cartridges?" Jem asks.

"I have another box in my saddlebags."

"All right, then. Get out of here, Kate."

I tighten the cinch on my pinto. She's antsy, sensing the tension in the air. She wants to run and she'll get her wish. I'm probably going to have to ride her to the ground.

"Easy, easy." I soothe her long enough for her to stand and I mount up.

"I'm coming too," says Gable, shoving his rifle into its sheath. "In case there's trouble on the way."

I gather the pinto in. She's throwing her head and making little starts forward. "I'll see you at the railhead."

I glance at Jem and Tagweiah and pull the brim down on my hat.

"Godspeed. We'll be following," says Jem.

I whistle up the pinto and the landscape blurs in swift-moving colors.

I should be afraid—afraid of the horse streaking across the hard, uneven ground, afraid of being a target and shot, afraid of what will happen if I do not reach the railhead in time.

But instead, my heart is pounding clear and strong in my chest. This, this is what it is to live.

I CAN SENSE something isn't right the moment I ride up into the Black Shaft Pass.

The tents and the traincars and workers are still there—to the eye, it looks normal. But the murmur of the crowd that has gathered for Archer Scott is low and uncertain, and the looks I get as I rein in are strange.

"Where is the governor?" I call. "I must see him! It's urgent!"

"Over yonder, where they do the blasting." A few arms gesture further in, out on the northeast part of the camp.

"Thank you." I cluck to the pinto and move her through the crowd. They are parting for us, but the noise, the unease, gets stronger the closer I get to the blast site.

Then I see his familiar figure. He is standing next to the railroad's vice president, Bracken, the loose-limbed fellow with the easy laugh.

"Governor Scott! Archer!" I dismount and run.

They turn to me—they were watching a couple men who are examining the rock wall intently.

"Kate, what is it?"

"I just came from the outlaw fight, there's word from Marshal Lacey—there's something amiss here, he doesn't know what, but he said to get out right now."

Good man, he doesn't hesitate.

"Get my horse for me?" he calls, waving down the nearest onlooker. They run off towards the crowded tents.

"Did everything go as planned?"

"Nearly. I didn't get a count or anything, Raymond is riding this way with the men."

"Good, good." He turns to Bracken. "I'm sorry this has to be cut short, I—"

The men at the rock wall pull out a match to light a lantern—oddly, I notice it with great, slow clarity.

The match strikes, once, twice, and then suddenly there's a great whoosh, like wind.

"No!" I see Bracken start forward, towards Archer. I duck instinctively, and I'm blown backwards into white nothing by a blast of hot air.

51

SIKES

I've been waiting for her. She comes near the end of the day when the time is almost fulfilled, when the air is tight and I can feel the rightness of it, the perfection of it, in my bones.

There are four men with her, armed with rifles and wearing tied-down guns. Men whose faces I do not recognize. Men who are, really, unimportant in the scheme of things.

I watch her from behind the curtain, readying herself on my doorstep. Watch her fingers, swift and nimble, clench and unclench, see the graceful lift of her neck and chin as she takes a deep breath and draws herself up.

She knocks, and the smile on her lips is thin and triumphant.

My dear girl, look at you stretch and bare your claws.

I open the door and step into the gap that is just enough for my narrow frame.

"Good afternoon, Mrs. Pike."

"Doctor Sikes." Her smile is genuine, but it is not a beautiful one.

"I've been expecting you. Will you come in?"

Something narrows, barely, in her eyes. "Thank you, yes."

I step back and open the door wide enough for her and her men to step in. She turns to two of them. "Go wait across the street. Watch the house." The wind catches at her black dress, waving it like a somber flag.

We go in, she and I, and the two gunmen.

"I set the front parlor for tea," I say, gesturing to the examination table, covered in a gingham tablecloth. "I made cake for the occasion. Lemon is your favorite, isn't it?"

She gives me a stiff smile that barely hides a sneer.

There are only two seats, so I pull out hers and seat myself across from her. The men I ignore. She waves them away to the slat-backed chair and the armchair across the room.

"I have come for you at last, old man," she says archly, as she pours out the tea. "You can no longer keep me at bay."

"Tea first."

She sets the teapot down, clattering the china lid. "Do you remember what you told me once?"

I do remember, but she wants to tell me.

She will not prove anything by it, except that I was right.

"You told me that I was nothing. You told me that these people were going to be great, but that I was just a girl playing with fire. Now you are going to watch as I burn down everything you love."

"Hm." I take a sip of my tea. "Is that all?"

"You pretend you are not afraid. But you and I both know that the more this territory is tamed, the more your grip on it weakens. And I have endured your presence long enough."

"My dear girl." I cut a slice of cake for her and hold out the plate. "It is not until you tame the wild places that the monsters come out. And they are coming, Maria. Even now they are coming."

A growl of thunder comes through the open windows.

"You are a fool. Who do you think the monsters are?" She leans her slim, white fingers against the gingham tablecloth and leans forward. "They are you and me. Just us. We could carve up the territory between us, or I get rid of you and leave it whole. One man or an entire territory. I'd rather keep it tidy."

"Maria, there are monsters of which you haven't dreamed in your wildest imaginations. Out here, we are all mere specks of dust trying to stand against the wind. That alone should make you want to stand with us and not against us. And yet, your pride prevails."

She takes a dainty bite of the cake and rolls it slowly in her mouth before swallowing. It is very good, and she hates that it is.

"This isn't about pride, Doctor Sikes. This is about the territory's potential. And instead of letting me join you as its protector, you told me that I and my vision were worthless."

"The problem with you, Maria," —I wipe the corner of my mouth with a napkin and fold it again— "is that you were never satisfied."

"As if you could know." Her eyes bore into mine with cold triumph. "I will still take away everything you've called your own."

"Indeed?" I urge, folding my arms.

"While you stood aloof from those you claim to protect, I entered their lives. Even now, Tora-Teth lures men in the west to their deaths in the wilds that are shrouded with mystery and legend. They will not come back to you. The Black Shaft Pass is full of crevices that spread strange airs that explode at the slightest flame and your appointed governor is there, any moment to be blown apart by a seemingly careless flame. The Swift brothers' fates are irrevocably tied to that of this territory, and you have not had the courage to tell them—but that is exactly what I will use to control them. And if I can tear apart the women's dreams—the sweet, fragile women whose lives have not yet been truly shaken—I can destroy their men. There are many ways to topple a castle, you see."

She takes another bite of cake and she takes her time savoring it.

"But the sweetest part of it all is that these silly, silly people think they are the reason for these misfortunes. They don't know that you are their downfall. You are the reason that I must destroy them. I have driven them out of Glory Mesa and into the wilds not to destroy them, but to destroy you. You can no longer protect them or yourself."

A clap of thunder sounds over the hills, and the wind presses against the windows, creaking the frames.

"Please." She laughs. "Don't tell me you are going to throw a tantrum, make a storm—a scene—here."

"No, I am not." I take a slow sip of tea. "Glory Mesa will have more storms than she can deal with before long. But remember, storms fly swift and dark over many hills, faster than a man can ride."

"Thank you for that beautifully petty threat." She laughs.

"I am not finished."

"Perhaps you are." She stands up, and her men rise in a rush.

"I said, I am not finished." A gust of wind hits the side window beside the armchair and the window shatters in, blasting the men with flying shards of glass. They scream, dropping their rifles, covering their heads. Blood runs down their faces and fingers, stains their sleeves.

I rise slowly, straightening my black coat.

"Maria Pike, I have heard you out, and you have said nothing to me that I do not already know as well, and yes, better than you. Why do you think that your efforts to lure Archer from Glory Mesa failed in the past? It is because those whom I have long protected have risen, as they were destined to, and met your schemes. Yes, the territory is being tamed, and with it, its need for my protection wanes. The monsters are coming forth in their last throes, and those heroes who are meant to meet them are rising even now. And mighty will be the struggle."

I see her tremble, ever so slightly, in the cold from the shattered window.

"What those men following Tora-Teth do not know," I continue, "is that they must soon play a part in things great beyond their knowledge. The actions of one of them will wake the long-sleeping curse-bringer, and the curse must swiftly be broken, or fulfilled. Against such powers, you can do nothing."

I lower my voice.

"Did you ever wonder why I told you that this course you desired, this thirst for power, was not for you? Did you ever once consider that I was trying to protect you?"

She takes in a deep breath, but she does not speak. Her face is white and her eyes burn.

"My aim was never to keep them from suffering." I shake my head slowly. "I have guarded them until they could stand on their own; and you may destroy their happiness, you may burn their homes and their dreams, but you will never have their hearts. And without that, your defeat is only a matter of time."

The silence is stark between us. Maria is nearly shaking with anger.

I reach down and begin to clean up from tea.

"What's more, there are men coming, right now, for you. Men you tried to kill and couldn't. If I were you, I would take what you can and run."

She leans across the table, clattering the dishes. She is so close that I can smell the perfume on her, strong and sweet.

"Hold your sweet, sweet pawns against me if you can, Doctor Sikes. I can still burn everything you love to the ground."

She stands up, bites out an order to her bleeding men. I regard them with a stony face.

They go out and she is following, slowly, reluctantly, as if weighing my words between bluff and truth.

But she knows I have never once lied to her.

"I hope you enjoyed the cake?" I raise my voice above the sound of the wind.

She laughs bitterly, and she is oddly beautiful in her anger, as if somehow it is where she feels most alive.

"It was magnificent." She is silhouetted in the doorway, the strong, pulsing wind tearing curls of dust from the ground. "Remember to make it for me again, when I return."

I stand with my arms folded.

"My dear girl, we shall not be seeing each other again."

52

BRITT

I MUST HAVE NICKED THE REPTILE BECAUSE A MILE OUT I start seeing a blood trail. He's heading clear north towards the wildest area, where the mountains tower high and hot steaming pools spread out below them.

I've never seen them myself, but I was in prison with a man who had. He spoke of a curse in that place and an untouchable ceremonial spear, put there by the Red Tree Clan.

Hang curses. I'd follow Tora-Teth into the heart of the earth.

Buck rides silently behind me, watching the same trail, following.

It's not until we're crossing the hills that lead into the great flats with the steaming pools, two days after we left the mustang camp, that Buck says, "Trail's getting stronger."

360

"Sure is. We'll have him today." I touch my pistol meaningfully.

"He's going into the forbidden place."

"It's not forbidden, Buck. Where'd you hear that nonsense?"

"The Red Tree clan. I lived with them five months, you recollect I told you."

"I recollect." I urge my horse up the steep path over the hill's summit, leaning forward to help him balance. "But we ain't Red Tree."

"They didn't say it was forbidden just to them."

"Then why is Tora-Teth going there?"

"He's a renegade. He doesn't believe in anything."

I don't answer that.

"He'll have to come out eventually," says Buck after the silence has stretched long. "We should wait for him."

"Are you superstitious?" I round on him.

"No, but legends like these happen for a reason. And I— I've got a bad feeling, Britt. Let's go after him another time."

"I ain't giving up this easy." I turn my horse around and look at him. "If you want to stay, that's your business. I'm going on."

"I don't like you going alone." Buck's voice takes on a stubborn edge.

"Well, I don't like you leaving when the going gets tough. You're an April, you're not a coward."

"That's not fair, Britt."

I ignore him and urge my horse into a canter down the

gently sloping side of the hill. There are fresh tracks: a single horse, unshod.

I don't look back to see if he's coming or not.

I ride out from under the sheltering pines and onto the flats. I have never seen anything like this place before in my life. There are great pools of water, ringed round with bright colors, yellow and rust red, green, and a blue bluer than the sky. The pools steam, and from what I can tell, the bottoms are too deep to see.

I dismount and step a little closer to the nearest one.

It's the strangest thing I have ever seen. A good distance away, one of the pools bursts into the air, spewing water upwards with a heavy hiss, like a steam engine.

A shadow flashes above me. I duck just as a knife skirts down the side of my neck and collarbone, with a thin, mean sting.

I swing arm around my assailant, trying to drag him forward, off my back and shoulder. He jerks and we fall to the gravelly ground.

I'm reaching for my gun but his hand is strong as steel, gripping mine like an eagle's talon, nails digging in, trying to stop me. I strain against his hand, push, push to a crisis, and then my arm gives and we flip on the ground.

I bang his head against the rocky ground, but he's slipped out of my hands like a snake, fingers fumbling for the knife on the ground.

I kick it hard and it falls into the steaming pool with hardly a sound.

The cut down my neck and chest is shallow, but it's bleeding down my arm, making my fingers slippery.

I get my hands on his throat. I am much longer and he cannot reach mine, though his fingers grasp. They find my arms instead, pushing and scratching.

He flails. I only have him half-pinned. My blood-slick hands lose their grip on his neck and he slides out from under me.

He's running, running as fast as he can past the pools, limping a little from his old wound. I am after him, reaching for my gun.

I pause to fire. He dodges this way and that. I cannot fire and chase him and stay out of the pools. I start instead to run, the gun gripped in my slippery fingers. I grip harder. The blood will dry soon and become sticky.

He rounds an outcropping of rock and I blaze after him. As I round the corner, he shoves himself back at me. I fall against the ground, the gun skitters across the ground and into the hot pool.

We're tumbling again, hands at each other's faces, throats, trying to gain some advantage. We're weaponless save for our hands.

The *isark* claw hangs from his throat still, white as aged bone. I reach for it and tear it off his throat. He lands a punch on my cheekbone and I shove him off with my knees to his stomach. He lands hard on his back.

I scramble to my feet, looking for a rock for a weapon, and my eyes light on the old, sun-bleached shaft of a spear, next to the outcropping of the mountain. Mere feet from my hand.

I seize it even as Tora-Teth scrambles to his feet.

"No!" I see fear in the man's eyes for the first and last time.

The spear comes up in my hands and I plunge it home.

Tora-Teth staggers backwards, a shocked, blank look in his eyes. Then he falls, dead, to the ground. A hard moment of silence follows, and then a roaring tears from the mountain.

The world rocks, heaves, and seems to steam and spin as the ground mingles with the sky. My ears are filled with the roaring.

The entire side of the mountain beside me gives way, just slides clean away, and dust and smoke choke the air.

Rocks are falling, sliding under my feet, moving for me like a sea wave.

I fall into yawning blackness.

FROM AFAR OFF, I hear the thud of steady drumbeats, pounding. From afar off, light finds its way to me, the darkness disappearing in chunks.

I feel arms, wet and slippery, around my chest, and suddenly it is as if a weight falls from my chest. Air floods my lungs. I gasp it in, choking.

The smell of blood is in my nostrils.

We go a long ways, I think, for the world closes in and

out like the ebb and flow of waves. At last, I feel the ground rise gently to meet me, as one might take someone into their arms.

I see Buck, covered in blood, kneel in front of me.

"You're bleeding," he says, in a soothing voice. "Here. Everything's going to be alright."

I feel hands at my side and pain like a faraway dream. But my vision spins. I cough and I feel it like something tearing at my insides.

"Easy now, easy—everything's going to be alright, my brother. It will be. Remember that."

His voice fades away, and I see him fall on one arm, gasping slowly, as the world closes in dark over me.

53

GABLE

THE BLACK SHAFT PASS IS A WRECKED, SMOKING uproar when I gain the top of the trail. Men shouting, horses screaming. I rein in and wheel my horse around to avoid a team running loose, covered in dust and blood, dragging half a wagon tongue behind them.

Whatever was supposed to happen just did.

I push my horse, already tired and lathered, into the milling chaos, moving toward the source of the smoke, the burning debris.

Either the governor was warned and isn't here, or Kate is going to need all the help she can get.

From the back of my horse, with the advantage of my height, I can see the source of the disaster.

A huge hole has been blown in the side of the rock wall. Around it, mingled with rock dust and rubble and blood, are slowly moving figures.

I spur my horse forward and dismount, my eyes searching for the governor. There are men all around, helping each other up, covering others with tarps, bending over the wounded, calling for help.

"Lesley Gable!"

One of the figures is starting to sit up, dazed. It's Kate Carnegie, almost unrecognizable under the dust and smears of blood where tiny pieces of rock smacked her face. Her hair is tangled and no longer what one could call tied back.

I rush over and hold out my hand. She grips it firmly and hauls herself up.

"Easy, easy now."

"Thanks." She brushes me off with brief thanks and begins to beat the dust out of her skirt.

"Are you all right?"

"I think so." She leans away and coughs, spitting dirt. "Where is Archer?"

"He didn't make it away?"

"No, but he nearly did." She pulls a handkerchief out of her skirt pocket and wipes her face as she moves towards the wreckage.

"The governor's been taken over there," a man nearby speaks up. "Not badly hurt, I think. But Bracken's done for." The man jerks his head to a figure on the ground. "He jumped on top of him. Man's a hero."

I walk over, my feet like lead, and crouch down next to the others who are crowded around Christopher Bracken with their hands covered in blood.

I glimpse his face and my heart's suddenly trapped in my throat, choking me. As his eyes meet mine there's a brief glimmer of recognition, a flash of pain and then something near and close as if he wants to speak.

And then he's gone. Just like that.

I feel alone—as alone as if I'm the last man on earth.

The earth has gone distant and blurry, all the sounds muffled. I'm aware of Kate coming up behind me, putting her hand on my shoulder.

I reach up and grasp it, grateful.

"I'm sorry."

"I am too." She's broken the spell. I feel as if my heart's made of broken glass, but the world is back and I am Lesley Gable, panting in the pale sun, shifting in and out of the clouds.

"Land sakes...." Kate grimaces again and tilts her head, tugging on her ear. "My ears won't stop ringing."

54

THATCHER

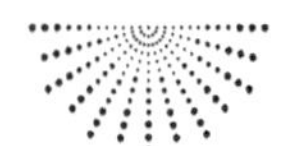

I think we're too late. There is a crowd in the streets of Glory Mesa. There's shouting and crying, and horses and wagons are already heading out, up the trail to the Black Shaft Pass.

Heavy smoke hangs over the horizon where the pass is.

"What is this?" Harrison mutters under his breath, reining his horse in sharply. Voices stick out like thin threads from the tapestry of the uproar.

"Explosion, up on the mountain!"

"It was too large to be the charges…"

"People hurt and killed. The governor—"

I lose the voice and my heart stands still.

"Come on." We ride down to the crowd, wading through slowly. I'm looking for a face I know and can trust.

Carson is standing on the porch of his saloon, his face white.

369

"Carson! Carson, what is going on?" He sees me and his face goes still. I like that even less.

"What is he doing here?" he demands, fixing Harrison with a look like death.

"What happened?" I demand, ignoring him.

"I said what is he doing here?" he demands again, bullishly.

"Helping me, now will you drop it?" I shout. "What happened?"

"There was an explosion up on the Black Shaft pass. Archer was there. The vice president of the railroad was there. Some of our men from the posse were there too—don't ask why, I only heard that. Some of them were hurt bad."

"Is Archer—? Raymond?"

"Archer's alive, they say, they didn't say how alive. Didn't hear Raymond's name particular, but where Archer is, Raymond usually is."

"What about Rosamund? Is she all right?"

"She didn't go."

"Is she at home?"

"I suppose so."

I don't wait any longer. I turn my horse and gallop up the street to their house. She's standing on the porch with her face white, her hands gripping the rail. Irene Sandler is with her.

"Jesse—" She comes running to me. I dismount and she throws her arms around me. "Jesse, please—"

"He's alive. I wasn't there, I don't know anyone's condition. I just heard he's not dead."

She bursts into tears on my shoulder. "Raymond?" she whispers.

I shake my head, regretfully. "I don't know."

I look up and Irene Sandler is gone.

"Now, Rosamund." I take her hands gently in mine. "I want you to go back inside and wait, and rest. I will go see what happened. I will bring him back to you or take you to him. Until then, stay in the house and don't come out for anyone until I get back, do you hear?"

"You'll hurry?"

"I promise."

"Thatcher," says Harrison warningly. Rosamund looks at him and goes still and her jaw hardens.

Harrison backs his horse off.

"Go inside," I whisper, and muster a smile for her. It almost fails me.

But she goes, and I hear the bolt slide.

"What is it?" I shove my foot into the stirrup and settle into the saddle.

"We need to find Maria, fast. It might be too late."

"Let's go."

We tear off to her house, but it's still and quiet and locked, neat as a button. The stables are empty.

"The restaurant?" Harrison suggests.

I dash off in that direction, not even waiting. The shutters are drawn, but I dismount anyway and wrap my horse's reins over the post. Harrison is following cautiously after me, his hand near his gun.

I step up to the door and try the handle. It's locked. I rap with my knuckles. Nothing.

"Hello?" I call.

A gunshot splits the air, whistles past my ear. I hit the ground before I even know I've reacted. Harrison is on the ground, firing upwards at the windows.

"I've got you covered, get back from the door!" he shouts.

Another round of shots, six, and a return from Harrison. I get back to my horse, ducking behind it as it pitches and pulls against the hitching rail.

"I'm covering, come on!" I call.

Harrison scrambles to his feet and joins me. But there's no further fire. I peer around the side of my horse at the front window.

I hear a scramble of hooves for a split second distinctly behind the restaurant before it's swallowed up in the clamor of the town.

"They're getting away!" Harrison leaps into the saddle and shoots off, laying hard on his horse side to side with the reins, shouting for it to go.

I mount and ride hard after them. There's six or seven of them, heading for the southern hills where Sikes goes to pick his herbs. They are all dark, swift figures mingled with flying dust, but there's one in the middle that seems as if I've seen it before, just so, streaking across the plain as if the devil was at her heels.

And I remember the woman riding alone in the rain, towards the mountains.

Harrison was right. It's been Maria. Maria this whole time, sowing grief, causing death. My stomach twists.

They're heading down towards a box canyon. Perhaps they don't know the way. If they enter it, we'll have them. There's no way out.

I whistle sharp so he can hear me, then signal for Harrison to go around the other side of the hill. This way, if they try to double back or skirt the hills, we'll see them.

I charge around the hill into the canyon, my gun drawn. It's empty and quiet.

I hold my breath and listen, for gunshots, for hooves, for something. But there's only the thin staccato of Harrison's horse as he rounds the corner, riding the leather off his horse.

He reins in sharply, his face darkening with confusion.

There was no other way out or around. They just disappeared. No trace, right into empty rock. It's still and hot and there's not a sound around us.

"Nothing?" he demands. He's covered in sweat and dust.

"They just vanished." I take off my hat and gesture helplessly with it.

Harrison throws his leg over his horse in disgust and drops down.

"How'd she know?" I ask, panting, trying to catch my breath.

"There was a roan with black legs. It belonged to one of my hands. When you came, he must have split off and come straight here, warned her." He stands there for a second, breathing hard.

"One of my own men—one of my own men!"

I let my breath out slowly. Sweat trickles down my face and into my collar.

Harrison slams his hat onto the ground with an oath.

55

NEWTON

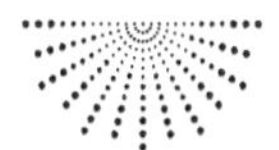

Dusk is falling in bright, fighting colors. The shadows of the fallen rocks cast deep shadows upon the rising steam of the hot pools. The entire area is changed; rocks cover places that were water, there are slopes where there were none before. Hills, gone.

Water splashes under my boots as I run over the jaggedly strewn rocks. Steam rises between them like a whispered warning.

Dark, dried blood is trailed thickly over the rocks, some of it in bootprints, in a hand held out to catch a fall.

A figure sits propped against the rocks, silhouetted against the vivid, dying light, still as if asleep. His head is slumped downwards.

"Britt? Buck!" I cup my hands to my mouth and shout.

The figure stirs slowly as if caught underwater, but he does not turn. I'm running now, my throat thick and choked.

There is another figure lying in the man's arms.

"Britt, Buck—"

It's Britt. His face is covered in rock dust and blood, and there are thick, dark streaks down his face and neck where sweat or tears have washed them partially.

Buck lies limp in his brother's arms. His face is peaceful and still but white as marble, and there are deep, bloody gashes over his body that have stopped bleeding.

"Britt." I kneel down beside him, look into his face. "Are you hurt?"

"See to him—" Britt nods shakily at his brother. There's dark blood trickling from his side. Too much blood.

I know the answer already, but I set two fingers under Buck's jaw.

"He's gone, Britt."

"He's not! He can't be." Britt's voice cracks; he doesn't have enough voice even to shout.

"Britt, you're bleeding. Let me help you."

"No, no—" He presses his forehead to his brother's, his bloody hands smoothing Buck's hair off his still face. "Please —he can't be dead."

"Britt." I peel off my shirt and tear it, wadding up half of it and pressing it against the wound.

He looks at me, clear as day, the first time he's looked at me without any kind of wall up behind those dangerous dark eyes.

"Listen. It's too late for me," he says, clearly and slowly.

"My brother dug me out and dragged me here with the last of his strength. He tied up this wound while he was dying. I haven't done anything worthy in my life, but he can't be forgotten."

"He won't."

He seizes my arm, hard. "Promise me."

"I promise." I reach out and take his hand. "Neither of you will be forgotten."

"I—I led him to this. He could have had any life—but he waited for me and he rode with me and he dug me out when I left him. What did I do to deserve that?"

"He loved you."

Britt takes a breath and his breath catches. He coughs and coughs. I hand him my handkerchief and he spits blood and wipes his mouth. All the color has gone out of his face.

"Bury us together?" he whispers.

"I will." I take his hand.

He starts to cough again, his body wracked with every ragged breath.

"Where are you?"

"I'm right here." I press his hand harder so he can feel it.

"Where's Buck?"

"He's right here."

His hand gropes around at the ground; I take it and set it on his brother's arm. His fingers close over his brother's hand weakly.

"I'm sorry, partner," he whispers.

And he's gone, remarkably gently, from the world with which he was so long at odds.

Dark has fallen. The stars are out, I swear, brighter than I've ever seen them.

5 6

IRENE

I'VE NEVER BEEN TO THE BLACK SHAFT PASS, BUT WITH the heavy, black smoke hanging like a cloud above it, it cannot be missed. Riders and buggies are rushing up the trail to it.

Time is gone from me—I have no idea how long it takes to get there. Every second, every heartbeat, is as real and separate as a day, yet the horse is blowing foam into my face with its effort. The acrid smell of smoke greets me before anything else. As I mount the path, clogged with people and wagons coming in and out, some bearing bloodied bodies, I can see the devastation before me.

There are still wagons and tents on fire, and suddenly I am back at the attack on the wagon train. My heart sinks to my stomach.

But if Raymond is here, I will find him. I know it.

I tie the horse up to a scrawny tree growing through the

rocks and press through the people coming and going, running through the tents and wagons, choking on the smoke.

"Have you seen Raymond Lacey?" I grab a young man's arm as he passes.

"The marshal? No."

"Have you seen Raymond Lacey?" I ask another. He just shakes his head.

Tears burn my throat as I run on. There's a lump so big I cannot swallow. I am coughing from the smoke but I press on.

There are wounded strewn around, men and women trying to help them as best they can. I am frozen where I stand, watching them, seeing the destruction with slow horror.

Smoke blows between the tents, and ragged pieces of them fly like banners in the wind.

A woman is coming by with a bowl full of bloody water.

"Excuse me, have you seen the marshal? Raymond Lacey? Tall man, mustache, deep—"

"Mrs. Sandler—Irene." A deep voice speaks behind me.

I turn slowly at the sound of my name, at the familiar voice.

It's Raymond. He's swaying with weariness, and his shirt is stained with blood and open at the collar above his vest. His hair may have been brushed down with his fingers, but it's still messy and part of it clings to his damp forehead.

My heart goes to my throat. I'm afraid. There is warmth in his eyes, and I am so afraid that my heart imagines it.

"What are you doing here?"

"I was looking for you." I'm breathless.

"For me?" His voice almost gives.

"They said that—well, I was afraid. It was all confusion down there in Glory Mesa. I thought you might be dying."

It sounds silly coming out of my mouth now, but worse, my voice cracks, breaks. If I speak again, I am going to cry.

"Ohh." The word comes out of his mouth like a sigh, and he reaches for me, takes my hand. It's real and whole and strong. I close my eyes and savor his realness down to the tips of my fingers.

"Come with me," he says, softly. "Let's get out of here— it's no sight for your eyes."

He leads me away from the burning wreckage, shielding my eyes from time to time, and up a small footpath to a flat lookout far above everything.

The sun is brilliant and golden, preparing to sink below the horizon. I can see the far-off rocks and hills north of us, soaked in golden light so that they almost disappear into it, see the green of the growing things along the Rio Jefe, see the blue of the open sky between the white and shadowy clouds.

Raymond takes his hat off with one hand, wiping his face on his sleeve. His other hand doesn't leave mine.

"I told you I loved this time of day," he says with conviction. I nod, but I cannot reply. Tears are streaming down my face so thick and hot that I cannot see. But it feels good and raw and healing with Raymond's hand in mine.

"Don't cry," he says gently. He lets go of my hand and puts his hands on my shoulders.

"It's all right. I'm crying because I'm happy," I manage. I try to wipe them away, but it does little good.

Raymond fishes a handkerchief out of his pocket and hands it to me. It smells of soap and sage. I dry my eyes and blow my nose, fold it, and hand it back, but he's not paying attention. His eyes are on my face and there's such tenderness in them that I am almost taken aback. I look down and tuck the edges of the handkerchief into a neater fold.

"Irene Sandler, will you marry me?" he whispers.

"What?" I look up at him, afraid I have misheard.

"Will you marry me?" He steps back and starts to go down to one knee, but I pull him back.

"I don't need that," I whisper, my voice failing me. "Just tell me you mean it."

"I mean it. Now and to the end of the world."

I wrap my arm around his and lean my head against his shoulder, hot tears soaking his sleeve, afraid he's going to disappear in my arms.

"Yes, Raymond. With all my heart, yes."

57

GABLE

I'M STACKING PIECES OF RUBBLE, CLEARING THE TRACK area, when Thatcher rides up in the fading light, dismounting before his horse is even stopped.

"Archer." He seizes his cousin by the shoulders. "I can't tell you how good it is to see your face. A man's got a lot of time to imagine the worst between Glory Mesa and here."

"Did word get down already?"

"It did. Record time, I think. How are you?"

"Bruised and bloodied up, but I'm fine. How is Rose?"

"Rose?"

"Did you see her?"

"Yes, she's worried."

Archer clenches his fists. "I must get down to her."

"I told her to wait inside, she won't be hearing gossip— Archer, I have some bad news to tell you about Maria Pike."

Archer isn't listening, he's scanning the nearby wagons

383

and posts. "Gable, is that your horse?" He points to my leggy bay.

"It is."

"May I take it? I'll pay you a rented rate for the trouble."

"Please, no, just take him."

"Thank you." He goes over and unties my horse.

"Archer—" Thatcher strides after him. "About Maria—"

"Never mind about her. I have to get down to Rosamund immediately, I can't have her worrying."

"She's waited for you far longer than this, Archer, she's a strong woman. What's gotten into you?"

"Gotten into me?" He turns around. I have never seen him look so frantic. "Thatcher, she is with child. I cannot leave her a moment longer than I must, wondering if I'm dead or alive."

He swings up into the saddle and spurs the horse into a gallop.

Thatcher stands in the swelling dust, staring after him in slow bewilderment. He peels his hat back off his head with a slow whistle.

"Well, of all the—" He shakes his head and collects his horse. He tips his hat to me briefly and he's gone, heading after his cousin.

It's late when I finally make it back to Glory Mesa. I catch a ride with a man I've never seen before, in a buggy.

He talked, I think, on the way home. I was dazed and too

tired to think.

I walk home, limping slowly, but I have had one thought and one thought only ever since I saw the disaster I was so nearly a part of.

Edith.

Standing on the porch, watching, she's wearing a pale blue dress. As I approach, she comes down and meets me at the gate.

She's staring at me in the twilight, with the purple night colors against her smooth, dark skin, tinting her black hair, and I don't think I've ever seen her more beautiful.

There are tears in her eyes.

"Edith." I reach out to her. "I've come back."

She comes to my arms and leans her head against me. "You look tired."

"I am. Horribly."

"Were you at the pass?"

"Yes."

"You could have been killed."

"I came after it happened. I rode from the outlaw camp with word, but Kate Carnegie was first. She saw it."

"Well," —she reaches up and smooths down my messy, dust-covered hair— "at least you had the outlaw fight."

I shake my head, the whole weight of the day on my shoulders. "No. I was on lookout, above the fight."

Her brow furrows. She doesn't move. "What do you mean?"

"The marshal asked me to take lookout duty."

She pulls away from me. "You told me that you were riding with the marshal to take down the outlaws. And—you hide on the rocks and watch?" She sounds as if I'd told her I no longer love her.

"Edith, darling, what is this?" I step closer to her out of habit and she backs away.

"You were supposed to fight. That is why you went," she hisses, the tears spilling from her eyes. "Lookout is a job for boys and the injured. It's not a position they give a competent man."

She couldn't have hurt me more if she had slapped me in the face. "Edith, take that back."

"I won't. It's true."

"Edith—"

"How can I face this wild, dangerous land you've brought me to if I can't even hold my head up around you?"

Her face is a mask of hurt and betrayal. She turns around and goes into the house, slamming the door.

It's strangely quiet.

I don't know when I opened the gate or how I stumbled up the lane, but the porch, freshly whitewashed by myself last week, is beside me, and I sink onto it, staring at the grass.

Does she really feel that way about the Western Territory? Did I do wrong in bringing her out here after all? After all this?

I put my head in my hands and stare at the ground.

Eventually, sometime in the night, tears come to my eyes, and I weep, and it is a relief.

NEWTON

I BURIED THE APRILS SIDE BY SIDE IN A PATCH OF SUN-speckled ground near a grove of pines. As Britt requested, they are together.

I cleaned their faces of the dirt and blood and wept to see that their faces were peaceful, as many in death are not.

And I spend a day hauling a gray stone to sit above their grave and hewing out their names on it.

Britt and Buck April. I don't know their dates.

TWO DAYS later I return to the mustang pens, where my men wait, and the smoke from the breakfast campfire rises in familiar welcome.

The place feels strange and empty without the brothers. I expect to see them walking among the rails, talking to the horses, their lanky frames leaning against the uneven, split rails.

I can see in my mind's eye the powerful horses bucking and pitching under Britt as he remains cool and steady as winter ice on their backs. I can see the way Buck stepped into a pen with a wild horse and it was as if the two spoke, kind to kind.

I can hear their laughter ringing off the canyon walls, the only place I ever saw them laugh.

"Sir, we're ready to take the horses out. I think they're ready for the trip. All except that one."

He points to a pale roan mare, running the fence, dark with sweat. Buck's pick.

"She's worked herself up in a sweat. She's going to hurt herself like this. She was creating such a stir we had to separate her out."

"What's wrong?"

"It's that young grullo. He jumped the fence three, four days ago, about dusk. But he keeps coming back for her, night after night. He's calling from those hills. Then she gets into these sweats and runs herself into a lather."

"Let her go."

"She's a good mare. We can shoot him or drive him off. She'll forget him eventually."

"Let her go." I stalk over to the corral and shove the rails back so hard they quiver.

"But, sir—"

"Out of the way! Didn't you hear me?" I grab him and

pull him back from the entrance. Her ears prick, swivel around. She snakes her head downward, looking for danger in the open gate. Then she gathers her muscles and tears from the corral into the hills.

The young stallion's bugle call rings out and she answers, mid-gallop.

They are two shapes, free and glad, in the golden morning sun, kicking up wild licks of dust in the still air.

For a moment the two meet, pausing to touch noses, arch necks, and then he's off, with her at his side.

"Sir, you look worn clean through. Come on back. We've got grub and coffee."

"In a bit. I'm not hungry."

I walk toward the far hill over which they disappeared. I follow their tracks, their settling dust, until I reach the summit, overlooking the valley.

I can see them, just specks of color against the green landscape. I remove my hat and wipe my forehead.

Somehow it seems fitting, standing as if I was at a funeral. I buried those boys days ago, but this right here feels like the true memorial. A fitting goodbye. The land stretching out as far as the eye can see in stark majesty, the rising sun covering it in gentle rays, the April boys' mustangs running free, running toward the quiet ground where they sleep together, undivided even by death.

From here, even the mountain is visible, a lone peak above the others, rising like a monument.

Something catches my eye, just above the mountain.

I squint and look again. This time it's unmistakable.
The mountain smokes.

ACKNOWLEDGMENTS

First thanks goes to my readers and everyone who read and loved *These War-Torn Hands* and waited so patiently for the sequel. You are the ones who kept me driving forward.

To my street team—you have been so helpful and supportive. I can't wait to share this book with each and every one of you.

To James Egan for the stunning cover; thank you for bringing my stories to life through your art. And to Essi and Emilie for the brilliant art that will go so well with this book, thank you.

To my real life Peter who does actually make the best coffee.

A huge thank-you to my intrepid proofreaders who really pulled out the stops on this one. You guys are the very, very best.

To The Inkwell and The Storyteller's Hall who sprinted

with me, encouraged me, and prayed for me. I hope we get to share many more hours of writing, storytelling, and living the author life together.

To Elisabeth, my editor, who has spent countless hours on this project and put so much care and love into the shaping of this novel, thanks doesn't cover it.

Finally, as always, thanks to my Heavenly Father who protected me and cared for me during the creation of this book. Truly, without Him, it would not have come into being.

ABOUT THE AUTHOR

EMILY HAYSE is a lover of log cabins, strong coffee, NASCAR, and the smell of old books. Her writing is fueled by good characters and a lifelong passion for storytelling. When she is not busy turning words into worlds, she can often be found baking, singing, or caring for one of the many dogs and horses in her life. She lives with her family in Michigan.

ALSO BY EMILY HAYSE

Crowning Heaven

Seventh City

The Last Atlantean

The Rivers Lead Home

These War-Torn Hands